meera vs meera

MADHAV HADA

Translator

PRADEEP TRIKHA

Vani Book Company

An imprint of Vani Prakashan Group

Vani Book Company
An imprint of Vani Prakashan Group
4695, 21-A, Daryaganj, New Delhi 110 002
Phone: +91 11 23273167 Fax : +91 11 23275710
India
Branches
Ashok Rajpath, Patna 800 004, Bihar
Coffee House Campus, Mahatma Gandhi Marg, Allahabad 211 001, Uttar Pradesh
Mahatma Gandhi International Hindi University, Wardha 442 001, Maharashtra
Motia Park Opp. Water Tank, Sultania Road, Bhopal 462 001, Madhya Pradesh
Goripur Taliya Para, 313, R.B.C. Road 24- Parganas (North) Kolkata 743 166, West Bengal

MEERA VS MEERA
Translated from the Hindi original
Pachrang Chola Pahar Sakhi Ri
Published by Vani Prakashan (2015)
by Madhav Hada
Translator Pradeep Trikha

ISBN : 978-93-88684-06-4
Criticism

Paperback First Edition 2020

Price : ₹ 399

Printed at Thomson Press (India) Ltd.

Vani Prakashan's signature motif is created by Artist Maqbool Fida Husain

In a work of unparalleled and original scholarly reconstruction, Dr. Madhav Hada's book on Meera, *Pachrang Chola Pahar Sakhi Ri*, made waves in its original Hindi imprint. I am very happy to see it in English now, ably and painstakingly translated by Prof. Pradeep Trikha. *Meera Vs Meera* will not only add to our understanding of Meera's extraordinary life and literary output, but re-kindle our interest in one of India's iconic and immortal heroines.

–Makarand R. Paranjape
Author & Director
Indian Institute of Advanced Study

Meera Vs Meera is a translation of a wellreceived book *Pachrang Chola Pahar Sakhi Ri* in Hindi. For centuries, the masses regarded Meera's poetry as a medium of expression of their feelings and emotions. Meera's poetry, though interpreted in multiple ways has dwarfed, weakened and gulfed her persona. The religious discourses and narratives festered with her religious aspect, whereas the European historians during the colonial period in India focussed on elements of love, romance and mystery in Meera's life. The Marxist critics and neo-feminist activists highlighted Meera's narratives related to her courage and selfdetermination, which she exhibited during her times. In this process the human aspects of Meera were completely side-lined which is far more evident from her poetry. Meera is a feudal, rebel, devotee, poet and much more. She led an eventful human life. She never felt alienated or free from womanly passions and was the creation of the society she lived in. Meera believed *'Soney kaat na lagey'* (Gold never rusts...). In *Meera Vs Meera* an attempt is made to conserve the 'real self' of Meera, left over by the multiple interpretations through the centuries.

Contents

Chapter - I

Life

1

The known and publicized life of Meera has been inferred, interpreted and at times even purposefully altered in myriad ways over generations. Many have concocted untrue stories about her in an attempt to demean or exploit her identity—during her lifetime and even to the present day. In the olden days, her courage and revolutionary thinking inspired a compendium of folk narratives about her. Later religious historians and devotees reconstructed her image in their hagiographies and spiritual genealogies. Despite carrying some elements of truth in the beginning, they lost factual integrity over time. During the colonial period, European historians focused on the elements of love, romance and mystery in Meera's life in their accounts. They added imagination to her stories, to serve their colonial interests of appropriating Meera's image, and to project it as they desired, in the eyes of their European peers as well as the Indian masses. Although several new records about Meera's life and her times have been discovered in the post-independence era, including some substantial information, (i.e., about her marriage) they were eclipsed by the conventional image of Meera as a saint poet—exuding love, romance, devotion, mystery and mystique, an image which has been further enhanced and diversified by literary and religious historians, critics, and finally, today's mass media.

On the other hand, quite a few Marxist critics and neo-feminist activists focused on the narratives related to Meera's courage and self-determination. Thus, researchers, whether Indian or from other countries, have interpreted Meera's life stories according to their own criteria, pre-dispositions, and standards. While taking advantage of the fact that there is little substantive evidence about her life, they have used their own methods and parameters of interpretation—leading to varied conclusions, forming new and desired images of Meera. As a result, many 'Meeras' have been created. For some, she may be a 'saint-poet'; for another, an extraordinary rebellious woman. For some, she is a woman shrouded in mystery and romance, 'addicted to love'. However, as we will be discovering throughout the book, in reality, Meera never negated life. She was neither a saint-poet, nor a female ascetic, never completely emancipated from the difficulties and 'illusions' of the world. Nor was she 'madly' in love. The images of her being oppressed, neglected and helpless are historically debatable. On the contrary, she belonged to the ruling class and her devotion, strong will and determination were not too inconsistent with the socio-cultural norms of her time. Moreover, the society in which she lived had given her the liberty to do what she desired. To a certain extent, she did not stray from the acceptable norms and most importantly, she was a woman of fame and considerable wealth, the latter being true, at least, in the initial phases of her life.

There is no unambiguous and verifiable consensus on Meera's life and times, owing to the few debatable records available on the same. Since she was neither a daughter nor a wife of a well-established ruler of Mewar[1], no information about her life was recorded in any *khayat* or *bahis* (traditional documents that recorded genealogies and timelines of rulers). It was a common practice among Rajput rulers of Rajasthan to register the names of royal ladies in formal birth and marriage records. Royal women also had their own bards, called *ranimangas*, who composed poems containing elaborate accounts of Queens and their offspring. While this tradition mainly involved women of ruling families, other Rajput women were excluded from it; and their mention was negligible[2]. However, it is widely believed that Meera's father Ratan Singh was the second son of Rao Duda, ruler of Merta. Being younger to Viramdev, he could not claim the *tikayat* (heirdom). Also, Meera's husband prince Bhojraj died when her father-in-law Rana Sanga still reigned Mewar.

Despite hailing from a ruling class, and also being married into one, Meera could never take pride in being either a daughter or a wife of any Rajput ruler and no *khayat* or *bahis* gloriously chronicles her life. Still, her name appears in works of Marwar's[3] Bhat Kehardan and Daudan[4]. Meera Bai also receives a mention in *Annals and Antiquities of Rajasthan*, which is a major historical work on India's Rajput states. It was written by Lieutenant-Colonel James Tod, an English colonial officer and a scholar. Based on the meagre available sources of historical information available to him during that time, combined with his deep-rooted European notions and interests he shaped Meera's image as a holy saint and mystic poet[5]. This image also caught the attention of historians and literary critics of the post-colonial era and influenced them greatly. Later, historians like Shyamaldas, Munshi Deviprasad, Harinarayan Purohit, Thakur Chatur Singh and Gaurishankar Hirachand Ojha collected a lot of new information on Meera's life and times. Then again, due to her already 'canonized' image which was quite popularized on strength of Tod's reputation in literature and media, their claims never received widespread acceptance[6] nor could move past Tod's glory.

As a result, little attempt was made afterwards to historically validate the popularized, idealized image of Meera. Most Marxist and feminist critics considered the accounts of Shyamaldas, Munshi Deviprasad, Harinarayan Purohit, Thakur Chatur Singh, Gaurishankar Hirachand Ojha and others to be influenced by royal patronage. Few people have given due acknowledgement to the research conducted by Munshi Deviprasad in his monograph *Meerabai Ka Jivan Charitra*[7]. In 1956, Hermann Goetz, the noted German art historian and oriental scholar delivered an important lecture based on his research on Meera Bai in Delhi, which was later published as a book by Bharatiya Vidya Bhavan, Mumbai[8]. Harinarayan Purohit, a distinguished Indian oriental scholar, did significant research on Meera's life and poetry, in collaboration with a historian and a paternal descendent of Meera, Thakur Chatur Singh[9]. The records obtained by them were mostly authentic but those were under-recognized due to the antipathy of the feminists and Marxist critics.

Meera may have little mention in historical writings, but she has a considerable presence in devotional legends and lores and also in religious biographical sketches. It seems that her life and work gained significance nearly a century after her death. Meera is mentioned in Guru Nabhadas ji's *Bhaktamal*, an anthology in the Braja language containing accounts of lives of devotees. Priyadas, a disciple of Nabhadas, in his commentary *Bhaktirasbodhini* provided one of the earliest biographical accounts of Meera, based on the oral legends available during his time[10]. Sukhsaran, the acclaimed critic of saint-poets, has devoted a complete independent document "Meerabai ki Parchi" to Meera bai, which can be considered a religio-historic record[11]. There is a mention of Meera in *Bhavishya Purana*[12]. In documents such as *Bhaktamal*, Meera is depicted as a woman with superhuman, miraculous qualities. It was based on the images of Meera as celebrated by devout worshippers, circulated through folk tales and legends. Owing to the lack of historical records, these traditional narratives about Meera have contributed greatly in shaping our understanding of her. However, these legends have not been recorded or comprehended in an unbiased, balanced fashion. People who claim to understand Meera have either accepted these legends to be fully authentic or have completely rejected them as false and fictitious. Popular legendary images are not completely false. We cannot forget that they were always a vital part of cultural discourses of their time—with their own language, origins, structures, grammar and dynamics, and some of them are true.

In order to understand any society, it is necessary to study and examine the grammar present within its cultural discourses. In the first half of the twentieth century, while hurrying to be 'modern' according to European standards, we became too skeptical to accept most of our country's traditional stories and knowledge as some of them fell outside the boundaries of logic or scientific reasoning. In order to understand Meera, we need to reconsider, analyse, and verify some of the legends that are rooted in our history and culture—the legends that bear testimony to Meera's struggle, suffering and her special form of devotion.

The main source of information about Meera's life and times is her poetry. One of the salient features of her poetry is that its original form is not fixed or restricted. There are many editions of her poetry, published in different languages. Her poetry has been sung for centuries and has also been revised along the way. Hence, many efforts have been made to discover the original compositions of Meera. For Harinarayan Purohit, it was his lifetime mission to search for and identify original poetic compositions of Meera. He tried to determine some criteria to judge the authenticity of her work, but before he could complete his research, he passed away. Later his compiled and edited volume was published by the Rajasthan Oriental Research Institute[13]. Apart from these sources, there are numerous *harjas*[14], or devotional songs shared as tradition, that depict some incidents of her life. The information available in

Meera's poetry and harjas may not be backed by some historical evidence but to reject them completely would be unreasonable.

Folktales or legends tend to deviate from actual facts over time, but they carry elements of truth. For centuries, oral narratives keep on rolling like pebbles in a river. Their shapes may change but their nature remains the same. Likewise, Meera's poetry has been passed down and evolved across generations, but it does inherit elements of its original version. Similarly, biographical details obtained from these poems and harjas may not be perfectly reliable but they are not entirely false. By aligning these 'clues' with available historical facts, we can arrive at the truth.

Many popular notions about Meera's life and times have been accepted as *argumentum ad populum*. These 'popular' notions rise from assumptions and speculations, so people might have judged her based on widely accepted, yet prejudiced parameters. Of her life history, critics and historians have often retained what fulfils their requirements and have side-lined other relevant pieces of information that might be inconsistent with their values and needs. They have also made their own discoveries to substantiate their argument. To show Meera as a saint-poet, certain critics have borrowed elements from scriptures and theories of poetry as suggested in ancient Indian texts. Meera's poetry, being flexible and diverse, and not being confined to historical bounds, allowed the critics to obtain what they were looking for. When they wanted to look for piety and righteousness to bill her as *sagun* exactly as scriptural texts ascribe, they found plenty of references in Meera's poetry. Her work also offered 'melody' when they wished to hear it. Those looking for *nirgun* attributes, were also not disappointed by Meera. Researchers have tried to identify mysterious, esoteric and stereotypical examples of the concepts and terminology of *yoga* in Meera's poetry. Linguists, classical and semi-classical critics have dwarfed and devalued Meera's poetry to align it with scriptures, and Meera did not disappoint them either. None who approached Meera was disappointed. Whoever studied her poetry, interpreted it according to their own perceptions. Meera always offered something or the other, to add to the intrigue of whoever approached her. But no one truly realized that Meera's poetry was not made to be 'taken' but to be earned. Its fluid elements come from folk lore and poetry, so her work cannot be held within the limits of any single tradition, religion, scripture or school of thought. Her poetry cannot be frozen in a groove. It is refreshingly new, contrary to the expectations of the critics, who conceived and popularized an extraordinary saintly, feminine image of Meera.

Critics also often portrayed her as utterly vulnerable and socially ostracised—who refused to accept patriarchal authority and defied social conventions of her time[15]. In reality, her society provided her enough space to express her feelings and emotions, and actively conserved her memories after she was no more. Surprisingly enough, neo-feminist thinkers considered the society in which she lived, to be stagnant and unprogressive. It must be noted that Meera was a high-born woman, a widow of a prince; so she naturally possessed enough resources for economic independence. It has been acknowledged that she used to shower generosity on fellow saints—by often distributing gold coins among those who entered the threshold, as suggested in Vallabha sect's devotional texts[16]. According to Harinarayan Purohit, Meera never promoted ascetic attire through saffron clothing[17].

Gopal Singh Meratiya, one of Meera's paternal descendants and a historian, suggests that it is wrongly conceived that Meera wandered unchaperoned, from one place to another, with a stringed instrument in her hand. According to Gopal Singh, being a daughter-in-law of Maharana Sangram Singh, she received the parganas of Pur and Mandal as a token to carry out her minor expenses. She never ran short of gemstones, jewellery or money. Accumulated cash and proceeds of the parganas enabled Bhagwati Meera Devi to donate money to saints, extend hospitality, and disburse salaries to her maids and servants. Whenever she went out on a pilgrimage, she was accompanied with a long trail of elephants, horses, chariots, vehicles, maids, and servants. She always exuded a royal splendour, being the Princess of Merta and daughter-in-law of the Ruler of Chittorgarh. It is, of course, another matter that she was a visionary and that she was aware of the connection of the soul with God. Gopal Singh further adds, unlike other queens, she would be more charitable on religious occasions and would interact with saints in their discourses on various religious matters[18].

In contrast to the opinions of neo-feminist critics, to a certain extent, Meera led an independent life. Common stories of injustice and oppression perpetrated on the saint-poet are far from the truth. She had a happy childhood and marital life. Although in Meera's poetry, she expressed dislike for some of her in-laws, she praised her father-in-law and husband. This is true that Meera suffered a great deal during the brief reigns of her brothers-in-law Ratan Singh (1528-1531) and Vikramaditya (1531-1536). Ratan Singh and Dhanabai, his mother, conspired to seize the throne; whereas, according to traditional history and folk legends, Vikramaditya was a frivolous, foolish and arrogant ruler, who could not gain much respect from the people of his kingdom[19]. After the demise of Vikramaditya, Meera's respect was restored in Mewar. In 1535, Bahadur Shah of Gujarat attacked Mewar, a fierce battle was fought, and eventually, the women inside the fort of Chittor had to commit *jauhar* when their husbands and male soldiers were defeated. They sacrificed themselves into a blazing fire, in order to protect their honour. The masses were convinced that this misery fell upon the kingdom, due to the harassment which Meera endured while living here. So, Rana Udai Singh sent Brahmins to Dwarka to get Meera back to Mewar[20]. Her fame kept spreading. It is believed that during the first half of the seventeenth century, the ruling King Maharana Jagat Singh had a dream in which Lord Jagannath himself appeared and commanded him to build his temple, since he had promised that Meera would return to Mewar.[21] In time, Maharana built a majestic temple of Lord Jagannath just outside his palace, which still stands as a famous Hindu temple located in today's Udaipur.

The deep, underlying tone of pain and sorrows in Meera's poetry were not mainly caused by any patriarchal injustice or oppression. It rather generated from a series of misfortunes that followed Meera. She lost many of her loved ones and had to wander from one place to another. She was married in 1516 and lost her husband Bhojraj by the year 1523. In 1527 the battle of Khanwa took place between Rana Sanga, ruler of Mewar and Babur, the founder of Mughal Empire, where Meera's father Ratan Singh and uncle Raimal died. Maharana Sanga, her father-in-law, died in 1528. After the death of Sanga, Meera's brother-in-law, Ratan Singh, inherited the throne. Meera increased her distance from Ratan Singh because he had conspired against Sanga. Ratan Singh was killed by the ruler of Bundi, Hada Surajmal. Then, Ratan Singh's younger brother Vikramaditya ascended the throne of Mewar, but he was an incompetent ruler. He also scorned Meera and made her life miserable in the palace. A crestfallen Meera went to Merta, where her uncle Rana Viramdev was ruling. But there too she did not have a peace of mind. In 1536 Maldev, the ruler of Jodhpur (Erstwhile Marwar) attacked Merta and destroyed the city. Viramdev had to leave his throne and travel from one place to another for many years. Meera accompanied Viramdev till Toda and then she left for Vrindavan and Dwarka. It is believed that in 1546, she died in Dwarka.[22]

The twentieth century saw the rise of mass media, popular literature, comics, films, TV series, cassettes and CDs. Initially, some effort was made to construct an image of Meera as an ideal, virtuous, docile woman representing Indian tradition and also reflecting the renaissance movement, where women had limited rights and mainly were expected to carry out the duties of a housewife. It also struck a chord with the Indian consumers especially those rooted in the middle-class. Publishing houses such as Gita Press: Gorakhpur and Amar Chitra Katha established Meera as a saint-poet and also an ideal Indian wife[23]. But, the new generations, who have been raised in a liberal, multi-cultural and economically progressive environment, have replaced the olden concept 'ideal wife' with a romantic, nonconformist and a fairly independent woman. Hence, the changing scenario and tastes resulted in the portrayal of Meera to be fiercely romantic who had defied the traditions of her time. A publisher of popular literature, Diamond Books, in its *Prem Deewani Meera* has presented her as middle-class, independent and somewhat unconventional woman[24]. Even in a film by Gulzar, it is clearly shown that Meera was an extraordinary devotee woman, languishing with love and desires for Lord Krishna, who went against the conventions of her time. In most popular music about Meera, her accepted image is that of a saintly, feminine, love-lorn woman. Meera who is widely popular in contemporary society has come a long way from the original Meera. These deviations are nothing new, they occurred ever since Meera came into existence. In fact, Meera still appears in folklores, devotional songs, historical accounts, religious narratives and critical discourses but now she is dwarfed, diminished and often divided.

Since we have meagre confirmed historical records depicting Meera's life, we rely on devotional texts and legends to know about Meera. However, there is a lot of information available about her kith and kin in *bahi-khata* and similar such systems. Muhnot Nainsi, a famous statistician, in his text *Marwar ra Pargana ri Vigat* includes the birth charts of Meera's father's elder brother Viramdev and his son Jaimal. Similarly, there are indisputable historical references regarding the birth and coronation of Meera's father-in-law Rana Sanga. The time and location of Meera's birth have been estimated using such references along with folklore and tales associated with her. It is believed that Meera was born around 1498 in Rajasthan as comprehended from the records of births, deaths and ascendancy of those belonging to the same period. Munshi Deviprasad, in his book *Meerabai ka Jivan Charitra* in 1898 mentions the dates of Meera's marriage and demise on the basis of available historical records; but he was unable to ascertain the time of Meera's birth owing to the lack of appropriate records to rely on[25]. In 1902, Thakur Chatur Singh, a paternal descendant of Meera and a historian of the Mertiya branch, in his book *Chaturkul Charitra* for the first time attributed Meera's birth to nearly Samvat 1555 (1498 AD)[26]. Har Bilas Sarda, an eminent academic, in the year 1918 in his monograph on Rana Sanga agreed with the information given in *Chaturkul Charitra* that 1498 is Meera's year of birth[27]; later, Gaurishankar Hirachand Ojha, Gopinath Sharma, and Hermann Goetz trusted the information given by Thakur Chatur Singh and Har Bilas Sarda[28]. To confirm this assumption, now we turn to written records of *Rani Manga Bhaton ki Bahi.* The copy of the original Bahi of Kehardan and Daudan was prepared in 1918. It has elaborate details of the Palaces of Marwar state from 906 to the reign of Jaswant Singh II (1838–1895). Though some of the details are inaccurate[29], most are credible. All of them confirm the event of Meera's birth to occur in Samvat 1555 (1498). In the *Rao Dudaji re Raniwasan ri Vigat*, it is mentioned :

Marajkunwar Ratan Singh ri beti Meerabai (kinchiyon ki dohti) hui, janam samvat 1555 savan ved brighuvar ro ne samat--1605 chait vad 3 ne Dwarka mein Ram kyo. Chittor re Rana Sanga re maraj kunwar Bhoj see ne parnai[30]

(Prince Ratan Singh is blessed with a daughter on Samvat

1555 (1498 AD) during the month of sawan on Thursday. And on Samvat-1605 chaitra vad 3 died in Dwarka. She was married to Prince Bhojraj, son of Rana Sanga of Chittor.)

Based on Rana Sanga's birth, some researchers have estimated the birth year of Meera's husband Bhojraj, and on the basis of that assumption, have tried to prove that Meera was born in 1504. According to them, if Meera was born in 1498, then Bhojraj must have been born in 1496. In this case, Maharana Sanga who was born in 1482 could not become the father of two sons in 1498[31]. It is of no use to argue over the exact date and time of Meera's birth because those *bahis* were prepared based on the memories of the queens. In most cases the Queen and others would link the dates with other major events that might have preceded or succeeded those years, thus the dates may vary by a few years. So, Meera's birth is considered to take place 'around' 1498, instead of exactly in 1498—which indicates that it may vary by a few years.

Accordingly, the rest of Meera's timeline is calculated including the dates and times of her marriage, demise etc. correlating them with important events of her life as well as of those around her. Using the birth charts of Viramdev and Jaimal from *Marwar ra Pargana ri Vigat*, it can be understood that Meera was born in 1498, as Viramdev was born in 1477 and Jaimal in 1507[32]. Meera's father Ratan Singh was younger to Viramdev therefore it is possible that his birth occurred earlier than 1477. Meera was elder to her cousin Jaimal so, the year of her birth could be around 1498. Meera's birthplace is mentioned in religious texts of that time which, however, do not contain the time period. Although Meera is regarded as the Princess of Merta, the place of her birth is believed to be the Kudki district of Pali. This confusion arose because Ratan Singh, Meera's father was bestowed with the fiefdom of twelve villages including Kurki, Bajoli and Chaukri. Munshi Deviprasad initially suggested that Chaukri was Meera's birthplace, but later, in consistency with Shyamaldas, Gaurishankar Hirachand Ojha and others he acknowledged Kurki to be her place of birth[33]. Even Harinarayan Purohit corresponded with the living descendants of Meera's family and he too considered Kurki as Meera's birthplace[34]. Later, Kalyan Singh Shekhawat claimed that Bajoli was her birthplace[35]. As mentioned earlier, Ratan Singh did have a fiefdom of twelve villages (Kurki, Bajoli, Noya, Ninvadi, Paladi, Akodia, Hakdhar, Nund, Pibhaniya, Motas, Dumdi and Sundri) but according to Udeibhan Champawat's *Rathoron ri khyat*, the estate was given to Ratan Singh in 1515[36], before which Meera was born in Merta.. Rao Duda (grandfather of Mira Bai) and Var Singh, his brother, laid the foundation of Merta. Later, Var Singh was poisoned and killed by Mallu Khan, the Governor *(subedaar)* of Ajmer. Var Singh's son Siha became the ruler of Merta. Since Siha was not a competent ruler, Satal, the ruler of Jodhpur, advanced against Merta to usurp the kingdom. Compelled by the crisis, Var Singh's widow and Siha's mother called Duda who was then in Bikaner, handing over Merta to him. Ambitious Duda killed Siha by strangling him while he was asleep. Siha's three sons (Jessu, Gaango, and Bhojo) made several attempts to reclaim Merta but as long as Duda was alive they could not succeed. After Viramdev came to power, they attacked Merta at the request of Maldev, the ruler of Jodhpur, but they were defeated. In 1555, their territories of Rayan and Kurki were annexed with Merta. Kurki was given to Ratan Singh[37]. It is possible that Meera spent her early years in Kurki, her father's territory. When Ratan Singh passed away, as he had no sons to inherit Kurki, it was given to Chanda, Viramdev's son, who was later subjugated by Maldev. This is why many devotional narratives refer to Merta as the birthplace of Meera. According to Nabhadas's *Bhaktamal Merte janam bhoomi, jhoomi hit nain lagey/pagey Giridhar lal , pita ki ke dhaam mein*[38]. In Raghavdas's *Bhaktamal* it is stated, *maat-pita janami pur merte, priti lagi hari peher mahin*[39]. In "Meerabai ki

Parchi" composed by Sukhsaran Merta has been recorded as the birthplace of Meera, *Meera janmi merte, bhagti karan kalukaal/ bina bajaya baji, mahlan sowan thaal.*[40]

2

There is hardly any perpetual consensus on Meera's paternal family and relatives. They often wandered from land to land in search of stability, territories, and power. Rao Duda, Meera's grandfather, was the courageous and ambitious son of Rao Jodha, the founder of Jodhpur. Rao Duda laid the foundation of a separate state, Merta but throughout his life, he struggled for power and sovereignty against the sons of Var Singh, his younger brother. Rao Jodha conferred on Duda and Var Singh the estate of Merta which used to be a desolate and forested territory. The brothers turned it into a prosperous, flourishing kingdom and in 1461 laid the foundation stone of a fort. Despite being a sibling, Var Singh was always apprehensive of Rao Duda's grit and ambitions, so he gave him a separate estate of Rayan. Discontented Duda left and went to Bika at Janglu (Bikaner)[41]. In Janglu, he accompanied Bika on several campaigns. He defeated Sarang, who was his uncle's killer[42]. He also attacked Mallu Khan, the Governor of Ajmer, who had abducted women from Teej (a religious fair) at Pipad and defeated him. During this campaign, he lost his brother Satal[43]. On the other hand, Var Singh's rule over Merta proved to be a challenging task. Mallu Khan deceitfully captured Var Singh and poisoned him[44]. Var Singh's son Siha came to the throne but he was utterly incompetent.

Meanwhile, Rao Suja, the ruler of Jodhpur, took advantage of the situation and made his mind to occupy Merta. Siha's mother was far-sighted enough to assess the situation, consult other kingdoms and jagirdars and she finally invited Rao Duda in Merta to take charge of the state affairs. Siha was so inebriated and inept as a ruler that Duda caught him off guard, got him tied to his bed and sent him off to Rayan[45]. Thus, after a long struggle in 1495, Rao Duda finally became the undisputed ruler of Merta[46]. After a successful reign, he died in 1515. He was not only a gallant ruler but also a religious man. He was an ardent devotee of Charbhuja (an incarnation of Vishnu) whom he built a temple of, in Merta. He had a liberal, inclusive nature. Due to his efforts, many peasants, traders and artisans from other states came and settled in Merta[47]. He had great regards for saints and devotees, which is perhaps the reason why many forms of Bhakti movement grew under his patronage and protection. It is also believed that he was a devoted Vaishnav. According to Thakur Chatur Singh, Rao Duda is regarded as a great Vaishnav and a firm devotee. In his capital city Merta, he constructed a huge temple of Charbhuja. Mertiya Rathores, his descendants, immensely revered the deity of the temple[48].

No clear proofs are available on Meera's mother and father—most inferences have been made based on folk narratives and Meera's poetry. However, some information regarding her father is available in *Muraridan Ki Khyat.* Among Rao Duda's five sons, Meera's father was the fourth. He was elder to Panchayan, and younger to Viramdev, Raimal and Raisal[49]. Duda's successor Rao Viramdev ascended the throne in 1515 after which he banished Bhoja, the grandson of his uncle Var Singh, and the son of Siha, from Kurki due to his despicable behaviour. Then Viramdev bestowed the estate of Kurki and twelve other villages upon his younger brother Ratan Singh. Ratan Singh was a fierce warrior; he attacked Sodawat Akha Panwar of Pisangan and killed him[50]. It is mentioned in *Marwar ra Pargana ri Vigat* that Ratan Singh gave Ratna, a misan charan, the village of Ratnavaas[51]. In 1527, Ratan Singh died in the battle of Khanwa which took place between Maharana Sanga and Babur. In this battle, Viramdev along with his younger brothers Ratan Singh and Raimal fought on the side of Rana Sanga. Viramdev was injured while Raimal and Ratan Singh breathed their last. There is no authentic evidence regarding Meera's mother. According to some scholars including Harinarayan Purohit, Veer Kunwari, Meera's mother was a daughter of Jhala Rajput, Surtan Singh of Gogunda in Mewar[52]. Another notion is also often held—Meera was born to Kusum Kunwar, the daughter of Kelan Singh Tak[53]. There are no reliable sources to confirm these two theories. The first theory may be correct because matrimonial alliances of Rathores and Sisodias took place with the Jhalas who hailed from Halvad state of Kathiawar, Gujarat. Maharana Raimal of Mewar married Ratan Kunwar, the daughter of Raj Singh, the ruler of Halvad. In 1506, due to a family feud, Ratan Kunwar's brothers Ajja-Sajja came to Mewar. They were bequeathed upon the estates of Gogunda, Delwara, Sadri among others[54]. Whether Ratan Singh's marriage into the Jhala clan was before or after Jhalas entered Mewar is uncertain. So far, most scholars agree with Munshi Deviprasad that Meera lost her mother during her childhood and Rao Duda brought her to Merta from Kurki—to raise her. According to recently discovered sources, Meera was born in Merta and according to the commentary provided on Nabhadas ji's *Bhaktamal*, Meera's mother was alive till Meera's marriage. It is clearly stated in the commentary :

Puchey maat-pita pat aabhran
lijiye ju, lochan bharat neer kaha kaam daam main

(The mother and the father told her to take anything along—clothes, jewellery etc., but not to be sad; with her eyes filled with tears, she said she needs nothing).[55]

Meera shared a close relationship with Viramdev, her uncle. After the demise of Rao Duda, Viramdev had ascended the throne in 1515. He married Gorjaya Devi, the sister of Rana Sanga[56]. He gave the estate of Kurki to Ratan Singh after seizing it from Bhoja, Siha's son. Viramdev, being a valiant warrior, never yielded to Maldev, the ruler of Jodhpur and throughout his life he struggled to keep his hold on Merta. Meera took shelter in Merta after her return from Mewar. Meera mentions him in her poetry as *babosa* (elder father). In 1527, along with his brothers he fought in the battle of Khanwa and was badly injured during the battle[57]. Viramdev died in 1544. Following the demise of Viramdev, Jaimal, Meera's younger brother ascended the throne. Like Meera he too was a great Krishna devotee. In *Bhaktamal*, it is said that he held other devotees in high esteem. It is believed that he was so devoted that he would climb a ladder to arrange for God's sleep, embellishments, etc. and then would remove the ladder. One day his wife sneaked in and found that God was sleeping[58]. Raghavdas' *Bhaktamal* too describes Jaimal's love for devotees[59]. Meera had a good relationship also with him because both were brought up together and both were great devotees. Many believe that Meera had given him a boon that he would never be defeated and his family would multiply. *(Bahut badhey tero parivaar: nahi hoy kajiya mein haar)*[60].

Like his father, Jaimal, too was a celebrated warrior. As his enmity grew with Maldev, he intuitively left Merta and he was given the fiefdom of Badnor in Mewar. He died in the battle that took place between Maharana Udai Singh and Akbar in 1567. To honour his extraordinary valour, Akbar erected a huge statue of him with Phatta on elephant outside the fort of Agra[61]. Jaimal too, after coming to power, tried to bring Meera, his cousin, back from Dwarka to Mewar[62]. According to Harinarayan Purohit, Gopal, an elder brother of Meera was born but he could not survive, after which her parents made a vow at Meeran Sahib's Shrine and Meera was born[63]. In Sukhsaran's "Meerabai ki Parchi" there is a mention of Anoopan, Meera's sister.[64]

3

Meera's childhood was happily spent in a huge and prosperous family. Rao Duda, her grandfather, faced a lot of uncertainty in the early phase of his life. Due to rivalry with Var Singh, his brother, he could not enjoy supremacy over Merta, as the result, he left Merta and went to Bikaner in search of a safe haven. But, again in 1495 he took over and ruled Merta until his demise. This was the period of Meera's birth and early childhood. Meera's father was the fourth among his five brothers. Viramdev, the eldest, had thirteen sons and three daughters[65]. Meera had a happy childhood. Except for the internal conflicts among Var Singh's sons, there was no reason for uncertainty or unrest in Merta. Meera might have been showered with great love and affection from her uncles and her grandfather. Rao Duda was a devotee of Charbhuja Krishna, an incarnation of Vishnu. It was a tradition of Rathores to worship Lord Dwarkadheesh Krishna. Siha, the first one among Rathores went on a pilgrimage to Dwarka and while returning he stopped at Pali. From there, his descendants first took over Mandore and later laid the foundation of Jodhpur[66]. The impact of Vaishnav worship in Duda's family was very profound in the successive generations. Viramdev and after him Jaimal were devoted Vaishnavites. Meera too had inherited her paternal lineage as Kaanthidhari Vaishnavites. *(pihariara log bhalero bandhey kanthi mala).* Meera had inherited her devotion to Krishna through her paternal ancestry. It is an incorrect assumption that before marriage Meera was so intensely devoted to Krishna worship. Had it been so, Rana Sanga would never choose her as a wife for his successor. Rana Sanga was not only the ruler of the largest territory of northern India. He was a clever diplomat and a valiant warrior. He could judge others' character well and this was perhaps due to the unfavourable conditions he met in life[67]. Could he have thought of choosing Meera, a bizarre and frantic match, always immersed in devotion for the future ruler of Mewar at the time when the kingdom was rife with inner conflicts, conspiracies and intrigues?

Along with Jaimal, Meera was educated under the supervision of Rao Duda, who was a great warrior himself. Her education had turned her into a fairly liberated and self-reliant woman. She might as well have the knowledge of politics, customs and ideas of her time. Keeping in view all this, Sanga might have decided to take her as his daughter-in-law[68]. During the medieval period, there was a tradition of informal education of girls belonging to feudal families. Brahmins used to teach them ethics, and religion through scriptures and discourses. The teachings were not entirely based on dogmatic religious scriptures alone. Necessary changes were made from time to time, according to the needs of the common people, and orthodox texts were simplified through forms of discourses, folk songs, bhajans and vrat-kathas. Those were some ways through which girls of aristocratic families were educated. Meera too was educated by Gajadhar, a Gurjar-Gaur branch of Brahmins. In her poetry, Meera describes the relationship between God and devotees, based on those popular religious discourses. Gajadhar also accompanied Meera to Chittor after her marriage. Meera honoured him, by conferring him with the title of *vyas* and also donated him two thousand bighas (a measure of land) land from her fiefdom of Pur and Mandal which she had received to meet her expenses[69]. Bhakti (devotion) in Meera was unfathomably deep ever since she was a child. There are several folk narratives available on the same. Legend has it that Meera, as a little girl, was once fascinated on seeing a well-embellished bridegroom in a wedding procession, she asked her mother or grandmother who would be her bridegroom. In order to satisfy her curiosity, she was told that Lord Krishna would be her bridegroom. She accepted this as a permanent truth of her life and chose Lord Krishna, in her mind, to be her husband[70]. Another folk narrative tells us, once Meera saw an ascetic with a small idol of Kishna, and she wanted to have the idol. The ascetic refused to give it to her, and went away. Meera was so sad that she stopped eating. Later, Lord Krishna himself appeared in the ascetic's dream and directed him to give the idol to Meera, so he understood his mistake and went to give it to Meera. After that Meera accepted

Lord Krishna as her groom and she adored him. There is yet another folk narrative regarding Meera's childhood, surprisingly it is similar to Andal, a female saint–devotee from the Alvaar sect. Once, Rao Duda, Meera's grandfather, assigned her the responsibility to perform rites and rituals during his absence. Accordingly, Meera offered food to the god, requested him to have it and drew a curtain before him. But when she lifted the curtain, the food was untouched, she kept requesting for two days. It was still intact. She was so upset that she decided to end her life. Finally, the god had the food. When Rao Duda returned he was overwhelmed by the miracle. Due to this incident in her childhood Meera's devotion became known to all.[71]

4

Meera was married to Bhojraj, the son of Rana Sanga, a brave and mighty ruler of Mewar. Most historians, by using pieces of circumstantial evidence, believe that it would have happened around 1516.[72] This marriage too was like any other conventional marriage of the feudal lords, but due to several political upheavals and internal conflicts, this marriage too had many ups and downs. After a long struggle with his brothers, Rana Sanga ascended the throne in 1509. He was the ruler of the largest state of Northern India in his time. He had twenty-eight queens and seven sons—Bhojraj, Karni Singh, Ratan Singh, Vikram Singh, Udai Singh, Parbat Singh and Krishan Singh.[73] Bhojraj was born to Solanki Raimal's daughter, Kunwar Bai, the queen of Sanga[74]. Bhojraj died at the time when Maharana Sanga, his father, was alive. Authentic records depicting Bhojraj's death are not available, but according to Gaurishankar Hirachand Ojha and many scholars, a few years after Meera's marriage (believed to be in between 1518-1523) Maharana Sanga was on a campaign to Gujarat or Malwa, where Bhojraj accompanied him. He breathed his last during this campaign[75]. Bhojraj never ascended the throne hence there are no detailed and authentic references regarding him, but according to *Jaimal Vansh Prakash*, he was a brave yet calm man[76]. Meera's marriage strengthened the relationship between Mewar and Merta. In fact, Sisodias of Mewar had a long history of matrimonial alliances with Rathores. Also when Rao Duda laid the foundation of Merta, this tradition continued and it enhanced the alliance between Mewar and Merta. Merta vigorously involved itself in all campaigns of Mewar.

Hansabai, daughter of Rao Chunda of Marwar was married to Maharana Lakha of Mewar. Following this marriage, the relationship between Mewar and Marwar brought a substantial change in the course of history. Rao Duda's sister who happened to be Rao Jodha's daughter—Shringar Devi, was married to Maharana Raimal of Mewar. Maharana Sanga, Meera's father-in-law was married to Dhanabai, daughter of Bagha, who was the son of Rao Suja of Marwar. Similarly, Viramdev, Meera's uncle was married to Gorjaya Kunwari, sister of Maharana Sanga[77]. Meera's marriage with Rana Sanga's eldest son thus was a continuation of this age-old tradition. Therefore it would not be correct to assume that Meera's marriage was solemnised only to strengthen diplomatic relations. It is also possible that Viramdev's wife who also was Rana Sanga's sister, Gorjaya Devi, Bhojraj's aunt, was like a mother to Meera. She might have had an instrumental role in the matrimony of Meera and Bhojraj.

The initial years of Meera's marriage were more or less pleasant except for some occasional conflicts and doubts. Her relationship with her husband was a traditional one. The expressions of antipathy towards 'Rana' in Meera's poetry was not about Bhojraj. Bhojraj could never ascend the throne and within Rana Sanga's lifetime, he died, so she did not refer to Bhojraj using the term 'Rana' in her poetry. 'Rana', which she used as a noun, refers to Vikramaditya (1531-1536) Meera's brother-in-law, who also happened to be an incompetent ruler. Historians have accepted this as a fact. Shyamaldas has added in a footnote in *Vir Vinod* that Meera endured the period of Vikramaditya and Udai Singh and it is revealed in her poetry that Maharana beleaguered her[78]. Gaurishankar Hirachand Ojha is also of the same opinion, that after the death of Maharana Sanga, Ratan Singh ascended the throne and he too died in Vikram Samvat 1588 (i.e. 1531 AD). Next, Vikramaditya ascended the throne of Mewar.

Meera had already gained admiration of the masses because of her religious poetry and absolute devotion. Vikramaditya was jealous and he started harassing her in a number of ways. It is widely believed that he even made a futile attempt to poison her[79]. Even during the short reign of Ratan Singh (1528-1531) before Vikramaditya, Meera did not have a happy time. Although Ratan Singh was a cousin to Rathores, it might just not be right to presume that he had a soft corner for Meera[80]. Ratan Singh and his mother Dhanabai, had feelings of resentment against Viramdev, therefore it is obvious that their relationship with Meera was not at all congenial. As mentioned earlier, Dhanabai was the daughter of Bagha, son of Rao Suja of Jodhpur[81], and she harboured the ambition of seeing her son as the ruler of Mewar. In her ambition, she was supported by the Rathores of Jodhpur. Despite the lack of historical records on the death of Bhojraj, many believe that he lost his life during Rana Sanga's campaigns against Sultanates of Malwa, Gujarat or during his fight with Ibrahim Lodi, Sultan of Delhi. After Bhojraj's death, Ratan Singh, being the eldest, ascended the throne. However, Sanga distrusted Rathores as they made an attempt to usurp Mewar during Lakha's regime. He was more inclined towards Vikramaditya and Udai Singh, the sons of Karmeti, sister of Hada Surajmal, who also happened to be a confidante of Rana Sanga and Samant of Bundi. Karmeti was also Sanga's favourite queen.

Although Maharana Sanga reigned one of strongest territories in Northern India of his time, his constant encounters with the Sultans of Malwa, Gujarat and Delhi left him drained and debilitated. In his battle against Lodi dynasty's Ibrahim Khan Lodi, he lost his left arm and was crippled due to an arrow piercing through his knee[82]. Incessant battles exhausted him. In order to avert an attack by Muzaffar Shah of Gujarat, he signed a treaty with him and gave one of his sons in his custody as a guarantee[83]. Since he was so much occupied with military campaigns and stayed away from the inner quarters of his palace, disputes arose over succession. Dhanabai, along with her supporters from Jodhpur tried to have Ratan Singh replace Sanga on the throne. Upon sensing the mounting tension, Sanga gathered his feudal lords and directed them to elect their new king. Although conspiracies against him were rising, Viramdev of Merta, Ratan Singh of Salumbar, Surajmal of Bundi and Prithviraj of Amer rejected the proposal for a new king. Viramdev and other feudal lords again joined Sanga and proclaimed him their king[84]. Sanga was a clever diplomat and a statesman. Often he was surrounded by adversaries, thus he was accustomed to dealing with them. He declared Ratan Singh his successor for the sake of balancing the power, but he weakened their antagonistic group from within, and tried to secure the future of Vikramaditya and Udai Singh. Before another conspiracy could rise, he sent Vikramaditya and Udai Singh along with their mother (Karmeti) to their maternal uncle Surajmal to keep them safe. Surajmal also was very brave and happened to be his confidante against the vile ambitions of Ratan Singh[85] He also gave his bejewelled crown which he had received as a gift from the Sultan of Malwa to Karmeti along with a waist-band made of gold.[86] Viramdev played an important role in strewing this plot for which he had to repay greatly. He was already not on good terms with Maldev of Jodhpur, as a result, Merta was attacked. Meera too had to bear the brunt of all this. Ratan Singh and Dhanabai, his mother, might have pestered her. However, these incidents during Sanga's life have not been assessed in an unbiased manner; Karmeti and Surajmal have been portrayed as villains, whereas Dhanabai herself just wanted her own son to ascend the throne; in this endeavour, as mentioned earlier, she had a support from the Rathores of Jodhpur. Munshi Deviprasad is of the view that, Meerabai witnessed the strange upheavals in the environment of her times. She had three brothers-in-law—Ratan Singh, Vikramaditya and Udai Singh. Ratan Singh ascended the throne of his father in kartik sudi 5 samvat 1584 (1527 AD), and in the fort of Ranthambore, Vikramaditya, declared himself as an independent ruler to have power over the district. The rift between them widened so much that one day a lawyer from one side would be sent to Babur's court and on the next day another lawyer from the other side would approach him and both would propose to offer Babur the fort of Ranthambore and he would support both of them.[87]

Although the repeated references of 'Rana' in Meera's poetry have been often attributed to her husband Bhojraj and it is assumed that their relationship was bitter and tense, it was actually not true. Bhojraj was a heroic, peaceful man of great nature and there are no reliable sources available depicting their conjugal conflicts. However, it has been mentioned in an episode of *Bhaktamal*, that Meera's relationship with her in-laws was tense and uneasy. After her marriage, Meera's mother-in-law insisted on her performing a ritualistic worship of a goddess, their ancestral tutelary deity, which Meera declined since her sole deity was Krishna and she would not worship the goddess.[88] This incident gave rise to several speculations. Some people believed that in Mewar there was a tradition of Shaiv worship and Ekling ji was the sole deity of the rulers, whereas Meera, belonging to the tradition of Vaishnavas, was a Krishna devotee and would not worship the goddess. It is also to be noted that Shaiva and Vaishnava both were classical forms of worship, and had not much distinct features in the day-to-day religious affairs of people of that time. Shiv and Vishnu both gods were revered equally. It is not justifiable to claim that in Mewar, only Shaiv devotion was prevalent. In Mewar, there was an old tradition of worship of Lord Vishnu after worshipping Lord Shiva, therefore Vaishnav worship had a deeper and broader significance in the masses.[89] It also may seem that Priyadas has exaggerated this episode while reconstructing it. During the medieval period some Vaishnav proponents, to establish their supremacy over others, used to oppose Shaiva and Shakta traditions vehemently. Priyadas was from the Chaitanya Gaudiya sect so he might have laid importance on his own rituals of worship.

After her marriage, Meera had a fairly comfortable and normal life. Some believe that Meera, hailing from a smaller territory, born of a lesser known man, might have felt a little uneasy in the inner-quarters (raniwas) of the palaces, as Bhojraj was the eldest son of Maharana Sanga, the ruler of the largest northern territory of that time[90]. However, this assumption is baseless. It is a fact that Mewar was a glorious, time-honoured state of suave values and culture, but in no way, Merta had any less honour or importance. As mentioned earlier, Rao Duda, its founder was the son of Rao Jodha of Jodhpur, a kingdom that already had a camaraderie with Mewar. There was a long history of matrimonial alliances between Mewar and Merta. There had been a continuous flow of daughters from each side to the other for marriages of rulers and their feudal lords. Before Meera arrived in Mewar, there is a possibility that several daughters of the feudal lords from Merta had already been present in the palaces. Lives, customs and traditions in the homes of Mewar, Marwar and Merta were quite similar to each other. The heir was known as *paatvi* which accorded the person a greater significance. The feudal lords and vassals would consider him of having 'big-feet' (higher status) and would respect and obey his orders. Apart from this, there were not many differences in their life or standards of living. Meera's marriage too was a traditional one; before her, many girls had entered Mewar palaces and had become part of the in-laws' clans, and many had left Mewar, and assimilated into Meera's clan too. Besides experiencing usual pangs of separation from her paternal relatives, the post-wedding experience was nothing unusual or novel for Meera. Having said that, she might also have suffered due to jealousies or conflicts that were common within the walls of the palaces in those days.[91] Maharana Sanga was a powerful ruler but he came into power after a long series of conflicts and battles. The struggle continued among his sons even while he was on the throne of Mewar.

The intrigues and jealousies that had existed within the inner-quarters were shortly revealed and the queens played an important role in the conflicts over the inheritance of the throne. Maharana Sanga had twenty-eight queens, he had seven sons and four daughters.[92] After his eldest son Bhojraj passed away, Rana Sanga was reluctant to pass on his throne to his next eldest son Ratan Singh, son of Dhanabai, who hailed from Rathore lineage of Jodhpur. Karmetan and Lakhu, were his other two queens who also were grand-daughters of the neighbouring Bhanda, the king of Bundi, and daughters of Narbad.[93] Karmeti, was ambitious and was also supported by Hada Surajmal, her brother. She was Sanga's favourite. She manipulated and usurped the domain of Ranthambore, for her sons Vikramaditya and Udai Singh which was against the wishes of Ratan Singh. She also conspired against Sanga in order to bring her sons to power. As a result, even the inner-quarters of Mewar were divided into two groups. After Sanga's death, his son Ratan Singh became the ruler. Apart from Dhanabai there were several other Rathore women in the palace, so they might have supported Ratan Singh's ascendency. On the other hand, under the leadership of Karmeti, other Hada Queens might have preferred Vikramaditya. Vikramaditya was a nephew of the Hadas, and unfortunately, he was foolish and arrogant.[94] Meera might have chosen to distance herself from all this, because of her firm loyalty to Rana Sanga. In Meera's poetry, one can find unfavourable remarks on Ratan Singh and Vikramaditya. Their reasons for their disapproval of Meera might vary, still, both of them heckled her as much as they could.

After marriage, Meera was not completely unsocial or cloistered. She was social and economically self-reliant. Provisions for her financial stability had already been made. Among feudal families, sufficient *stree dhan* or wealth was given to the bride by her relatives at the time of her marriage. Meera too had received sufficient *stree dhan* from her parents. Most feudal lords ensured economic self-sufficiency of their wives and daughters. They were given estates. Management, income and expenditure were independently controlled by their operatives. Feudal lords never interfered in such economic affairs. Maharana Sanga had made ample arrangements for monetary security of his daughter-in-law, after her marriage. Meera was bequeathed with the estates of Pur and Mandal of Mewar to carry out her expenses. There is a mention of it in the Khyat of Gurjar Gaur Brahmin and in the shloka *(Shri Chitrakoot Murlidhar naam murtivarayasanam dwijrai Goyadharai/ Pradati Menan patyu sqwaysarthkaama tasyanvyakaljana prathamo hi Vyas)*. Two thousand bighas of irrigated land along with the rank of *vyas* was accorded to Pandit Gajadhar by Meera. It said that their descendants still have the land.[95] From the accumulated wealth and revenues collected from her properties, Meera generously rewarded saints and devotees, paid salaries of her operatives, paid for her own pilgrimages etc. She did not depend on anyone for her day-to-day expenses. These provisions for economic self-reliance of aristocratic women were seen as traditional rights that cannot be taken away or reversed. If anyone did not follow it, the subordinate communities would raise questions and it would mean dishonour for the family. There might have been some disruptions in the flow of income from Meera's lands, during the reign of Vikramaditya, otherwise this never invited any troubles. It is believed that Meera had set up a granary in Dwarka, based on her income from the estate, which even sustained till Udai Singh's reign and even later.[96]

5

Meera's life as a widow was quite eventful and filled with grief and sorrows. Between 1523 and 1540, the security of both the kingdoms—Mewar and Merta were robbed of vitality due to repeated internal conflicts, fights for succession and assaults of invading forces. During the initial years of Meera's widowhood, security was never a major issue. During 1518-1523, the atmosphere of the inner-quarters of the palace was toxic. As stated earlier, Sanga's palaces housed a legion of twenty-eight queens, paswans, daughters-in-law, and daughters. Due to Sanga's prolonged absence from the palaces, the competitions in the inner quarters intensified. Dhanabai, who hailed from Jodhpur, a big and powerful state, wanted her son Ratan Singh to succeed Rana Sanga (after Bhojraj's death), while on the other hand, Hada Rani Karmeti too was trying to raise her son Vikramaditya to power with the connivance of her brother Surajmal. Against the wishes of Ratan Singh, Karmeti was successful in convincing Rana Sanga to give her the estate of Ranthambore under the guardianship of Surajmal for her sons. So, hate, envy and intense rivalries ran deep in the inner quarters of palaces. In all this Meera, due to her indifference towards political power and supremacy, might have suffered, as she was caught amid the fierce rivalry between Dhanabai and Karmeti. Both parties might have criticised Meera, for being alienated from the power play, and their attitude towards Meera was anything but favourable.[97] Since she declined to be a *sati*, a section of the inner quarters might have also despised her.

The practice of *sati* was not mandatory and more or less it was voluntary.[98] Dhanabai might have seen Meera as an impediment in her ambition to see Ratan Singh as the ruler because Meerabai's family had constantly supported Maharana Sanga. No woman of Maharanas had committed *sati* since the reigns of Hammir to Rana Sanga, the only exception being the death of Prithviraj, Sanga's elder brother, when sixteen women committed *sati*.[99] It seems even Meera was insisted on committing *sati*. References in Meera's poetry and underlying religious accounts suggest this to be true. Meera says : *Bhajan karsyan sati na hosyan man mohyo ghannami.*[100] (Will sing devotional songs and will not commit *sati* since my mind is immersed in God's name). This reference also occurs in Nagaridas's *Pad Prasang Mala*. It says :

Yeh jag prasidh hi so kitnek din Upraant kahoo samay rana ke va bhai ko dehant bhyo, aru rana hutey so Meerabai dukh paye rahey hi hai, ye vaishnavini ko Sat Sang karite yatei va samay rana ne kahee, jo yeg awsar hai, tum bharta ke sang Sati hou. Tab Meera agey lagiy hai, tyohui lagey rahey ya samay kuch bhed mani nahi, aru ya baat ke uttar to ek vishnu pad nyo banay rana ko likh pathayo. Pad bahut prasidh bhyo so veh yeh pad :

Meera ke rang lagyo hari ko, ab aur rang atak pari,
Girdhar gasyan, sati na hosyan man mohyo dhan nani
jith bahu ko nato nahin rana ji, hun sewag yeh syami
churo dobro tilak ju mala, seel barat sringaar.
Aur sringaar bhavey nahin ranaji, yun gur gyan hamar.
Koi nindo, koi bindo, gun gobindra gasyan.
Jin marg ve sant pahuton, tin marag meh jasyan,
Chori karan na jeev satasyan, Kain karsi mahro koi
Hasti chari gadhey na chara, ya to baat na hoi
Raj kartan narak padesi, bhogila jam ke liya
Bhagat kartan mukt pahuntan, jog kartan jiya
Girdhar dhani, kudumbo girdhar, maat pita, sut, bhai
thaen therey, meh mihvey ho ranaji, you kahey Meera bai[101]

(It is a popular belief that when Rana's brother passed

away, he sent a message to Meera, while she was busy interacting with Vaishnava saints, that she should commit *sati* following her husband's death. Meera opposed him, writing a Vaishnav verse in response. The verse became popular.

Meera is drenched in colours of the Lord and no other shade affects her.

She would sing in his praise and will not commit *sati*.

Because her mind is occupied with Lord's name.

Relations like 'brother-in-law' and 'daughter-in-law' are meaningless, as now she serves Krishna.

She has renounced all sorts of ornaments,

That has been professed by her teacher...

The path on which saints go, she too would follow,

She would never commit any theft nor inflict sufferings on any living being.

It is of no use, who mounts elephants or who mounts donkeys, issuing diktats will lead to hell it only breeds indulgence.

Worship alone leads to deliverance,

Renunciation leads to life,

Girdhar alone is my husband, family, parents, and brother too, He is neither yours nor mine, this is what Meerabai has to say.)

Meera's refusal to commit *sati* might have invited a lot of scorn when Ratan Singh, her brother-in-law died, and three among four of his wives—Renukunwar, Sankhla, Ratnakunwar and Hada Kunwarabai performed the ritual of *sati*[102]. As the result of the growing censure and hatred, Meera was further isolated and took refuge in devotion. Despite the feelings of loneliness and alienation during the reign of Maharana Sanga, Meera was not insecure but after his demise, complications in Meera's life had increased manifold. Due to potential hindrance in Dhanabai's ambitions and Meera defying the custom of *sati*, the suppressed anger, and condemnation against her grew around her. With the death of Ratan Singh and Surajmal, it further worsened the doubts, tension and hostility in the inner quarters of the palaces. In 1531, Ratan Singh was assassinated without leaving any sons as successors. Vikramaditya came to the throne but he was incompetent and foolish. He patronized seven-thousand wrestlers and body-builders. He began to ignore, insult and neglect the feudal lords, and chieftains, as a result, they receded to their respective feudal areas and joined hands with his enemies. This led to anarchy in the state with spreading doubts, hostility and distrust everywhere[103], Vikramaditya and his mother already disliked and resented Meera. The resentment kept growing because she was solely interested in devotional songs, interacting with saints and ascetics, and all this was against their family conduct and customs. Vikramaditya imposed several restrictions on Meera. His attempt to poison her has been mentioned in Meera's poetry many times, and it has been substantiated through various religious texts and folk narratives. Meera in her verses records: *Pyala rana ji bhejyo, dyo Meeran na va jaay. Kar charnamrit Meeran pee gayi, koi aap jano reghunaath.*[104] (Rana sent a bowl of poison, so that Meera dies. Meera, drank it like a divine nectar and left the rest to the Lord) In another verse she says : *Visra pyaala Ranaji.... dojyo Meeran re haath Kar charanamrit pee gayi Meera bheju ju reghunaath.*[105] (Rana offered a bowl of poison to Meera, she drank it like a divine nectar, while singing devotional songs in the praise of her Lord).

Several attempts were made to assassinate Meera. It was mentioned in Nabhadas ji's *Bhaktamal* and Sukhsaran's "Meerabai ki Parchi". It is stated in *Bhaktamal, Drushtani dosh vichari, Mrityo Ko udhyam kiyo/baar na banka bhyo, garai amrit jiyon piyo*[106] (The evil-minded conspired to kill her. Nothing happened to her. She drank the poison as a divine nectar). In "Meerabai ki Parchi", there is a mention of Dayaram, the caretaker of the temple who was directed by Vikramaditya to offer Meera a bowl of poison.[107] Numerous attempts to poison Meera have been remembered through folk memories for centuries. It is also believed that Vikramaditya ordered a person from Vijayvargia, a merchant (Vaishya-Baniya) community to poison Meera. The merchant, in turn, included two Brahmins from Gurjar Gaur and Dahima communities in this conspiracy. Many have abhorred these three conspirators and this episode has been widely believed to be true. It is remembered as: *Bija bargi baniyoo, diyo gujardaud, teejo meley jo dahimo karey tapro chor.*[108] (A Vijayvargiya, along with Gurjar gaur, Dahima among Brahmins—is a deadly combination because they can make a house crumble). Meera was intrepid, she never shied away from criticizing Vikramaditya for his foolishness and crude behaviour. She openly confronted him.[109] The feudal lords were not fond of Vikramaditya and it had already been revealed to the masses that he was an incompetent, weak ruler. So, Meera received a lot of support. Some narratives spread—expressing anger against Vikramaditya's disapproval of Meera and glorifying Meera's courageous resistance. Now, let us see what brought Vikramaditya to the throne.

Meera's life as a widow was gravely affected by a series of tragic events in Mewar and Merta involving endless invasions from external forces, internal feuds, and deaths of her loved ones. As mentioned earlier, a fierce battle was fought between Maharana Sanga and Babur at Khanwa, Maharana Sanga's defeat in the battle of Khanwa was a conclusive one and this laid the foundation of Mughal rule in northern India. This incident led to a rapid growth of conspiracies and intrigues in Mewar-Merta regions. Rao Viramdev's army had taken part in the battle and he was badly injured. Ratan Singh (Meera's father) and his brother Raimal died.[110] More tragedies were about to follow. An injured, crestfallen Maharana Sanga was poisoned to death by his own feudal lords[111]. Meera was indeed shattered by the death of her father and father-in-law.

Even before Maharana Sanga's death, struggles for

succession had been brewing at home, after Sanga's death—they came to a boil. Rana Ratan Singh II ascended the throne after his father Sanga's death. At the same time, Karmeti requested Babur, to help her son ascend the throne.[112] Ratan Singh was worried about Karmeti's plans, which she hatched with her brother Rao Surajmal. In an attempt to get rid of Rao Surajmal, Ratan Singh tried to kill him during a hunting expedition, but they both ended up killing each other.[113] Ratan Singh had no heir, so, Vikramaditya Singh (his surviving brother) was crowned as the ruler of the Mewar kingdom. His relationship with Meera was sour, he pestered her often. Moreover, his crude temperament and incompetence led to unrest in the state. In 1532, Sultan Bahadur Shah of Gujarat took advantage of this situation and attacked Mewar. At the culmination of his first campaign against Mewar, Bahadur Shah signed a treaty and returned, but then again he attacked in 1535. Mewar was not ready for a battle as the discontented nobles did not want to support Vikramaditya in his fight, and retreated to their respective fiefdoms while some of them even joined hands with the enemy himself—Bahadur Shah, to defeat Vikramaditya. The attack was brutal, many feudal lords lost their lives and Karmeti, along with many elite/royal ladies committed *jauhar*. This battle is also known as 'war of second shaka'.[114] It is believed that during these attacks, Meera was in Merta. Had she been in Mewar, she too would have committed *jauhar*. The relentless hostility that she faced within the palace in Mewar might have compelled her to leave the kingdom before the second attack of Bahadur Shah. Her poetry clearly reflects that she requested Viramdev to call her to Merta. She says, *Mahra babosa se keyjyo, mahney vega leva ave*.[115] (Go and inform my babosa [her father's elder brother] that he should come to fetch me). According to Thakur Chatur Singh "In Vikram Samvat 1589, during Vikramaditya's rule, she suffered a lot for one or two years. Around this period, Rao Viramdev ji and Prince Jaimal ji called the princess (Meera) to Merta considering her plight, or else, when Viramdev Ji came to Chittor to fight against Bahadur Shah, he might have taken her with him".[116]

Meera, being tired of hostilities from her brothers-in-law Ratan Singh and Vikramaditya, returned to Viramdev, who was like a father to her, in her paternal home, but there too, she found no rest or peace; invasions by external forces and internal conflicts were inescapable. Maldev, the eldest son of Rao Ganga of Jodhpur (erstwhile Marwar) and Viramdev had not been on good terms, which only got worse over time. To Viramdev, dignity and sovereignty were of utmost importance, so he could not subjugate to the authority of Maldev. During Sanga's lifetime, he had prevented Dhanabai, and her Rathore allies from crowning Ratan Singh. As a result, in 1536, Maldev, a scion of the Rathore clan himself, annexed Merta, following which, Viramdev had to wander powerless for many years. Meera too, after being so unceremoniously uprooted, travelled with her family members from one place to another. They went to Ajmer, where he was confronted by Sahsa Rathore of Riyan, the descendant of Var Singh. In the battle, he lost his brother Raisal. Maldev once again attacked him in Ajmer, he escaped to Didwana, Jet and Kumpa, Maldev's forces did not let him stay in those regions peacefully either. Viramdev kept moving on—from Chatsu, Lalsot, Toda, Banawali, Malarava to Ranthambore and eventually reached Agra to meet Sher Shah Suri, the founder of the Suri Empire. In 1543, Sher Shah Suri defeated Maldev in the Battle of Giri-Sumel and Viramdev again became the ruler of Merta.[117] Meanwhile, Meera had moved on and travelled to Vrindavan and then Dwarka. Her poetry suggests that Viramdev had accompanied her till Toda. In one of her lesser-known verses, it is recorded: *Jaan na di ji yarre kurne re ja Meeran Todare base motee hoi.*[118] (It is a known fact that Meera grew in Toda). Hukum Singh Bhati, in *Yashodhar Charitra* suggests that Meera might have lived in Toda with Viramdev until Maldev occupied Toda in 1538.[119]

Meera was not a saffron-clad holy woman with a halo, or an ascetic as she appears to be in popular literature and modern media. She went on pilgrimages and long journeys in far-off places, on her way she used to mingle and interact with saints and ascetics but she never adopted their attire or looks. According to Thakur Chatur Singh, a historian and paternal descendant of Meera, "A monarch of great valour, Maharana Sangram Singh, was the ruler of a territory generating ten crores in annual income *(Tuzk-e-Babri)* therefore being his daughter-in-law (Meera) should have had a huge wealth including cash, jewellery and property. From her accumulated wealth and income from the estates [parganas], Bhagwati Meera met all her expenditures including alms, hospitality of sages and holy men, salaries to the servants and other workers, and also her pilgrimages. She never embarked on any journey singing and holding veena in her hand, unlike her image as perceived by several scholars of the medieval period and of recent times. Whenever she went on a pilgrimage, she was accompanied by her royal retinue that included brave servants, Kshatriyas, caretakers, a large number of men and women, elephants, horses, chariots and similar such vehicles etc. aligned with her grand status of being a princess of Merta and wife of the eldest son of the owner of the largest territory (Bhupaal), of Chittor."[120] Tracing back her historical lineage, it does not seem that Meera assumed the attire of an ascetic. Ramkaran Asopa, a historian, published a coloured portrait of Meera in *Madhuri*. It was drawn from the palaces of Jodhpur and perhaps was taken during the reign of either Udai Singh (who had the sobriquet Mota Raja) or Sur Singh in the Marwar kingdom. The portrait [Meera's] is a beautiful one in royal robes.[121] In Nabhadas ji's *Bhaktamal* and Priyadas ji's commentary (tika) along with another seventeenth century manuscript is preserved in Rajasthan Prachya Vidya Pratishthan, Udaipur. A vintage portrait of Meera is available in that manuscript as well. Here she does not appear to be in ascetic robes, but she is sporting traditional attire and ornaments.[122]

For centuries, it has been a common belief that Raidas was her spiritual mentor. The same is also recorded in her poetry. The cenotaph near the Kumbha Shyam temple in Chittorgarh is believed to be dedicated to Meera's saintly Guru Raidas. Shobhalal Shastri's Sanskrit script of 1932 also concurs:

Shir Nand nandanam-pada-mbhurahsya bhringi Meeran hare nirlaya muchhmim chakar/ya syaa gritao lasti mandipaka tarastham/ tsya gurushcharnam pankaj-yum-chinham. (Meerabai, the ardent dear devotee of nand nandanam [Krishna] got a huge Vishnuji temple constructed in front of which there is a cenotaph preserving spiritual mentor's footprints).[123]

There have been a lot of speculations on Meera's relationship with Raidas. Mahendra Bhanawat, a folk art scholar, has travelled to various places associated with the folk memory of Meera. According to him, it is a common belief that Raidas hailed from Piploda village in Jodhpur and he belonged to one of the so-called 'untouchable' communities. He was possibly illiterate, yet had immense spiritual knowledge. Meera left Chittor with him and travelled a great deal before finally reaching Dwarka. In Dakor, she proclaimed that he had been her mentor. It is also a common belief that Raidas was not only her spiritual mentor, but also her scholarly Guru. He supported her, gave her moral sustenance in her pursuits and accompanied her till the very end.[124] In western Rajasthan, Meera's harjas (devotional hymns) that have been sung for centuries, suggest that Raidas was her mentor.[125] Similar folk narratives, which still linger in Gujarat, indicate that Raidas had settled in Sarsai village near Girnar and Meera too was present there.[126] Her verses indicate that she accepted Raidas as her Guru. She says, *Khojat phirun bhed va ghar ko, koi na karat bakhani Raidas sant miley mohi satguru, dinih surt sehdani mero man lagyo hariji su, aban rahungi atki Guru milay Raidasji, mahne dini gyan ki gutki.*[127]

(Searching for a secret and a home, no one educates me,
Ever since I met Raidas
My heart is immersed in God [Hariji],
Now I won't deviate,
I have found Raidas—my Guru,
Who made me realize the ultimate truth).

Here is another example with similar indication: *nahi main peehar sasrey, nahi piyaji ri ka saath Meera ne Govind milaya ji, guru milaya Raidas.*[128]

(I am neither with my parents or in-laws, nor with husband;
Meera has met Govinda, and accepted Raidas as her Guru).

Raidas was Ramananda's (the 14th-century legendary Vaishnava poet-saint) disciple and a contemporary of the mystic saint-poet Kabir. According to his followers (Raidas-panthis) he lived between 1376 and 1506.[129] As noted in *Bhaktamal*, a Jhali Queen of Chittorgarh, the capital of Mewar, went to Kashi to meet him.[130] The name of the queen was not mentioned there but Hermann Goetz and some other scholars suggested that she was Ratan Kanwar, who hailed from Jhala Rajput clan of Halvad in Kathiawar, Gujarat who was married to Raimal (1473-1509), Maharana Sanga's father, the Rajput ruler of Mewar. Her devotion might have been born out of her family traditions in Saurashtra, the peninsular region of today's Gujarat, which was at that time a Bhakti movement hub; the vicinity where Narsinh Mehta, the Bhakti poet-saint and similar others were active those days. Having carried forward this tradition of faith and devotion, Meera might have received some support from the Jhali queen while she lived in the inner-quarters of the palaces of Mewar.[131] The Jhali queen also invited Raidas to Chittor, and it was Chittor where he breathed his last. Raidas was revered and respected far and wide. Surprisingly, even those who opposed the monopoly of brahmins in socio-religious spheres, spread the message that Raidas, in his previous birth had been a brahmin pandit himself and in the present one, he was born a saint-devotee. According to some, he had non-vegetarian food in his previous birth, which is why Raidas was born in a lowly caste. There are also other additions to this tale. Once Chittorgarh's brahmins refused to sit and eat with Raidas and asked him to prove that he had been a Brahmin in his previous birth. To prove the same, he ripped off his skin to show his holy thread (*janeu*, which is donned by Brahmins).[132]

Nonetheless, some scholars say that Raidas had already passed away even before Meera was born, so, she could not be his disciple.[133] Since Meera was from the ruling class and was much revered by the masses, adherents of Raidas (Raidas panthis) with other sects might have had a twinge of envy for her and they possibly have made up this story to exalt his greatness further. Still, the relationship between Raidas and Meera has been eternalized through the folk memory and devotional songs, especially in northern India, so it cannot be completely denied that Meera might have known Raidas in some way or the other. Raidas might have belonged to an earlier period, still, most scholars are not yet sure about the exact time period of Raidas.[134] In devotional texts or oral tales, no authentic details regarding his birth and death have been found. Also, there are no trusted records that prove Meera had a formal consecration of their guru-disciple relationship. Saints and devotees in general, were adored and venerated by a large population during the medieval Bhakti movement. Mystic saint-poets also had a great influence on common life with their simple words. Saint-devotees in this movement did not necessarily belong to superior castes. There was a rising inclination towards embracing diverse devotees with equal respect and all obstacles, and setbacks previously faced by different classes were slowly disappearing. In the Mewar-Marwar regions of Rajasthan, there were quite a few similar saint-devotees who enjoyed great respect and acceptance among the common people as well as in the elites.[135] The Jhali Queen herself was probably consecrated by Raidas, which reveals that saint-devotees from different classes were not a taboo.

Perhaps, Meera, after being encouraged by Ratan Kanwar, the Jhali Queen, also regarded Raidas as her saintly Guru. However, many legends were woven around their special relationships and many verses acknowledge it.

Uda Bai, Meera's sister-in-law, has been mentioned in her verses, in the form of dialogues. Uda Bai asks Meera to renounce the path of devotion and satsang. She suggests that Meera should behave in a stately, respectable manner, and should not disregard the traditions and customs in her family. Meera firmly refuses and says that her only faith rests in the path of devotion. Uda Bai argues that what she is doing is not permissible in royal families, and it has also displeased Rana. Meera further replies that she has entirely submitted herself to Lord Krishna. Family honour or societal acceptance are of little importance to her, irrespective of its consequences.[136] However, no reliable records are available to substantiate this event. In Badva Devidan's khyat, Uda Bai has not been mentioned among other daughters of Rana Sanga. On the basis of the khyat, the modern historians Shyamaldas and Gaurishankar Hirachand Ojha regard Kanwara bai, Gangabai, Padambai and Rajbai as four daughters of Rana Sanga.[137] There is also a possibility that this verse was not a composition of Meera herself, but was created by the common people, to match their own understanding of the hostility Meera faced in the palace, and how her in-laws tried to dominate her spirit and determination. However, like other lores, there might be some elements of truth in the verses. Uda Bai possibly was a powerful real figure to have earned a mention in the popular verses, and she probably left no stone unturned to deviate Meera from her path of devotion. Existing texts offer some hints that she might be Meera's sister-in-law.

As stated by Jagdish Singh Gehlot, the historian, "When Rao Surajmal of Idar's son Rao Raimal left the throne threatened by Bhim, his uncle, and sought refuge under Rana Sanga. Rana offered Uda Bai, his daughter's hand to Raimal for marriage.

Bhim was succeeded by his son Bharmal. Raimal defeated Bharmal in Vikram Samvat 1571 with the support of Rana Sanga and reclaimed the throne. Rao Raimal of Idar's wife was Uda, who was Meera's sister-in-law."[138] This statement is partly supported by Shyamaldas and Gaurishankar Hirachand Ojha. According to Shyamaldas, "Rao Raimal married the daughter of Maharana Sangram Singh-I of Chittor."[139] Ojha too has noted, "Rao Bhan of Idar had two sons—Suryamal and Bhim. After his death, Suryamal inherited the throne but he, too, lost his life after ruling only for eighteen months. Suryamal's son Raimal was to inherit the throne, but he was too young, so his uncle usurped the throne. Raimal was protected by Maharana Sanga. Maharana Sanga sanctioned his daughter's engagement with him. After a while, Bhim died and his son Bharmal came to the throne. Raimal was still very young. He regained Idar with the help of Maharana Sanga."[140] Uda Bai's link with Idargarh is also manifest in Meera's verses. Once, Uda Bai chastises Meera for bringing dishonour to their family and says, *Bhabi Meeran kul ne lagai gaal, Idargarh te ayaa olma*[141] (Meera, Sister-in-law, has been a disgrace to the family honour, complaints have poured from Idar too.) In Sukhsaran's "Meerabai ki Parchi" as well, Uda Bai is said to be Meera's sister-in-law. It is also noted there that she was a widow. In one of the popular narratives, Meera's mother-in-law says that *devi* (goddess) blesses women by giving a long life to their husbands, and Meera raises a question, if this is true, why is Uda a widow? *(Swaagh bhag Devi ke sarey, to kyun Uda vidhwa gharan tumhare)*[142]

6

Meera spent the last phase of her life in Vrindavan and Dwarka. Before going to Vrindavan, Meera went on a pilgrimage to Pushkar—which reflects several times in her poetry.[143] She was possibly compelled to leave her homeland and go on pilgrimages, as Merta and Mewar—both kingdoms were going through a challenging time. However, in that period, widows from the royal families often chose to go on pilgrimages, utilizing the revenue generated by their respective estates. Mewar had comfortable *havelis* (rest houses)[144] located at its most frequented pilgrim centres; during their visits women would give out alms, carry out restoration of temples and construction of water reservoirs *(bawarees)*[145] In those days Vrindavan was the heart of Krishna devotion because many established sects of Krishna devotees were active there; and the places where Meera lived were not very far from Vrindavan, therefore she must have reached there as well. Her fond memories of Vrindavan had been expressed in the devotional narratives about Meera as well as in her own poetry. She says, *Vrindavan n nij dhaam dekhyo ri Vrindavan nij dhaam/ shri jamuna jyonke nikat vehat hai sum vidh puran kaam.*[146] (I have seen the splendour of Vrindavan, the place of pilgrimage, the river Yamuna flows near it, it fulfilled all my desires). Meera's stay in Vrindavan is also acknowledged in religious texts that recount her meeting with Jiva Goswami, the Gaudiya Vaishnava scholar and legendary saint of Vedānta tradition. Meera is believed to have broken his vow of never being in a woman's presence.[147] This incident might be real, because it is cited by Priyadas, closely associated with Jiva Goswami and also with Chaitanya Gaur sect; as well as Nagaridas of Vallabh sect.[148] Since Meera belonged to a powerful family and was revered by many, different established Krishna devotee sects of Braj Mandal (regions of Braj) claimed Meera's association with their respective sects. The followers of the Vallabh sect were in touch with Meera. Jiva Goswami was one among the six prominent scholarly disciples of Chaitanya Mahaprabhu and he resided in Vrindavan. It is said that Chaitanya Mahaprabhu had visited Vrindavan around the year 1516[149]. His devotion was tender, yet ardent, grounded in ecstatic love and reverence for the Lord. He was charismatic enough to carry anybody off their feet.[150] As Mewar and Merta waded in a state of constant crises, Meera's love for Krishna grew deeper, penetrating with stronger roots in her heart. Her faith might have taken her to Jiva Goswami. Priyadas and others have narrated this incident with some variations. After being dethroned, without having any stable, secure roof over their head, Viramdev and Meera had been wandering helplessly, till they reached Vrindavan, in search of peace and comfort, but sadly, there was none. Despite being geographically separate from Mewar, Vrindavan was not disconnected from it. Agra was a vital political domain, which was quite close to Vrindavan and information regarding Meera's activities in Vrindavan was conveyed to Mewar quite easily. Toxic power struggle had already reached new highs in Mewar. Vikramaditya's attitude towards her had no improvement.

In 1536, Vanvir Singh, a Paswan son of Prithviraj (Rana Sanga's elder brother) decided to kill Vikramaditya. He also wanted to kill his younger brother Udai Singh II—he somehow escaped the murderous clutches of his uncle and ran away to Kumbhalgarh.[151] Meera's devout association with saints, her unshakable love for Lord Krishna, and her different way of life would have infuriated both—Vikramaditya and Vanvir. Each of them wanted to uproot Meera from Vrindavan—which is clear in many devotional narratives. In Priyadas's commentary, we can see, *Rana ki malin mati dekhi basi dwaravati.*[152] (Rana's cruelties compelled her to move to Dwarka). Many people agree with this notion as it is recalled in many harjas, in one of them, she says: *Amba pakya, Kalhar kairi, nimbora mahney des/ Udaipur ra rana kin vidh choryo des, mevari rana kan par chodyo des.* (Mangoes might've ripened; unripe mangoes too have appeared, my place has cultivated lemons. Rana of Udaipur! Only you have not realized why I left my homeland).[153]

Meera spent the last few years of her life in Dwarka and Bet Dwarka, Gujarat. She was occupied with *bhajan-kirtan* (songs of prayers), religious congregations and similar devotional activities.

This has been commonly accepted in most traditional narratives and available records. Due to its simplicity, inclusiveness, and its philosophy of non-discriminating love and devotion, Bhakti movement was accepted with great respect extensively in Gujarat. Narsi Mehta, Isardas and several other saints had considerable influence on royals, nobles, as well as the common people. Places like Girnar, Junagadh and Dakor etc., flourished into eminent devotional hubs. Saints from different regions started gravitating towards those places. It is said that Raidas, Meera's Guru also had settled in a village called Sarsai near Girnar.[154]

There are a few reasons that are attributed to Meera's coming to Dwarka. First, by this time, the Bhakti movement was already popular in Gujarat. Then, she was also safe here because this region was ruled by one of the clans from the descendants of Rathores, from her paternal ancestry—Wadhel (Wadher). Last but not least, Dwarka was known to be the abode of her sole deity Krishna.[155] It is said that Meera first travelled to Junagadh in Saurashtra. From Junagadh she shifted to Sarsai, Somnath, Gorakhmani, Madhavpur, Gerh, Sudamapuri, Porbandar and then, via Niyadi reached Arambhara. Shiva Sanga was then the Wadhel ruler, who was a descendant of Rathore Veravalji Beejal, who in thirteenth century, had migrated from Marwar and occupied a small territory in the desert of Kutch, near river Vedmati. They settled in the northern Dwarka on the banks of a bay in Arambhada and established their rule.[156] Shiva Sanga himself was a Krishna devotee. Naturally, Meera stayed in Arambhada for quite a while.[157] Then she went to Bet Dwarka, where she got a temple constructed; as revealed first by Lt. Col. Tod in *Travels in Western India.* In 1822, Tod left Udaipur to go back to England. He travelled through Abu, Sidhpur and Patan etc. and then reached Dwarka. While describing Bet Dwarka, he wrote that the temple which proved to be the centre of attraction for him had been constructed by Lakha's queen, the famous Meerabai who belonged to his land, Mewar.

It is a temple of Gopal Devta of Saursen, in which He is the lover of nine, his original form, and that Rajput queen (Meera), was his greatest devotee.[158] This mention must be based on his research which he carried out while he was in Mewar. When he personally went there, looked at the physical temple and marvelled at its beauty, his conviction was further strengthened. The temple's history has been uncovered using some authentic records of Bet and also some age-old folk narratives. In *Introduction to Dwarka/ (Dwarka Parichay)* which was grounded on various archaeological and historical sources, it is mentioned that "Meerabai reached Arambhara, it was ruled by Shiva Sanga, a Vaadher King. Like Meerabai he too was a devotee of Ranchhod (Krishna) and belonged to Meera's paternal lineage. Meera stayed in Arambhada for a long time. She inspired him to get Dwarkadheesh temple built in Bet."[159] It is likely to be true. As mentioned earlier, women of noble, royal families helped build temples and water reservoirs at distant places of pilgrimage and also contributed a lot in their restoration. It is also believed that in Chittor, Meera got a Krishna temple built next to the Kumbha Swamy temple. In *Udaipur-Chittaur Patnaam* there is an account of the construction of a temple supported by Meera and expenditure incurred on it.[160]; It is also believed that Meera restored a temple at Dwarka that had been completely destroyed. As noted by Hermann Goetz, the present temple of Dwarka was built by Gopal Nayak Tambekar during the eighteenth century. Meera reached Dwarka in 1537, when the main Krishna temple was in ruins, and it was possibly rebuilt by her support. The original one, rebuilt by her, was comparatively smaller than the present one.[161] Besides restoring the temple, she also built a food area (a store room) to feed devotees and pilgrims. After Meera's death Maharana Udai Singh along with his family went on a pilgrimage to Dwarka. He was accompanied with Surjanji Hada who built another granary similar to the one that Meera had built.[162]

During the autumn of her life, Meera had immersed herself in devotional activities in Gujarat. She is also counted with Narsi Mehta—to be two major fifteenth-century Gujarati poets of devotional literature. Meera belonged to Rajasthan as well as to Gujarat; many of her verses are composed in Gujarati. It may seem surprising now. Before the colonial era, Rajasthan and Gujarat were not very different from each other culturally or linguistically. The colonial rules drew bolder lines between the linguistic identities of distinct states of northern India, otherwise, the languages and dialects were better interwoven and exchanges were quite common earlier.[163] Gujrati and Marwari (Rajasthani) were fairly similar but for some regional inclinations. According to Krishanlal M. Jhaveri, an early scholar and expert of Gujarati literature, modern Gujrati has two dialects—Kutchi and Marwari. Gujarati has a blend of Marwari and Brajbhasha (a dialect spoken in the area of Mathura, Vrindavan, Agra and Bharatpur) and it is understood by the Marwari-speaking people in most part of the region.[164] Therefore, Meera composing poetry in Gujarati is nothing unusual.

Although there are no authentic historical records that there were conscious efforts to bring Meera back to Mewar, there is a series of popular narratives, religious biographies and secondary evidence that support this fact. After Vanvir's rule declined, the kingdom was gradually recovering from the lawlessness and dissatisfaction. On the other side, following a long struggle in Merta, Viramdev finally took the throne, and after him, his son Rao Jaimal inherited it. Jaimal and Meera—the cousins were on good terms. Simultaneously, The fall of Mewar was seen as the effect of afflictions thrown on Meera after she was compelled to leave her homeland. People in the kingdom had a firm belief that a curse fell on them, as Meera had to leave home, move to Vrindavan and then to Dwarka. Consequently, Udai Singh and Jaimal tried to reinstate Meera back in the palace. They had sent a few nobles and Brahmins to Dwarka for the same reason. However, Meera refused to return to Mewar-Merta.[165] Her followers believed this incident to be true and disseminated the same information with slight alterations. First, this was recorded in a commentary in Priyadas ji's *Bhaktamal*. It is mentioned that Rana, upon realizing Meera's pure, pristine nature of devotion was ashamed of all the wrongdoings on Meera. He asked some Brahmins to request her to return. The Brahmins conveyed Rana's plea and sat in a protest at her threshold when she was refusing to return. Then she went inside Ranchhod's (Krishna's) temple and merged into the statue. The Brahmins searched for Meera everywhere but they could not find her.[166] This episode is also noted in Nagaridas's *Pad Prasang Mala*. Nagaridas records it this way:

So ya bhaanti manorath karat yeh pad gavat Dwarka pahunche, tahan koi din rahe ta pache Meeranbai ke sung prohit adik je rana ke lok hain, tin kahyo ab bahut din bhaye hain, ab des ko chalon, rana ki agya hai, aisey dwe, teen din to kahyo, phir Meerabai par dharna kiyo, tab Meerabai thakur ranchodji au vida habey to naam le mandir mein akeley hi jaye maharti sahit hi nayo pad baney gaiyo so veh yeh pad

Hari harahu jan ki peer,
Draupadi ki laaj raakhi, tum badhayo cheer,
Bhakti kaaran roop narsingh, dharyo aap sareer
Harinakashyap maari lino, dhryo nahin dheer
Budhte gaj grah taryo, kiyo bahir neer daasi
Meera lal giridhar, dukh jahan tahan peer.

So yeh pad gayen hun utte na dharey, tab maha arti prema ves sahit ek aur pad banayo gaayo, tabhi thakur aap mein unko yahii shareer tey leen kri leen dehu narahi, so ja pad gayen leen bhaye, so woh pad hai,

Sajan jiyon sudhi jaaney juyon leejay
Tum bin mere na aur koi kripa rawri kijey
Deyos na bhookh, raen nahi nidra, yeh tan pal, pal cheejey
Meera prabhu, giridhar nagar ab mili bichuran nahi keejey.[167]

(In this way with a cherished purpose, and songs, Brahmins

and Rana's men reached Dwarka. They informed her that it had been too long, requested her to return, and also said that Rana had himself commanded them to accompany Meera to home. They kept pleading for two to three days, then they sat in protest; Meerabai went inside the temple of Ranchodji to seek His permission. She sang a new verse :

O lord, take away all malaises,

You saved Draupadi from dishonour by blessing her with a long robe,

Devotion has made you appear as Narasimha avatar, in a corporeal form,

[You] Killed [the demon] Hiranyakashyap, with patience.

Ward off evils, comfort the King.

O Giridhar [Krishna]! I am a humble servant, at your feet,

Only you can cure all worries with your grace.

After the verse, she again sang another verse, then Thakur Ji allowed her body to amalgamate with Him, while she was immersed in her prayers. The verse is:

O My Beloved! recognise me.

Except you none shall confer their grace upon me.

No hunger during the day, sleepless nights or weakened body.

Meera, at your feet. If we meet, may we never depart.)[167]

It is still unclear how and when Meera passed away. Many devotees firmly believe that inside the temple of Dwarka, Meera disappeared while being absorbed in her prayers. Munshi Deviprasad and Gaurishankar Ojha have found in a speech of a panegyrist of Bhurdan from the village Lunvey of Merta, that Meera breathed her last in 1546[168] while according to Har Bilas Sarda, Meera died in Dwarka in the year 1549.[169] According to Mertiya Rathores and Kalyan Singh Shekhawat's *bahi* based on other available information, 1547 was the year of Meera's demise[170] whereas according to Kehardan and Daudan's *Rani*

Manga Bhaton ki Bahi she died in 1548. In the *bahi* it is recorded that *in samat 1605 Chait Vad 3 ne Dwarka mein ramkiyo.*[171] This is the period when Meera's disappearance is believed to have occurred. This information was circulated in Mewar-Merta by the Brahmins who had previously pleaded to get her back, with some variations in the dates and years of the event. According to literary and historical sources of Gujarat, it can be inferred that Meera was nearly thirty years of age when she reached Saurashtra. In 1540, Jadejas dynasty of Kutch arrived there, founded the town of Jamnagar and they also built a Jagat-temple in 1560 on the insistence of Isardas, a charan devotee in Dwarka. At that time Meera's age was sixty and she was in Bet Dwarka.[172]

Meera possibly accepted *jal samadhi* (buried herself in water), or she went along and lived on her own—these are some theories that arise from the shroud of her mysterious disappearance. In Dwarka and Saurashtra, she was regarded as the saint-devotee from Mewar who had renounced her aristocratic power and comforts to seek refuge in Lord. Back in that time, saint-devotees were believed to possess miraculous, supernatural attributes. They were considered to be different from the common people and ordinary events of their life such as birth, death, marriage etc. were publicized as extraordinary events. Since Meera was accepted as a saint-devotee, the event of her death might have been exaggerated to make it more extraordinary. It is also possible that certain people didn't want Meera to be associated with *brahma-hatya* or the sin of killing brahmins, as the lives of the Brahmins might be in peril being part of a strict protest to bring her back. So, they popularized the image of her having entered into the temple of Ranchhod to seek His consent and there, she became one with the idol. As a result, some of her robes were left behind.[173] Even today while adorning the idol of Dwarkadheesh, a robe is always left hanging, which carries the same symbolic significance.

According to some Gujarati sources, Meera too, like Jaidev, Vallabhacharya and Isardas entered jalsamadhi.[174]

7

Although this was a popular belief that Meera assimilated herself in the statue of Ranchhod Ji (Krishna), scholars suggest that she possibly died due to some mishaps, severe illness or by entering jal-samadhi. However, most of her devotees still regard this event as a heavenly miracle. Since this possibly happened around 1546, the tales of Meera's meeting with Akbar, Man Singh, Tulsidas, Tansen and Birbal are considered to be imaginative, non-historical and based on sheer folklore[175]. However, certain researchers are of a contrasting opinion that Meera did not pass away in 1546. Age-old sources indicate that Meera died at the age of sixty-five or sixty-seven, so, if she was born in 1498, her death might have occurred around 1563-1565. Some believe that the story of Meera's immersion into the statue was created by the Brahmins of Mewar, in an attempt to conceal their failure in convincing Meera to return. Hermann Goetz, who chronicled the major events of Meera's life, believes that Meera had escaped from Dwarka. According to Goetz, following her disappearance from Dwarka, Meera might have gone on pilgrimages in the southern and eastern parts of India and might have lived there. However, this claim is neither validated by history, nor recognized by common people, or traditional tales.

Meera's presence can be traced back to the court of Raja Ram Chandra Baghela (1555-1592) of Bandhavgarh (Rewa) in northern India. It was also believed that after her short stay at Bandhavgarh, she went to Amer and Mathura, moreover, during this period she met Tansen, Tulsidas, Akbar, Man Singh and Birbal.[176] Although this notion is very easy to reject as a concocted story, just in case, had Meera's death not taken place in 1546 and had she been alive during 1563-1565, this would not have gone against the events and background of that time. Hermann Goetz is of view that, all these public narratives, as they are, utterly foolish but if accepted, in comparison with historical perspective, they seem to concur.[177]

The reasons behind Meera going on long pilgrimages were obvious. She never wanted to return to Mewar. She still felt that the atmosphere in Mewar was not conducive to her path of devotion. Meanwhile, most feudal lords had accepted Udai Singh II as their ruler but his claim on Mewar was still not free and uninterrupted. His actual status had been nothing more than one of the feudal lords of Sher Shah Suri. After defeating Maldev in 1543 in Ajmer, Suri turned towards Chittor, Udai Singh, to prevent further damage and loss of power, offered him the keys to the fort and signed a treaty. Sher Shah came to Chittor and returned without a fight, but he left a representative behind.[178] Udai Singh's competence as a ruler is debatable, for example, according to Gaurishankar Ojha he was too indulgent and lacked courage.[179]

Meera's passion for the Bhakti movement might have ignited her longing for travelling to southern India, moreover, her interactions during her pilgrimages with other saint-devotees had sparked her curiosity about that region. Ramananda, Raidas's mentor, was from the south India; both Chaitanya and Vallabhacharya had travelled to the South. Perhaps, Meera concluded her long journey via Puri and Nadia at Bandhavgarh, the abode of Raja Ramchandra Baghela. In 523 or 626, one Ramchandra Baghela from Gujarat laid the foundation of this dynasty. He was from the lineage of Vyaghra Dev.[180] His court was a haven for saint-devotees, artists and poets of the medieval period. He appreciated art and poetry. Even Kabir is believed to have travelled to Bandhavgarh. In the forest reserve of Bandhavgarh, there is still a temple that was built in honour of Kabir. Vitthalnath, the son of Vallabhacharya, while returning to Jagannath Puri stayed here.[181] Among the folks of

Mewar-Marwar, there was a hearsay regarding Meera's stay with Baghela, which is also reflected in her verses. In a verse, Uda, Meera's sister-in-law asks Rana to find out from the Baghelas if Meera of Merta is alive or dead *(Ranaji ra Waghela the liyo ne miran ji ri khabar, mueeki jivey miran mertee).*[182] Perhaps this was the period when Meera met Tansen. Till 1560, Tansen was in the court of Ramchandra Baghela, later Akbar took him to his court. Mahesh Das, popularly known as Birbal, was also in the court of Ramchandra Baghela, so there is nothing extraordinary in considering that Meera could have come into contact with him too. Chitrakoot, which was devoted to Ram worship, was not very far from Bandhavgarh, and was known for exquisite beauty and brilliance. Tulsidas (1532-1623) lived in Chitrakoot.[183] Meera could have met him there. Tulsidas, who was quite young during that time, was not yet renowned. After her short stay at Bandhavgarh, Meera might have moved to Amber and Mathura; at Amber she possibly came in touch with Man Singh, the adopted son of the king Bhagwant Das of Amber.[184] Man Singh and Birbal both were favoured by young Akbar, therefore, it wouldn't be surprising if she met Akbar (1542-1605) through them. Akbar, during his early phase, had started visiting Hindu mystic saint-devotees.[185]

Meera's familiarity with the rulers of Amber is nothing surprising. Rajput rulers of that time were rather liberal and progressive. Their policies and ideas were similar to those of Meera. Bharmal, the King of Amber, had attended the crowning ceremony of Akbar and young Akbar was impressed by this action.[186] Later in 1562, he set matrimonial alliance with Akbar by offering Harkhabai, his daughter's hand to Akbar for marriage.[187] Akbar conferred the title of Mariam-uz-Zamani on his Hindu-Rajput queen. Besides working together with Akbar, the Kings of Amber also played a vital role in the formation of Akbar's policies for Rajputs. They were also impressed by the reformist, new-age ideas of the rising Bhakti movement. They constructed temples of Ramdevji, Govind Dev Ji and Radhavallabh in Braj, Govardhan and Vrindavan; by tradition, they were all Krishna devotees.[188] Prithiviraj, father of Bharmal, was a disciple of Krishnadas Payhari and a loyal Krishna devotee. His name has been mentioned in *Bhaktamal* as well[189]; Prithviraj supported Rana Sanga in the battle of Khanwa against Babur; Bala Bai, a Rathore queen of Prithviraj, like Meera, was a Krishna devotee[190]; Also Man Singh, might have been influenced by Meera to a great extent. In 1568, Akbar attacked Chittor, along with Bhagwant Das and Man Singh on his side. This attack was very destructive, but Man Singh safely carried the idol of Giridhar ji (Krishna) that Meera used to worship. Later, Bhagwant Das and Man Singh constructed a magnificent temple of Jagat Shiromani in Amber and established the same statue of Giridhar ji there.[191] In Vrindavan as well, Man Singh constructed a great temple of Govind Dev Ji, that flaunts a fusion of Mughal and Indian architecture. It is obvious that Meera had an association with Man Singh.

It is said that Vrindavan was covered with forests. In about 1516, after the rise of Chaitanya Mahaprabhu, this area was developed. In this region, Chaitanya discovered several places mentioned in Bhagavad Purana. After staying there for a while, Chaitanya Mahabrabhu returned, but later he sent his two disciples—Rupa and Sanatana. After some time, Rupa Goswami's nephew—Jiva Goswami and Sri Chaitanya Mahaprabhu's disciples—Gopal Bhatt, Raghunathdas and Raghunath Bhatt also went there. The six disciples of Chaitanya recovered several idols of Krishna from Vrindavan. Owing to the fear of Muslim invaders, they hid them in some houses, or possibly buried them. Govind Dev Ji's idol was excavated from Goma mount in Vrindavan. Rupa Goswami died in 1563. In 1590, Man Singh placed the same idol in the temple of Govind Dev Ji in Vrindavan.[192] Perhaps, Jiva Goswami was a member of Rupa Goswami's family. It is possible that he might have met Meera and also was amazed at her. Although Meera was no more at the time when the idol was set up there, maybe, due to Man Singh's familiarity with Meera, he might have started admiring Jiva Goswami and Rupa Goswami. Nothing is known regarding Meera's influence on Akbar but it is highly possible that he was charmed by those who had come into her (Meera's) contact. Some say that Harkha Bai, Akbar's first and the foremost Hindu queen, also known as Mariam-uz-Zamani, was Meera's follower[193]. It must be noted that this queen had a profound influence on the Mughal ruler's policy and ties with Hindus and Rajput kings. It is worth mentioning that right from the start, Akbar had open and affable policies towards other rulers, Hindus and Rajputs. In 1562, when he was twenty years of age, he abolished the practice of enslaving prisoners of war. In 1563, he abolished the pilgrimage tax imposed on Hindus by former Muslim rulers. Furthermore, he abolished the notorious *jizya* tax against non-Muslims in 1564. He even started wearing garments like Hindus and expressed his disapproval of non-vegetarianism. Muslim historians of that time, had recorded it as an influence of Hindu princesses in young Akbar's harem.[194] After Meera's death (1563-1565) once again, conservative Ulemas started exercising their influence on Akbar.

8

Meera was a simple feudal woman, but the unique circumstances and events during her lifetime made her journey of life extraordinary. As pointed out earlier, power thirst, constant fights, invasions and insecurities that she had faced, gave her several turning points in her life. To recapitulate her whole life once again, we must remember that around 1498 Meera was born, although it is not possible to make exact, irrefutable calculations of the date and time of this event. Those are based on the folk memory and inferential records—so they cannot be categorically agreed upon by one and all. According to newly discovered sources it is somewhat certain that she was born in Merta. It is also confirmed by devotional narratives as well as popular recollections. Ratan Singh, Meera's father was a gallant warrior; after Meera's birth he got the *jaagir* (estate) of twelve villages along with Kurki. Her mother belonged to the Jhala clan. Her mother's existence has not been proven by historical records, still, according to folk narratives and popular verses, she had been alive at the time of Meera's marriage. Viramdev, who was a father-figure to Meera, showered her with great love and affection; he also happened to be Rao Duda's successor. Meera had a happy childhood; she was brought up in a prosperous joint-family. During the medieval period, informal education was imparted by the Brahmins for developing life skills and learning customs in the feudal families, Meera was educated in the same way. Krishna devotion was a tradition in her family, thus she too had inherited the same nature, as claimed by several folk narratives. Duda, Meera's grandfather was an eminent diplomat, a great politician and a valiant warrior of his time. He might have raised Meera as a confident, self-reliant woman, well-prepared for contributing to the socio-political relations of Mewar, Marwar and Merta. Raidas was not a formal mentor of Meera, neither was she consecrated by him, but she might have nurtured great faith in Raidas—as suggested by many folk narratives. Meera was married to Bhojraj, the eldest son of Maharana Sanga around the year 1516. It was not a benefit-seeking diplomatic matrimonial alliance. There was a long tradition of marriages in Mewar, Marwar and Merta. Initial phases of Meera's marriage were happy, except for minor conflicts and day-to-day jealousies and distrusts common within the walls of the palace. Her relationship with her husband was conventional. After Bhojraj's demise, her life as a widow was sad and eventful. History as well as some of her verses reveal that Meera's sister-in-law Uda often pestered her for mingling with saints and ascetics. At that time, the custom of *sati* was not widespread, rather it was voluntary. However, in turn of events,

Meera was persuaded to become a *sati* but she turned it down. After the death of Bhojraj, Meera had a plight of facing internal conflicts between two groups—who fought for taking the throne after Sanga—on one hand, Ratan Singh and his mother Dhanabai, the Rathore queen and on the other hand, Vikramaditya and Karmeti, his mother, the Hada queen. Her relationship with both brothers-in-law Ratan Singh and Vikramaditya was sour. Due to her commitment to her relatives of Merta, and her unique way of life, both Ratan Singh and Vikramaditya heckled her. During their reigns, several attempts were made to kill her. She lost many of her relatives including her father. Due to a constant state of grief she might have immersed herself more into love and devotion for the Lord. In search of security and stability Meera went back to her family in Merta, but here too she could not avert attacks from invaders. As she wandered along with her family like a destitute, she might have decided to go on pilgrimages. Meera first went to Vrindavan, as it was the centre of Krishna devotion, and multiple forms of time-honoured religious sects were active those days. Initially Meera, being a woman faced resistance, but later, she was recognized, accepted and revered. From Vrindavan, she went to Dwarka. It was not unusual for feudal women to go to Dwarka. The people of Gujarat were inclusive and generous, the Bhakti movement was flourishing here; therefore Meera fully adapted herself to it. She also received support from the feudal lords of her own caste; Meera spent her time in religious discourses, congregations and in support of saint-devotees. She also built a temple here. It is said that around the year 1546, she merged into an idol of Ranchhod Ji (Krishna). Meera was seen as the feudal woman who turned into a saint-devotee, and then immersed in the Lord himself, so the masses accepted this miraculous incident and popularized it greatly. Some people believed that she sneaked away from here and went on a journey to South India. After a few years of pilgrimage, Meera appeared in the court of the north Indian ruler, Ram Chandra Baghela;

here she possibly met Tansen, Birbal and Tulsidas. From here she went to Amber and Mathura, where she possibly came in contact with Man Singh and finally Akbar. After 1546, the life story of Meera is entirely based on legends and lore. If all this is true, Meera died around 1561-1563 at the age of 63-65 years. There are several misconceptions regarding Meera. She was not a woman occupied in pagan-divine devotion, nor was she a love-fanatic. Her upbringing was like that of a modest young woman. She was fairly educated, empowered with sufficient wealth and some family support, who had seen the ups and downs of life. She was not even the helpless, saffron-clad, ascetic saint devotee that the world loves to see her as. The reconstruction of Meera's life should be carried out only based on her real life. To fathom and investigate her realities is certainly a daunting task. Meera's life, which might deviate from her life as seen by the masses, more clearly, was carved out of their expectations, dreams, wishes, and thus something or the other keeps on adding or being removed from her actual life till this very day.

Notes and References

1. Mewar was a former princely state which was merged in Rajasthan after independence. Its ancient name was 'Medpat', which was later tweaked into Mewar. It was the largest state of northern India during the medieval period. Earlier the Gehlots among Rajputs and later their branch--the Sisodia dynasty ruled Mewar. Chittorgarh used to be its capital and later, during the medieval period, Uday Singh established the city of Udaipur which became its capital. Its geographical boundaries have changed from time to time. Chittorgarh, Bhilwara and Rajsamand districts have always been parts of Mewar.
2. See: Devi Lal Paliwal, ed., *Mewar ke Raja, Raniyon, Kunwaron Kunwarion ka Haal - Badva Devidan ki Khayat,* (Udaipur: Sahitya Sansthan, Rajasthan Vidyapeeth, 1985).
3. Marwar was a former princely state which was merged in Rajasthan after independence. The districts of Jodhpur, Pali, Balotra, Barmer etc. of present Rajasthan used to be parts of

this kingdom. Rathore, a Rajput branch dynasty ruled Marwar. Mandor used to be its capital. Later Jodhpur was built at the time of Jodha and became the capital of Marwar.

4. Mahendra Singh Nagar, ed., *Ranimanga Bhaton ki Bahee - Marwar ka Raniwas,* (Jodhpur: Maharaja Mansingh Pustak Prakash Shodh Kendra, 2002).
5. James Tod, *Annals and Antiquities of Rajasthan,* ed. William Crooke (Delhi: Motilal Banarsidass, reprint edn. 1971, London: 1st edn. 1920), 2:337.
6. Kumkum Sangari, *Meerabai aur Bhakti ki Aadhyatmik Arthaneeti,* Hindi trans. Anupama Gupta (New Delhi: Vani Prakashan, 2012); Parita Mukta, *Upholding the Common Life: The Community of Mirabai* (Kolkata: Oxford University Press, 1997) & Madhu kishwar and Ruth Vanita, "Poison to Nectar: The Life and Work of Mirabai," *Manushi,* no. 50-51-52 (January-Jun 1989).
7. Munshi Deviprasad, *Meerabai ka Jivan Charitra* (Kolkata: Bangiya Sahitya Parishad, 1954, 1st edn.1898).
8. Hermann Goetz, *Mira Bai: Her Life and Times* (Mumbai: Bharatiya Vidya Bhavan, 1966).
9. Harinarayan Purohit, "Meera Prakaran" *Parampara* (Special Issue on Vidyabhooshan Harinarayan Purohit), no. 63-64 (1982).
10. Nabhadas & Priayadas, *Shri Bhaktamal - Shri Priyadasji Praneet Tika-Kavita Sahit,* ed. Sitaramsharan Bhagvan Prasad Roopkala (Lucknow: Tejkumar Book Depot (P) Ltd., 11th edn. 2011).
11. Sukhsaran, "Mirabai ri Parchi," *Parampara,* no. 69-70 (1983).
12. *Bhavishya Mahapuranam,* (Allahabad: Hindi Sahitya Sammelan, 1997), 2:716.
13. Harinarayan Purohit, ed., *Meera Brihat Padavali,* Vol.1, (Jodhpur: Rajasthan Prachaya Vidya Pratishthan, 3rd edn. 2006).
14. Most of the *Harjas* (Devotional songs) of Meera have been compiled by Jalpal Singh Rathore. All of these *Harjas* are published in coherent form in *Loor* (Special Issue on Meera), no. 2, (Jodhpur: Rajasthan Folklore Study and Research Society).
15. Sangari, *Meerabai aur Bhakti ki Aadhyatmik Arthaneeti*; Mukta, *Upholding the Common Life: The Community of Mirabai* & Kishwar and Vanita, "Poison to Nectar: The Life and Work of Mirabai."
16. Goswami Gokulnath, *Chaurasi Vaishnav ki Varta* (Nathdwara: Shree Vidhya Vibhag, 1970), 239 (The text of this work is authentic. But the author of this is disputed. There is a presumption in Vallabh Sect that Goswami Gokulnath narrated the *Vaartaas* and those were scripted by Harirai. The work begins

like this: *Vaarta Shree Gokulnathji Prakat Kiye taakaun bhaav Shree Hariraiji kahat, so likhyate.*

17. Purohit, "Meera Prakaran," 92.
18. Gopal Singh Mertiya, *Jaimal Vansh Prakash Badnor* (*Mewar*) (Jodhpur: Rajasthani Granthagar, 2nd revised edn. 2012), 2:421.
19. Gaurishankar Ojha, *Udaipur Rajya ka Itihas* (Jodhpur: Rajasthani Granthagar 1996-97, 1st edn. 1928), 394.
20. *Lagi chatpati so bhup bhakti so saroop jani, atii dukh mani, vipra shreni le pathai. / Baigi lakey aao moko pran de jivaavo ahoe gaye dwar daharno de vintiti sunaiayay.* - Priyadas, *Shri Bhaktamal*, 722.
21. This legend has been written and it is displayed at the main entrance of the Jagdish temple in Udaipur, Rajasthan.
22. Hukum Singh Bhati, *Mirabai: Aitihasik aur Samajik Vivechan* (Jodhpur: Ratan Prakashan, 1986). 16-20.
23. Hanuman Prasad Poddar, *Bhakt Nari - 2* (Gorakhpur: Gita Press, 2001).
24. Giriraj Sharan Agrawal, *Prem Deewani Meera* (New Delhi: Diamond Pocket Books Pvt. Ltd., 2003).
25. Deviprasad, *Meerabai ka Jivan Charitra*, 9.
26. Thakur Chatur Singh, *Chaturkul Charitra Itihas* (Nasirabad: Edward Printing Press, 1902), 1:78.
27. Har Bilas Sarda, *Maharana Sanga*, (Jodhpur: Suryanagari Prakashan, 2008), 77.
28. Ojha, *Udaipur Rajya ka Itihas*, 335; Gopinath Sharma, *Bhakt Meerabai* (Udaipur: Meera Kala Mandir, 1990), 10 & Hermann Goetz, *Mira Bai : HerLife and Times*, 4.
29. *Rani Manga Bhaton ki Bahi*, xxvi.
30. Ibid., 16.
31. Bhati, *Mirabai: Aitihasik aur Samajik Vivechan*, 9.
32. Muhnot Nainsi, *Marwar Ra Pargana ri Vigat*, ed. Narayan Singh Bhati (Jodhpur: Rajasthan Prachya Vidya Pratishthan, 199) 3:336.
33. Deviprasad, *Meerabai ka Jivan Charitra*, 9.
34. Purohit, introduction to *Meera Brihat Padavali*, 1:2.
35. Kalyan Singh Shekhawat, *Meera ki Pramanik Jivani* (Jodhpur: Rajasthani Sahitya Sansthan, 2006), 10.
36. *Udeibhan Champawat ri Khyat - Muraridan ri Khayat* Manuscript), Accession no. 15675 (Jodhpur: Rajasthan Prachya Vidya Prathishthan), 574.
37. Ibid., 575.

38. Nabhadas, *Shri Bhaktamal,* 714.
39. Raghavdas, *Bhaktamal - Chatur Das ki Tika Sahit,* ed. Agar Chand Nahata (Jodhpur: Rajasthan Prachya Vidya Prathishthan, 1965), 99.
40. Sukhsaran, "Meerabai ri Parchi," 17.
41. Nainsi, *Marwar Ra Pargana ri Vigat,* 2:41.
42. *Khap Champavat* (Manuscript), Accession no. 74/11 (Bikaner: Rajasthan State Archives).
43. *Khayat Bhainsara Bada* (Manuscript), Accession no. 11/33 (Bikaner: Rajasthan State Archives).
44. Nainsi, *Marwar Ra Pargana ri Vigat,* 2:46.
45. Ibid., 47.
46. Mertiya, *Jaimal Vansh Prakash,* 1:61.
47. Nainsi, *Marwar Ra Pargana ri Vigat,* 2:46.
48. Chatur Singh *Chaturkul Charitra Itihas,* 1:23.
49. *Udeibhan Champawat ri Khyat,* 574.
50. Ibid.
51. Nainsi, *Marwar Ra Pargana ri Vigat,* 2:109.
52. Purohit, introduction to *Meera Brihat Padavali,* 1:3.
53. Swami Anand Swaroop, ed., introduction to *Meera Sudha Sindhu,* (Bhilwara: Yatindra Sahitya Sadan, 1942), 8.
54. Ojha, *Udaipur Rajya ka Itihas,* 341.
55. Priyadas, *Shri Bhaktamal,* 714.
56. Mertiya, *Jaimal Vansh Prakash,* 1:99.
57. *Udaybhan Champavat ri Khayat,* 574.
58. *Merate basal bhoop, bhakti kau saroop jaanaun, jaimal anoop jaakee katha kahi aayai hain.*
    Karee saadhuseva reeti priti ko prateeti bhee naee ek sunau hari kaisaikai ladaaye hain.
    Neeche maani mandir so sundar bichaari baat, chhat par bangala kai chitr le banaaye hain.
    Vividh bichauna sej raajat udhauna panadaan dhari sauna jaree parada sivaayai hain.
    Taaki daaru seedhi, kari rachana, utaari dharain, bharain doori chaukee, aap bhaav svachchhataee hai.
    Maanasee vichaarain, laal sej pag dhaarai, paanakhaan lai ugaar daarai, paudhai sukhadaee hai.
    Tiya hoonabhed jaanai, so nisenee dharee vaanai, dekhai ko kishor soyau phiree bhor aaee hai.
    Pati ko sunaee, bhee ati man bhaee, vaakau kheejhi darapaee, jaanee bhaag adhikaee hai. - Priyadas, *Shri Bhaktamal,* 714.

59. Raghavdas, *Bhaktamal*, 151.
60. Mertiya, *Jaimal Vansh Prakash*, 2:427.
61. Ojha, *Udaipur Rajya ka Itihas*, 417.
62. Chatur Singh, "Meera Prakaran", *Parampara*, no. 63-64 (1982): 70.
63. Purohit, introduction to *Meera Brihat Padavali*, 1:2.
64. *Ratan raav dooda ko jaayo, jin ek kudakee nagar basaayo, Jin ghar janamee meeraambaee, bain anopa or na bhaee.* - Sukhsaran, "Meerabai ki Parchi", 18.
65. Sharma, *Bhakt Meerabai*, 11.
66. Gaurishankar Ojha, *Jodhpur Rajya ka Itihas* (Jodhpur: Rajasthani Granthagar, 1997), 1:287.
67. G.N. Sharma, "The House of Mewar" in *A Comprehensive History of India*, eds., Mohammad Habib and Khaliq Ahmad Nizami (Delhi: People's Publishing House, 1970), 5:802.
68. Goetz, *Mira Bai: Her Life and Times*, 8.
69. Mertiya, *Jaimal Vansh Prakash*, 2:422.
70. Sharma, *Bhakt Meerabai*, 12.
71. Mertiya, *Jaimal Vansh Prakash*, 2:422.
72. Ojha, *Udaipur Rajya ka Itihas*, 358.
73. Ibid., 384.
74. Ibid.
75. Ibid., 359 & Sharma, *Bhakt Meerabai*, 13.
76. Mertiya, *Jaimal Vansh Prakash*, 2:423.
77. There had been a long tradition of marriages between Sisodiya's of Mewar and Rathores of Marwar-Merta: (1) Hansabai, daughter of Rao Chunda (1394-1423 AD) of Marwar, was married to Maharana Lakha (1382-1420 AD). (2) Shirangardevi, daughter of Rao Jodha of Marwar (1453-1487 AD), was married to Maharana Raimal (1473-1509 AD) of Mewar. (3) Dhanabai, daughter of Rao Bagha of Marwar, was married to Maharana Sanga (1509-1528 AD) of Mewar. (4) Gorjaya Kunwari, daughter of Maharana Raimal (1473-1509 AD) of Mewar, was married to Viramdev (1515 AD-1544 AD) of Merta. (5) Meera, daughter of Rattan Singh, the son of Rao Duda (1495-1515 AD) of Merta, was married to Bhojraj, son of Maharana Sanga, of Mewar.
78. Shyamaldas, *Vir Vinod*, Part-II (Delhi: Motilal Banarsidass, 1986, Ist edn. 1886), 1:2.
79. Ojha, *Udaipur Rajya ka Itihas*, 360.
80. Bhati, *Mirabai: Aitihasik aur Samajik Vivechan*, 17.
81. *Mewar ke Raja, Raniyon, Kunwaron Kunwarion ka Haal*, 8.
82. Sarada, *Maharana Sanga*, 49.

83. Muhammad Qasim Hindu Shah Firishta: *Tareekh-e-Farishta*, trans. Narendra Srivastava (Lucknow: Uttar Pradesh Hindi Sansthan, 2005), 2:400.
84. Sarada, *Maharana Sanga*, 50.
85. Ojha, *Udaipur Rajya ka Itihas*, 360.
86. Ibid., 389.
87. Deviprasad, *Meerabai ka Jivan Charitra*, 12.
88. *Devi ke pujaayabe kaun kiyau le upaay saasu,*
Bar pai, pujai suni vadhoo pooji bhaakhiyai.
Bolee joo bikaayau maathau laal giradhaaree haath,
aur kaun nav, ek vahee abhilaakhiyai. - Priyadas, *Shri Bhaktamal*, 716.
89. Madhav Hada, "Mira ka Samay aur Samaj," *Banas Jan*, Jan. 2012, 37.
90. Alamshah Khan, *Meera: Loktatvik Adhyayan* (Udaipur: Sanghi Prakashan, 1997), 7.
91. Sharma, *Bhakt Meerabai*, 14.
92. *Mewar ke Raja, Raniyon, Kunwaron Kunwarion ka Haall*, 9.
93. Ibid., 7.
94. Ojha, *Udaipur Rajya ka Itihas*, 394.
95. Chatur Singh, "Meera Prakaran," 68 & Mertiya, *Jaimal Vansh Prakash*, 2: 427
96. Chatur Singh, "Meera Prakaran," 70.
97. Sharma, *Bhakt Meerabai*, 14
98. Hada, "Meera ka Samay aur Samaj," 37.
99. Ojha, *Udaipur Rajya ka Itihas*, 342.
100. *Meera Brihat Padavali*, 1:316.
101. Nagaridas, *Nagaridas: Granthavali.*, ed. Kishori Lal Gupta (Varanasi: Nagari Pracharini Sabha, 1955), 2:363.
102. *Mewar ke Raja, Raniyon, Kunwaron Kunwarion Ka Haal*, 9.
103. Shyamaldas, *Vir Vinod*, Part II, 1:25.
104. *Meera Brihat Padavali*, 1:43.
105. Kalyan Singh Shekhawat, ed. *Meera Brihat Padavali* (Jodhpur: Rajasthan Prachya Vidya Pratishthan, 1975), 2:82.
106. Nabhadas, *Shri Bhaktamal*, 713.
107. *Dayārāma piṇḍō ēka nāmā, rājamindara sēvau aṭhajāmā,*
Sīsōdyō bauhau bhānta sikhāyau, yūṁ kahijyau caraṇamati lāyau.
Gupta dāna vākūṁ lē ghālyau, sō māraṇa mīrān kūṁ cālyau,
Piṇḍō kahai bhāga dhina rāṇī, jiṇa prabhu kī bhākta pichāṇī.
Harijī kī agyā bahī mīnai, cāramati bhējyō tone,
Kai lēvō kai pūṭhō phērō, binā liyāṁ paṇa jēhai tērō.

Jāṇyau jēhaira maraṇa kē kājai, binā piyāṁ mērō biṛada lājai,
Charaṇāmr̥ta suṇ seese līyō, rāma bharōsē pyālō pīyō. – Sukhasaran, "Meerabai ki Parchi", 47.

108. *Report - Mardum Shumari Raj Marwar, 1891 - Marwar Census Report - 1891*, ed. Rai Bahadur Munshi Hardayal Singh (Jodhpur: Rajasthani Granthagar, 2010, 1st edn. 1894), 440 & Mertiya: *Jaimal Vansh Prakash,* 2:425.
109. *Mhe to sumaraya chhai madanagopaal, raanaajee mhaara kaanee karasee.* (p. 227)
Raanaajee thaaro desadalo rang roodo,
Thaare mulak mein bhakti nahin chhai, log base sab koodo. (p. 248)
Raanaajee the kyaanne raakho mosoo bair,
Raanaajee mhaane aisa lagat hai, jyoon birachhan mein ker. (p. 248)
Raanoon maharo kaanee karailo raaj, mhe to chhaandee kul kee laaj. (p. 257)
Raanonjee mevaado mhaare daay na aavai,
Giradhar mhaarai man bhaaya, bholi maay. (p. 258) - *Meera Brihat Padavali,* Vol.1.
110. Shyamaldas, *Vir Vinod*, Part-II, 1:1.
111. Ojha, *Udaipur Rajya ka Itihas*, 383.
112. Zahiru'din Muhammad Babur Padshah Ghazi, *Baburnama,* Hindi trans. Yugjeet Nawalpuri (New Delhi: Sahitya Akademi, reprint edn. 2012), 405.
113. Ojha, *Udaipur Rajya ka Itihas*, 392.
114. Ibid., 399.
115. *Meera Brihat Padavali,* 2:75.
116. Chatur Singh, "Meera Prakaran," 74.
117. Mertiya: *Jaimal Vansh Prakash*, 1:77.
118. *Meera Brihat Padavali,* 2:48.
119. Bhati, *Meerabai: Aitihasik aur Samajik Vivechan*, 20.
120. Chatur Singh, "Meera Prakaran," 69.
121. Ibid., 92.
122. Nabahadas & Priyadas, *Bhaktirasbodhini Sangrah* (Manuscript), Accession no. 2092 (Udaipur: Rajasthan Prachya Vidya Pratishthan).
123. Shobhalal Shastri, *Shree Veer Bhumi Chittorgarh* (Udaipur: Mohanlal Dashora Advocate Publisher, 2nd edn. 2013), 41.
124. Mahendra Bhanawat, *Nirbhay Meera* (Udaipur: Muktak Publications, 1994). The book is based on the memories of Meera.

Bhanawat conducted research tours to most of the places related to Meera from 1982 to 1987.

125. Mukta, *Upholding the Common Life: The Community of Mirabai,* 105.
126. "Meerabai ka Jivan Charitra" in *Dwarka Parichay,* eds. Bharat C. Sukhpariya, Pradeep R. Madhvani and Girish V. Ganatra (Dwarika: Ravi Prakashan, Hindi edn. 2005), 97.
127. *Meera Brihat Padavali,* 1:207 & 220.
128. Ibid., 201.
129. Dharmpal Maini, *Raidas* (New Delhi: Sahitya Akademi, 2008), 14.
130. *Basat chittaur maanjh raanee ek jhaalee naam, naam bin kaan khaalee aan shishy bhee hai.* – Priyadas, *Shri Bhaktamal,* 477.
131. Goetz, Mira Bai : Her *Life and Times,* 11.
132. Viyogi Hari, ed., *Sant Sudha Saar,* (New Delhi: Sasta Sahitya Mandal, 3rd edn. 2004), 155.
133. Sharma, *Bhakt Meerabai,* 19.
134. *Sant Sudha Saar,* 155.
135. Hada, "Mira ka Samay aur Samaj," 37.
136. See: Verse-345 & 346, *Meera Brihat Padavali,* 1:163.
137. *Mewar ke Raja, Raniyon, Kunwaron Kunwarion ka Haal,* 9.
138. Jagdish Singh Gehlot, *Meerabai ka Jivan aur Kavita* (Jodhpur: Hindi Sahitya Mandir, 1973), 24.
139. Shyamaldas, *Vir Vinod,* Part-I, 354.
140. Ojha, *Udaipur Rajya ka Itihas,* 347.
141. *Meera Brihat Padavali,* 1:63.
142. Sukhsaran, "Meerabai ri Parchi," 39.
143. *Meera Brihat Padavali,* 1:198.
144. Sharma, *Bhakt Meerabai,* 18.
145. Hada, "Mira ka Samay aur Samaj," 31.
146. Meera Brihat Padavali, 2:93
147. *Vrindavan aaee, jeev gusaeen jee son jhileen, tiya mukh dekhibe ko pale chhutaayo hai.* - Priyadas, *Shri Bhaktamal,* 721.
148. *Tā pichai mīrāmbā'ī gaṅgādika tīratha karirkai aru śrī vr̥ndāvana hū ā'ē, tahāṁ jīva gusā'ījī kō praṇa strī kē na dēkhibē kō chuṭāya sabasōṁ guru gōvindavata sanamāna satyasaṅga kahi dvārikā kō calē, uhāṁ bāsa karibaiṁ kē liyaiṁ.* – Nagaridas, *Nagaridas Granthavali,* 2:364.
149. Mertiya: *Jaimal Vansh Prakash,* 2:426.
150. Rupa Goswami, *Bhakti Rasamrta Sindhu,* Hindi trans. & eds., Nagendra & Vijendra Snatak, (Delhi: Hindi Department, University of Delhi, 1963), 10.

151. Ojha, *Udaipur Rajya ka Itihas*, 401.
152. Priyadas, *Shri Bhaktamal*, 722.
153. *Harjas* are sung by the singers of Meghwal caste in western Rajasthan, during the night of awakening. This section has been taken from the *harjas*, sung by Padmaram, one of noted folk singers.
154. *Dwarka Parichay*, 79.
155. Ibid., 80.
156. During the 13th century or so Rathore Rajput brothers, Veeravaliji and Bijlaji of the Vadhal dynasty of Okhamandal reached Dwarka from Marwar. In that region, a dispute between Hiron and Chavada Rajputs was going on. The conflict ended with the victory of Rathod Rajputs and Chavadas were completely routed from the region.
    They captured the surrounding territories and established a small but strong estate. Now the Rathores started using the surname as Wadhe/Wadheral. Veeravalji conquered the territory till the river Vedmati near the small desert of Kutch. He established a new capital in the north of Dwarka that is at Arambhada a small settlement in the village as a centre of power. After his death Vikamsi, his son, came to power and after him nine descendants one after the other became Ranas. They all ruled for about 120 years. Among the lineage of Vikamsi, one Sanganji also came to power, and expanded his territory to Jamkhambhaliya. Sanganji had defeated Rao Mandlik by attacking the Shankhodwar Dweep. Sanganji came into conflict with the Wagheras of Manik Avantak, this had become quite regular therefore he signed a treaty that Okhamandal that it shall be ruled by Wadheras and Wagheras shall rule on Dwarka. He also made this kind of an agreement that both of them should remain in harmony, so that their strongest enemy could never destroy them. Since then both the tribes have been living together. After Sanganji, his son Bhimji came to power. During the reign of Bhimji's, Mahmud Baghera attacked his territory on the behest to check the looting pirates due to its proximity with Dwarka and defeated Bhimji, eventually establishing Muslim rule in the region. But later, the Wadheras consolidated the entire army and reclaimed the entire state from Mahmud Baghera. In 1592 AD under Akbar's pressure, Vader Rana sought refuge with Shiva (Savji) of Wadher.
    At the same time Mughals attacked, Shivaratna sacrificed his life in battle with him. As the result of which the state of Okhamandal

came under the control of Muslim rule, under the Mughals. At this time, Shivrana's son Sanganji escaped towards Sindh but he forced the Malla, Muslim rulers to abandon their arms and run away. Samana Manek went searching for Sanganji in Sindh He brought him back, then a fierce battle took place and the Muslim army was completely destroyed. After the war, the coronation of Sanganji a new dynasty started. After Sanganji, Akheraj, his son, came to power. He was just a young lad and was imprisoned by his brother-in-law Navanagar, then Patramail, the son of Manek, of Dwarka, with the help of Wagher army rescued Akehrej.

In 1664AD, Akheraj died and his son, Bhoj Raj came to the throne. His prince Vajerajji had a quarrel with his other six brothers, so Bhojraji entrusted him and his posterity with the administration of Poshitar. In the years 1715 and 1718 AD, the Wadhers along with the peasants of Vadaara and Poshitar burgled some places in Saurashtra with the help of Waghers of Dwarka. Then the armies of Navnagar, Gaudal and Porbandar clashed to suppress them. On this occasion they had to leave the territory of Navanagar which the Wadhers had captured. Their rule confined to the region of Okhamandal. When Wajarajji was given the manor of Poshitra, it was divided into- Dwarka and Vasai. All four of them were self-proclaimed kings but in case of any external threat or attack they stood together.

Quoted from Rasiklal Pariakh, *Gujrat ka Rajkiye aur Sanskritik Itihas* (Mughal Period), 138-140.

157. Purohit, Introduction to *Meera Brihat Padavali*, 1:16.
158. James Tod, *Paschimi Bharat ki Yatra,* Hindi trans. of *Travels in Western India* by Gopal Narayan Bahura (Jodhpur: Rajasthan Prachya Vidya Pratishthan, 2nd edn. 1996), 442.
159. *Dwarka Parichay,* 80.
160. *Mahārūṇī jī śri mīrāṁ kanvarī rāṭhauṛa mēṛatā rā dūdā bhāramalōta jōdha'uta kī nē mandara karāyō śrī nārā'īṇa cārabhujājī kō jī kō samōratha sammata padarasē cavadā sē kāmacalatō huvō sammata 1514 kā mahā sudī pañcamī rē dana nīma dīdī gaṛha cittauṛa uparē bhagavā śrī kumbha śyāma kō mandara rāṇā jī śrī kumbhājī karāyō jaṇī mandara nakhē rāṇī mīrāṁ kanvarī nē karāyō sammata padarāsē chatīsā tā'ī huvō barasa bīsa mahē huvō sammata 1536 tā'ī huvō. Jī kī kharacadā'arī kā rupiyā 404799 udīyāpaṇa kā rupīya bābvana hajāra nasē cautīsa lāgā 52934 cītaupara ā'ī ṭhāṇā mandara kā cha jī su sagalā su sagasa kāma mīrābā'ī kā mandara huvō. Akandara rupīyā*

pāñca lākha navasē tētīsa lāgā 500933 udīyāpaṇa huvō. Sammata padarāsē chtīsā baraṣē 1536 kā māha budī āṭhama guruvāra kē dana udīyāpaṇa huvā. (Here the Queen of Maharana Sanga has been written as Meera, which is incorrect, in the same way the dates given are not historic.) - *Udaipur-Chittaur Patnaam,* ed. Manohar Singh Ranawat (Sitamau: Shree Natnagar Shodh Sansthan, 2003), 156.

161. Goetz, *Mira Bai : Her Life and Times,* 31.
162. Chatur Singh, "Meera Prakaran," 70.
163. Bhalchandra Nemade, *How Much Space Does an Indian Writer Need?* (New Delhi: Sahitya Akademi, 2013), 9.
164. Krishanlal M. Jhaveri, *Milestones in Gujarati Literature* (New Delhi: Asian Education Services, reprint edn. 1993), 35.
165. Chatur Singh, "Meera Prakaran," 70.
166. *Rānā kī malīna mati, dēkhi, basī dvārāvati, rati giradhārīlā, nita hī laṛā'iyē,*
Lāgī caṭapaṭī bhūpa bhakti kō sarūpa jāni, ati dukha māni, bipra śrēṇī lai paṭhā'iyai.
Bēgi lēkē āvau mōkō prāna dē javāvau ahō gayē dvāra dharanau dai vinatī sunā'iyai,
Suni vidā hōna ga'ī rāya ranachōra jū pai chāṇṛau rākhau hīna līna bha'ī nahīṁ pā'iyai. – Priyadas, *Shri Bhaktamal,* 722.
167. Nagaridas, *Nagaridas Granthavali,* 2:365.
168. *Dwarka Parichay,* 26 & Ojha, *Udaipur Rajya ka Itihas,* 360.
169. Sarada, *Maharana Sanga,* 74.
170. Kalyan Singh Shekhawat, *Meerabai ka Jivan Vrit evam Kavya* (Jodhpur: Hindi Sahitya Mandir, 1974), 46.
171. *Rani Manga Bhaton ki Bahi,* 16.
172. *Dwarka Parichay,* 97.
173. Deviprasad, *Meerabai ka Jivan Charitra,* p.26
174. *Dwarka Parichay,* 80
175. C.L. Prabhat, *Meera: Jivan aur Kavya* (Jodhpur: Rajasthani Granthagar, 1999), 153.
176. Goetz, *Mira Bai: Her Life and Times,* 33.
177. Ibid., 35.
178. Abbas Khan Sarwani, "Tarikh-i-Sher Shahi" in *The History of India, as Told by Its Own Historians,* trans. & ed. Henry Miers Elliot (Allahabad: Kitab Mahal, 1992) 5:404.
179. Ojha, *Udaipur Rajya ka Itihas,* 422

180. A. Cunningham, *Reports of Tour in Rewa, Bundelkhand, Malwa, and Gwalior, in 1884-1885* by Archaeological Survey of India (Calcutta: Superintendent of Government Printing, India, 1885), 103.
181. J.M. Shelat, *Akbar* (Mumbai: Bharatiya Vidya Bhavan, 1964), 218.
182. *Meera Brihat Padavali*, 1:16.
183. Mataprasad Gupta, "Tulsidas: Jivan Vrit aur Kritiyan & Ramcharit Manas" in *Tulsidas*, ed. Sudhakar Pandey (Delhi: Radhakrishna Prakashan, 1972), 9.
184. According to Jagdish Singh Gehlot, Man Singh was the son of Bhagwant Das, the younger brother of Bhagwan Das - *Kachhwon ka Itihas* (Jaipur: Unique Traders, revised edn. 2004), 91.
185. Shelat, *Akbar*, 211.
186. Ibid., 195.
187. Vincent A. Smith, *Akbar: The Great Mughal, 1542-1605* (London: Oxford University Press, 1917), 57.
188. Gehlot, *Kachhwon ka Itihaas*, 91 & 101.
189. Priyadas, *Shri Bhaktamal*, 724.
190. Devi Singh Mandava, *Kachhwon ka Itihaas* (Jodhpur: Rajasthani Granthagar, 2nd edn. 2010), 15.
191. *Progress Report of the Archaeological Survey of India, Western Circle, 1910*, Accession no. 22181 (New Delhi: Central Archaeological Library), 47, https://archive.org/stream/in.ernet.dli.2015.70436/2015.70436. & Gehlot, *Kachhwon ka Itihaas*, 23.
192. Ashim Kumar Roy, *History of Jaipur City* (New Delhi: Manohar Publishers, 1973), 161.
193. Goetz, *Mira Bai : Her Life and Times*, 37.
194. Henry George Keene: A *Sketch of the History of Hindustan* (Delhi: Idara Adabiyat, 1972), 98 & Shelat, *Akbar*, 211.

Chapter - II

Society

Some believe that the society during Meera's lifetime was a rigid, repressive, and non-progressive one. This notion was primarily a creation of colonial-era historians, critics and neo-feminists. They also tried to repeatedly establish this as a fact based on their preconceived notions. Scholars who consider rationalism and a skeptical attitude to be a hallmark of a progressive society, believe that during Meera's life, her society lacked a true understanding of 'progress'. They insist that the society was governed by rather archaic features—such as religion, spiritualism, romanticism and mysticism. Perhaps, this way, some of them made an attempt to devalue not only Meera's society but India as a whole. However, the oriental scholar Lieutenant-Colonel James Tod, in his major work *Annals and Antiquities of Rajasthan Volume-II*, has shared his point of view of Rajasthan of that time, which was uniquely his own. His inferences are based on certain 'realities' of society at that point, rather than on the 'ideals'. In his book, he makes a remark, …(the society) in terms of customs, rituals and social behaviour, remained unchanged[1]. ...It was an eventful period across the country and in Rajasthan, there were surprising changes, new principalities were emerging replacing the older ones. Capital cities were destroyed, flourishing towns were abandoned, and these changes had a great impact on the lives of the people in multiple ways. However, there were hardly any changes in their rituals and customs.[2] A lot of records in history and literature in the following periods support Tod's observation. It was believed that the society adhered to the sacred texts and Puranas. Neo-feminist thinkers do appreciate Meera's courage, as well as her revolutionary attitude, but they also portray her as a helpless, ill-fated figure against the backdrop of a suppressive society. According to them, Meera was an extraordinary woman, who went against the tyrannical values and practices in a world of male dominance. They also suggest that the society was saddled by authoritarian Brahmanical 'sacred' texts. It is also assumed that, when the middle ages dawned upon India, the instructions in the Smritis including the Puranas perhaps were not accepted as stringent laws, still, based on those ideologies, the customs and identities of Rajput ruling clans were built.[3]

However, these notions may not align with the truth. It seems that certain western scholars and feminist thinkers could not remove themselves from personal feelings and opinions. They could have presented a more objective and impartial account of the society. It is highly possible that the 'realities' of Meera's society were distorted, or contaminated by 'Eurocentric' thoughts. They might have deliberately side-lined the rational, liberal aspects of the society and in turn, shifted their focus to its religious, spiritual, romantic and mystical facets. In contrast, Colonel James Tod has presented far more coherent and unbiased interpretations of the feudal culture and the status of women in medieval Rajasthan, but at the same time, he has overlooked the fluid, progressive, and inclusive aspects of the new day that was dawning. He has elaborately described Brahmanical domination in multiple spheres of common life, but these descriptions cannot be treated as verifiable records. Moreover, neo-feminists condemned the wrong-doings of some sections of the population and held the entire society accountable for the same. It is true that the status of women during the middle ages in India, was not the same as that of men, of course, there were cases where they were oppressed, discriminated against and also exploited, but we cannot deem them to be the salient features of Indian society at that point of time. Some commentators tend to limit their views by either totally depending on, or finding faults with dogmas and doctrines which they believed, were the main contributors in shaping the social policies of that time. They fail to keep a balanced perspective, and end up straying from the truth. To understand customs such as sati, widowhood, widow-remarriage in Meera's times, researchers often depend on the orthodox principles laid down by Brahmins, whether they are verifiable or not. Meera, receiving popular support and veneration through folk narratives, devotional songs, herself is proof that the community adored her because she rejected certain prevailing injustice and discriminations, and also that it offered a fertile ground for such resistance to grow. The community in general, respected Meera for her courage to be vocal against the social superiority and moral authority of the elites, and provided opportunities that encouraged her to live life on her own terms. Parita Mukta, in her research on Meera, has made some opinionated observations on Meera's acceptance in her society and community. According to Mukta, even the memories of Meera were forbidden in the Mewar-Marwar region and people there regarded her as a black sheep, a 'disgrace' to her society[4]; this observation is one-sided. The society in which Meera lived was not an ideal one but certainly, it was dynamic. Despite having a lot of shortcomings, it helped Meera realize her ideals and to communicate them to a large audience. Some obstacles did come along the way; they spurred, lashed, and went on till their energy petered out. Objections raised against Meera were personal in nature, not propagated by any organised body of persons. Traditions lay at the root of the society, but they were not stifling or exploitative. The society was "…as lively as the day-to-day affairs in the lives of men and women and their behaviour"[5]. The belief system rested on a fairly uncritical acceptance of authority, as well as moderate tolerance and respect for diverse viewpoints. In medieval India, Due to constant invasions and internal conflicts of succession, family dynamics saw a shift. Most critical research related to Meera has side-lined this important aspect of her society and ignored the political climate of the time. So, an attempt has been made here, to capture a comprehensive and accurate picture of Meera's society and her community, navigating their political landscape and socioeconomic context.

1

The Rajputs, associated with Kshatriya clans, gained political importance starting from the ninth century. The origin of the Rajputs has been debated by most historians. Some believe that they are descendants of foreign invaders like the Scythians or the Hunas.[6] They invaded parts of northwest and north India and settled along with native Kshatriyas, adopted their customs and lifestyle and soon were assimilated into them. Before those invasions, Rajasthan was divided into smaller diplomatic territories.[7] Later, these ethnic groups proclaimed themselves to belong to the 'solar' or the 'lunar' race, or some, 'born out of fire'. Some commentators say that such claims were made to conceal the fact that they were outsiders. The Chandravanshi clan was said to be born from the Moon and the Suryavanshi, born from the Sun. There are four Agnivanshi clans: Chauhans (Chahamanas), Parihars (Pratiharas), Parmars (Paramaras) and Solankis (Chalukyas). They established their rule in the respective territories and often fought with each other for political supremacy. For them, "fighting had become part of the bravery".[8]

After the Delhi Sultanate came to power, its rulers wanted to establish India as their empire. The Sultanate successfully merged smaller Rajput states by extending semi-independent status to their respective rulers. Even during the peak period of the Sultanate, the Gohils of Mewar and Rathores of Marwar managed to sustain their freedom and authority. Consequently, by the end of the fourteenth century, with the fall of the Delhi Sultanate, almost all these regional rulers declared their kingdoms as independent states[9]. During this episode of history, Mewar and Marwar emerged as two major powers in northern India. Merta was Meera's parental state and Mewar, the state of her in-laws. Despite being neighbours, each had an autonomous political status. Mewar was an eight-hundred years old established state, while Merta was a part of Marwar, and was struggling to seek an independent status as a state. Despite constant foreign attacks, Mewar was the only state in northern India which had succeeded in preserving its existence and honour[10]; it was believed that the rulers of Mewar were descendants of Lord Rama (Raghuvanshi), also that, Sumitra, a powerful ruler was the descendant of Kusha, the son of Rama. King Sumitra's descendant Gohil, a glorious king, came to power around the year 560, who founded the Gohil dynasty in Mewar.[11] After about two hundred years later, Bappa Rawal (often referred to as Kala Bhoj) ruled Mewar from 734 to 753. Bappa's reign had the landmark achievement of defeating Mauryas and conquering the fort of Chittor. He ruled a vast kingdom, with superb autonomy. Multiple gold coins, attributed to Bappa's period have been found.[12]

Bappa was succeeded by Khuman, Allat, Narvahan, Samar Singh and others. After Samar Singh, his son Ratan Singh enjoyed a brief reign, then Alauddin Khilji, the Sultan of Delhi, invaded Chittorgarh, Ratan Singh gave a tough resistance to Khilji. It took him six months to conquer the fort. Ratan Singh was killed in the battle along with his chieftains, and his Queen Padmini, along with her retinue and other noble women inside the besieged fort, committed *jauhar* (sacrificed their lives in fire) to avoid enslavement or worse. Later, Alauddin Khilji handed over Chittorgarh to Maldeva Sonigira. After the decline of Delhi Sultanate around the year 1326, Hammir, a Gohil, usurped control of Chittor from Maldeva. He is often thought to have established the rule of the Sisodia dynasty in Chittorgarh.[13] He was indeed a powerful ruler. After his coronation in Chittorgarh, he accepted the title *Maharana*. He was succeeded by Kshetra Singh (Kheta), Lakshya Singh (Lakha) and Lakha's son Mokal. Mokal was the youngest son of Hansabai, the sister of Rathore Ranmal. Mokal's eldest brother Chunda considered himself to be the rightful heir.[14] Mokal had seven sons, Kumbha, his eldest son, ascended the throne in 1433. He was a valiant ruler; he expanded his empire by defeating the rulers of Mandu, Delhi, Gujarat, Nagaur and Malwa. Kumbha was a learned person, a man of refined taste; connoisseur of music and fine arts. His son Udai Singh I (Also known as Udah) killed him and took the throne, but he was soon banished from Mewar by the nobles for committing patricide. Udah's younger brother Raimal, another son of Rana Kumbha, is believed to have avenged his father's death by killing Udah. He became the ruler of Mewar. His last phase of life was marked by his sons' conflicts for the throne. However, in 1509, a scion of the Sisodia Rajputs, of Suryavanshi lineage, Rana Sanga, succeeded his father, Rana Raimal, as the king of Mewar. In *Tuzk-e-Babri*, Babur's memoirs, he notes that due to his extraordinary ethics and military prowess, Rana Sanga had acquired so much power that none of the Sultans of Malwa, Gujarat or Delhi can defeat him alone.[15] Maharana Sangram Singh (Rana Sanga) joined forces of Rajputs in Rajasthan. He also formed a coalition with Afghans under Mahmud Lodi, the son of Sikandar Lodi of Delhi. This alliance fought against Babur in the Battle of Khanwa, sadly, it turned into a disaster. Rana Sanga's Rajput confederacy was awfully beaten. Mughal victory was further established.

Sanga spent his entire life fighting battles. As mentioned earlier, he had twenty-eight queens, and from these marriages, he had seven sons—Bhojraj, Karan Singh, Ratan Singh II, Vikramaditya Singh, Udai Singh II, Parvat Singh and Krishna Singh. In 1516, Meera was married to Sanga's eldest son Bhojraj.[16] Probably between 1518 and 1526, Bhojraj passed away[17] while Sanga, his father, was still alive. Sanga confronted Babur, for the second time, in the Battle of Chanderi (the aftermath of Khanwa), but even before the war began, some conspiring chieftains who had previously opposed Sanga on several occasions, slain Sanga by poisoning him. In 1528, Ratan Singh took the throne of Mewar, but his reign too was not a bed of roses. Political instability and vicious conspiracies were the order of the day. After the assassination of Ratan Singh by Hada Surajmal, his younger brother Vikramaditya Singh ascended the throne. He was an incapable, weak ruler. Consequently, Bahadur Shah, the Sultan of Gujarat attacked Mewar, thousands of Rajputs were killed and Hadi Rani Karmeti committed *jauhar*, along with many other women. After a while, Rajput rulers once again united to re-establish their authority in Chittor and they accomplished in doing so. However, Vikramaditya's incompetence and depravity showed no signs of improvement and it was a reason for concern among Rajput chiefs. Vikramaditya also afflicted Meera in a number of ways[18]. In Meera's poetry a weak, incompetent ruler's coming to power, satirically refers to the same person. Vanvir Singh, supposedly, the son of Prithviraj and a maid, assassinated Vikramaditya and usurped the throne of Mewar. Vanvir also wanted to kill his (Vikramaditya's) adolescent brother Udai Singh, but Panna Dai (his nursemaid), replaced the prince with her own son Chandan who was killed instead. An arrogant and condescending Vanvir Singh, despite coming to power in Mewar and Chittor, could never win the confidence or admiration of other Rajput Chiefs. Moreover, he was not a highborn prince (the son of Prithviraj and a maid), therefore not respected by them. The Rajput Chiefs gathered at Kumbhalgarh and declared Udai Singh as the Maharana of Mewar. In 1540, Udai Singh along with Rajput lords and warriors defeated Vanvir, recaptured Chittorgarh and inevitably was pronounced as a legitimate heir to the throne of Mewar. Then, tragedies clouded over Mewar again. During his reign in 1567, Akbar invaded Chittorgarh and defeated Udai Singh's army, many were killed, while countless women and children performed *jauhar*.[19]

In comparison with Mewar, Merta was a small and newly established semi-independent state of Marwar. In Merta, the reign of Mertiya Rathores also had its challenges. During the thirteenth century, Rao Siha came here from Kannauj. Among one of his descendants, there was Rao Jodha, the son of Rao Ranmal (Ranamalla) of the Rathore clan. Rao Jodha is credited with the establishment of Jodhpur in 1459. He had two sons, Var Singh and Duda, born to Rani Songari Champa. Merta was jointly bestowed upon the two brothers.[20] Both established and populated the city with the help of Jats and Rajputs from Pali, Nagaur, Phalaudi, Bikaner and Ajmer.

Var Singh and Duda were joint owners of the state of Merta. But when the town started flourishing, the differences between the brothers increased, so Duda deserted Merta and went to Bikaner. After the death of Var Singh, his son Siha ascended the throne, but Siha was not a capable ruler, which made Merta vulnerable. His mother invited Duda back from Bikaner and divided Merta into two equal territories and shared among them. But Siha was still not able to control his area competently, as a result, Satal and Suja of Jodhpur started interfering with Merta. Duda, in turn, offered Siha a small territory of Rayan, in order to establish his own control over Merta.[21] Duda had five sons Viramdev, Ratan Singh, Raimal, Raisan and Panchayan. In 1515, Duda was succeeded by Viramdev. In order to curb the vicious advances of his uncle's grandson Bhooja, Viramdev banished him from

Merta. He gave the confiscated twelve villages to his younger brother Ratan Singh.[22] Meera, born in 1498, was the only daughter of Ratan Singh. She was brought up under the supervision of Rao Duda. She was married to Bhojraj, the eldest son of Rana Sanga of Chittor. Viramdev's life, however, was always engulfed in crises. Maldev, an ambitious and ruthless descendant of Rao Jodha attacked Merta, wreaked havoc on it, destroyed its palaces, dwellings etc. and strangely enough, he ordered to grow nothing but the radishes.[23] For fourteen years, Viramdev was banished from Merta. His family too fell apart.[24] At the same time, in Mewar too, the unrestrained behaviour of Vikramaditya might have compelled Meera to return to Merta. Perhaps, during this period, she too along with her family members had left Merta for Ajmer and Shekhawati. From here, they lived an insecure, unstable life. Later she went to Dwarka. Around 1546, it is believed and said that Meera disappeared mysteriously from Dwarka. This incident of her life propagated in form of a legend.[25]

After the demise of Viramdev, his son Jaimal inherited the throne of Merta. Initially, Jaimal's reign was peaceful and trouble-free but due to internal conflicts in the royal family of Jodhpur, which had continued for over ten years, Jaimal too faced tough challenges, as a result, he left Merta and went to Mewar. Later, he was given the state of Badnor. Nonetheless, Jaimal was a brave warrior. In 1567, during the battle between Maharana Udai Singh and Akbar, Jaimal, his loyal Chief, lost his life in the battle-field.[26] Ratan Singh, Meera's father, was also killed in the Battle of Khanwa, which was, as already mentioned earlier, fought between Rana Sanga and Babur.[27]

2

While Meera lived, certain customs and traditions abided by Kshatriya clans had become an accepted code of conduct of the society. However, against the ever-shifting political winds, these traditions were adjusted and altered according to the needs of the masses. Still, some Kshatriya dynasties had deep, strong bonds with their values and traditions. They obeyed the rules laid down by their ancestors, to such an extent, that they were always prepared to sacrifice their lives for the sake of protecting their values, traditions and other aspects of their identity and culture. They condemned those who would even think of violating them[28]; the violators were often socially ostracised, and sometimes, severely punished. Temptation of women was considered as a weakness because the warrior clans believed that, the more attracted a man is to his women, the more he would turn his back on battles, which went against their core values of sacrifice and honour. Women were often used for pleasure; wives for looking after the home. During the days of peace and leisure, chiefs, or lords were amply showered with sufficient entertainment, food and of course, women. The maids, mistresses and servants were trusted with the responsibility of raising the children of nobles or lords. The children had formal, occasional interactions with their actual parents. The longing for succession among male children would also be ignited at an early age, because of all this, perpetual feelings of anxiety and insecurity overcast their joys of growing up.[29]

Rana Sanga of Mewar had to withstand conflicts with his brothers over the throne. With the apprehension that he could be killed by his brothers, he went on a self-exile along with the Panwars of Ajmer[30]. After Rana Sanga, his successor Ratan Singh too was afflicted by conspiracies of his step-mother Karmeti and his step-brothers Vikramaditya and Udai Singh. Eventually, he was slain by Hada Surajmal, Karmeti's brother.[31] Since the struggle for power spread within the vicinity of the palaces and forts, Kshatriya clans began to develop formal, cold family relations and ruthless rivalries. In Mewar, Udah, came to the throne by assassinating his father Rana Kumbha, though later was removed from throne by the Rajput chiefs for the heinous crime of patricide.[32] Even Maldev had killed his father Ganga to seize Jodhpur.[33] There were many instances of patricides and fratricides in the ruling class. In Mewar, sons of Raimal fought with each other ferociously for ascension. Rana Sanga lost an eye, injured by a blow from Prithviraj. Similarly, in Marwar, two sons of Rao Jodha fought for power. Bika had established a new state of Bikaner, due to which he was not bothered by ascension of Satal, but after Satal passed away, Suja ascended the throne, as a result, Bika was anxious and he attacked Jodhpur.[34] Meera's grandfather Rao Duda and Var Singh were siblings and due to their joint efforts the state of Merta was established, but because of a widening rift between them, Duda left Merta for Bikaner and returned only after the death of Var Singh.[35] The grandsons of Var Singh and the sons of Siha were ambitious too. They conspired in connivance with Maldev against Duda's son Viramdev for overthrowing him.[36] The rulers of Jodhpur (Marwar), and Merta were siblings, yet, Rao Ganga's son, Maldev, ruler of Marwar, who had a Machiavellian nature, wreaked havoc on Merta.

Yes, on one hand there were countless instances of betrayal, and treasons, while on the other, there were great examples of loyalty, integrity, sacrifice, and extension of help and charity—including the protection of refuge-seekers. The Umrao-chieftains of Mewar had such a great sense of loyalty for the state. They were ready to offer their lives for Mewar.[37] They rather considered it as a matter of honour and pride to accept food from the dish of the rulers of Mewar even before setting off to have their meals.[38] The brave and loyal Umrao-chiefs were often awarded *jagirs* (estates) to rule. During the exile of Rana Sanga, his guard Karam Chand, was bestowed with Ajmer, Parbatsar, Mandal, Phulia, Banera and several other parganas.[39] Meera's own relatives were loyal to Mewar. Perhaps because of this, when Jaimal was in exile from Merta, he was offered the state of Badnor.[40] Especially the rulers of Mewar considered it their solemn duty to protect refuge-seekers and even were eager to wage wars in their favour. Raimal, the son of Suryamal of Idar, was deprived of the state, and he sought shelter under Rana Sanga. As a result, Rana set up a battle against the Sultan of Gujarat and helped Raimal to reclaim Idar.[41] Sanga also helped another Rajput chief Medini Rai and bequeathed him the regions of Gagron, Chanderi and more. Furthermore, Sanga incarcerated Mahmud, the Sultan of Malwa, and his state[42]. Sanga also gave safe haven to the Prince Bahadur Shah, the son of the Sultan of Gujarat, Sanga's mother treated the prince like her own son, but later this proved to be dangerous for Rana Sanga.[43] Sanga gave away the estates of Delwara, Sadri and Gogunda to yet another refuge seeker, Ajja-Sajja who was the son of Jhala Raj Singh, the ruler of Halvad of Kathiawad. Ajja-Sajja came to Sanga's territory owing to the growing hostility among siblings at home[44].

On the other hand, Maharana Kumbha was assassinated by his son Rao Udah, who sought to take over the throne. Prithviraj, Jaimal and Sanga, sons of Raimal of Mewar also fiercely fought with each other. Rao Jagmal of Sirohi, poisoned his brother-in-law Prithivraj to avenge his disrespect.[45] Maldev, the ruler of Jodhpur, pushed his father Ganga through the window and killed him. Similarly, sons of Siha conspired with Maldev to overthrow Meera's paternal uncle. Var Singh was poisoned to death.[46] He was a brother of Meera's grandfather Rao Duda. There was a throng of conspiracies and treasons against Meera's father-in-law Rana Sanga due to which, the decline of the Mewar Empire was inevitable. Rana Sanga's favourite Hadi Rani Karmeti manipulated her brother Surajmal (the ruler of Bundi) to help her sons (Vikramditya and Udai Singh) become the successors. To achieve her ambition, she even went to the extent of soliciting help from Babur, a Mughal emperor and an enemy of Mewar. After Sanga's death, Ratan Singh, the ruler of Mewar and Karmeti's brother Hada Surajmal had a precarious relationship, which turned lethal during a hunting trip where they took each other's life. After Ratan Singh, it was Vikramaditya who became the ruler of Mewar. Since Vikramaditya was a clumsy ruler, the state's conditions deteriorated. After his assassination, a Paswania son of Prithviraj (allegedly the son of Prithviraj and a maid), Vanvir, laid his hands on Mewar as a ruler. He even wanted to eliminate Udai Singh, but the quick-wittedness of Panna Dai (the loyal nursemaid of prince Udai Singh), saved the prince.

In the politics of Mewar-Marwar, Umrao chiefs had an important role to play in sustaining the power and prestige of the ruling clans. Their consent was indispensable in taking vital decisions related to state affairs. If a ruler went against the tradition, Umrao chiefs would come together to protest. Rao Udah, the murderer of Maharana Kumbha was dethroned by the Umrao Chiefs and in his place, they accepted Raimal from Idar as the ruler of Mewar.[47] In another incident, upon being pleased with Ganga's hospitality, Umrao Chiefs declared Ganga as the King of Jodhpur instead of his elder brother Viramdev.[48] In Mewar too, Umrao Chiefs had fiercely opposed the wrongdoings of Vikramaditya. His disgraceful behaviour made most of the Chiefs recede back to their estates to bar themselves from providing him any support. They also insisted on the purity of lineage. Though the Paswania son of Prithviraj, Vanvir successfully achieved the throne in Mewar, Umrao Chiefs never accepted him as their ruler. They declared exiled Udai Singh, who took shelter at Asha Devpura's place at Kumbhalgarh, as the legitimate ruler of Mewar.[49] *Musahib kamdars* (royal retinue) in the prince's convoy too was an important element in the administration, though they had a negligible mention in historical records. Mahajan Asha Devpura was from the merchant class, but he was the leader of a battalion in Kumbhalgarh, he along with Panna Dai helped Udai Singh to escape from the clutches of Vanvir. Both Panna and Asha Devpura nurtured, looked after Udai Singh and later helped Umrao Chiefs to induct him as the ruler of Mewar.[50]

In Marwar, the merchant class too, had a significant role to play in the administration of the state. They were basically managers and account-holders working for the estate-owners and other ruling classes. During Jodha's reign, Bhandaris came from Godbad; Jain managers too had a great influence on the day-to-day functioning of the state. During the reign of Ganga, they migrated from Sirohi, they too were an influential community in Marwar for years together. They had the status of *bakshi*[51] (pay-master). It was also a period during which there was a great influence of mystic-saints or sadhus among the masses. In order to validate Sanga's claim on the throne during the years of power struggle, a charan fortune-teller played a decisive role, she was then shown as a miraculous goddess.[52]

3

The society during the middle ages was not resistant to reforms. Before colonial rule, the society was evolving with amalgamation of clans and creeds, changing lives and livelihoods—which is suggestive of the fact that Brahmanical ideologies really did not govern day to-day affairs of the common people because there were other priorities. Although their religious knowledge and interpretation of scriptures were at the heart of any rites and rituals taking place in the communities, they did not weigh down on the life of the masses. In fact, those who have tried to interpret or understand the Indian caste system have not comprehended the nuances of customs and rituals completely[53]. It has more been interpreted in the light of ideals prescribed in scriptures and less on the basis of actual social reality. It was a social reality that marriages during this period used to take place in accordance with the natural order (anulom). In times of crises, and also occasionally in the interest of the state, blending of different castes or ethnic groups was highly possible. It is also indicated in *Srimad Eklingpuranam*, a religious text composed during the reign of Rana Raimal (1473-1509) in Mewar that Brahmins expressed concerns on the inter-mixing of castes. While describing the Kaliyuga (dark era) the composer points out: "Among the four ages, Kali Yuga is a shudra (the ones at the lowest rung of the indo-aryan society) era, so even pure races such as brahmins, kshatriyas and vaishyas too would live and behave like shudras." (Yatha Varanashch chatvar' Kritidhenyashish tathaa yugaa/Attaa shudra shudracharaa durijatyaa).[54] Castes traditionally placed at the bottom of the society might seek to gain higher status by following the rituals and practices of the upper or dominant castes. Sociologist M. N. Srinivas in the 1950s, used the term *sanskritization* to describe a form of social change through which a lower Hindu caste, or a tribal or other clan, changes its customs, ritual ideology, and way of life to raise itself in the direction of a higher caste.[55] Such changes were consciously introduced in day-to-day life to claim a higher position in the caste hierarchy. One example of sanskritization was the adoption of practices prevalent in the higher classes, such as vegetarianism, by people of the locally acknowledged "low castes" who, by tradition, did not dislike non-vegetarian food. In this way, practices and beliefs kept percolating from the apex to the bottom of the social ladder. On the other hand, in times of political instability or financial crises, there was also a downward mobility of individuals in the hierarchy. People from so-called higher castes and communities, in order to sustain, adopted a set of rituals, customs, ideologies and even professions traditionally associated with 'lower castes'. To continue to exist in tough times, they became craftsmen, farmers and merged into smaller ethnic groups and sometimes also formed new groups.

During the medieval period, fights were common in Kshatriya clans in a continuous struggle to expand and control their territories. Adding to their home-grown plight, endless attacks by the Mughals and the Turks left a great, deep wound on Mewar. Being deprived of their land rights, Kshatriya warrior groups would often turn violent and plunder their own territories, this phenomenon was termed as *bikha.*[56] It must be noted that some Kshatriya communities in those regions also merged among traders, farmers, craftsman, and tribal castes. After defeat in battles, or propelled by political reasons, some Kshatriyas even converted to Islam. Munshi Hardayal Singh, the Census Superintendent of Marwar State points out, countless attempts were made to convert Rajputs into Muslims. It all started with the attack of Mohammad Qasim—the Arab invader, in samvat 770, and it concluded with the death of Aurangzeb in samvat 1762. Over a thousand years, millions of Rajputs were converted to Islam during Muslim invasions. After a battle was lost by Hindus, especially any of the martial Rajputs clans, they would be offered a chance at life by accepting Islam. If they refused, they were massacred so that none of them would rise again to wage a war against Muslims conquerors in future. To avert such catastrophes, some Rajputs would leave their weapons, abandon their warrior clans, merge into lower castes and accept their professions too. 'Rajput' became a melting pot of castes, kin bodies, and local groups, because, at that point of time, many had chosen to accept other castes, clans and lineages. Some became Muslims to survive, and became appointed as *sepoys* (soldiers).[57]

Several Kshatriya clans abandoned their arms and armour, and chose a vast range of occupations. Only in their religious rites and rituals, they carried along their traditions. Many sub-ethnic groups were formed, which is evident in the western Rajasthan. It is said that 24 groups of Rajputs of Khari-Khabar region, after being defeated by the Turks gave up their arms and took refuge under Kanhadadeva, the ruler of Jalore. They developed a different community and with the permission of Kanhadadeva, they took up agricultural activities in the land as their new profession. Gradually they merged into the existing groups in the area and formed matrimonial alliances to establish their bonding further. In the hilly regions of Rajasthan there are some ethnic groups and sub-groups who earlier were warriors. Some communities, at the bottom of the social stratification, often claim to be Kshatriyas, who reveal that many Kshatriya warriors, at times of attacks, had entered the claimants' communities in order to save their own lives (a claim also backed by some genealogists). After such amalgamations, in 1200s, the community heads resolved to declare themselves as independent classes, developed a comparatively new set of rituals and customs for their posterities.[58]

Shyamaldas, one of India's first unbiased historians, has described: With the advent of Buddhism, most of the Rajput clans, out of fear of conversion, stowed away into the Aravallis. And with the passage of time, they came in touch with the bheels of the region, but it is difficult to ascertain the time period.[59] The folk memories of these ethnic groups do not indicate the monopoly of any single indigenous leader, they did have their respective leaders. Shyamaldas in his book *Vir Vinod* gives an account of some of the major tribal groups of Mewar in the light of folk memory. Some among them believed that they were the descendants of the panwar king of Dhar, while others had faith that their lineage was issued from some powerful Kshatriya clans. Since they came to live with the tribal communities and had marital relations with them, they themselves became part of those communities[60]; similar indication is made in *The Census Survey of Marwar 1891*. According to certain genealogists, as Allauddin Khilji captured Jalore in samvat 1342, Rao Kanhadadeva, and his son Viramadeva, were killed in the battle field and their sons and brothers—Rao-Satal, Bhojraj and Moolak Dev along with the entire clan took refuge in the hills, seized the lands of tribal people to rule over them, and eventually became part of the tribal community.[61]

Some farmer tribes belonging to the hilly areas of Rajasthan claim Rajput descent, without having any matrimonial alliances[62]. This is a distinct community that had multiple sub-groups in erstwhile Mewar. They possessed *jagirs* of hilly areas, were primarily engaged in farming and agriculture, but if need arose, they also supported the crowned rulers of the kingdom by offering martial assistance, accompanied with tribal clans. Their early lineage consisted of Rajputs that had ranked high in the social order, and it is said that due to constant struggle and crises, and loss of control over their respective territories, they took shelter in the hilly regions, and were subjugated by higher-order Rajputs. This can be found in two books of leases, during the reign of Maharana Raj Singh of Mewar. Rajendra Prasad Bhatnagar, a researcher and scholar, reveals: Before the reign of Rana Sanga, ancient dynasties were suppressed due to the emergence of new clans, to such an extent that they could not live among higher-caste Rajput families, but still, they retained their land. Due to a rise of new clans, their former' access to the powerful classes was diminished. For the sake of livelihood, they started tilling and cultivating the land, which gradually turned into their main occupation. Though they were hard-working farmers yet, they never gave up the skills of arms and warfare.[63]

As discussed earlier, certain ethnic groups of the western Rajasthan considered their ancestors to belong to higher-order Rajput communities and because of the change of occupation, they deviated from their original trajectory. According to their panegyrists, Raja Siddhraj Singh of Sidhpur in Gujarat, built a huge temple of Rudramal, in order to carry on the work through the night, many oil extractors were employed, but it required excessive work and labour, so they ran away. In turn, the same work was handed over to civil servants who earlier used to supervise oil extraction. Some Kshatriya groups too, were engaged in the work, as a result, other Kshatriyas severed all ties with them. Later they were compelled to establish and maintain a separate caste.[64]

Morganatic marriages (refers to marriages, in which neither the partner belonging to lower social rank, nor any offspring can claim the properties of the spouse of the higher rank), and widow remarriages also contributed to the ethnic diversities. Marriages mixed several ethnic groups of higher-order into the lower ones, new castes emerged. *The Census Report-1891* sufficiently revealed the formation of new castes and the ethnic homogenization.[65] Women from some newly founded castes believed that their ancestors were Brahmins, so, they abstained from having alcohol or meat and even kept their utensils separate from those of the other members of the family to maintain their racial purity.[66] In Mewar, new castes grew a number of branches. In Rajasthan, many morganatic marriages took place, and even some of the higher-caste descendants were found to have links with tribal communities or other disadvantaged castes. Having a superior lineage placed them in the higher social rank. They would allow their sons to get married to women from lower castes but would never approve their daughters to be married to them. Even some Hindu and Muslim communities formed matrimonial alliances.[67]

In the Brahmanical model of an ideal matrimony, widow remarriage was prohibited, but, if we see history, it was not very effectively implemented. During the medieval period, widow remarriage was prevalent in craftsmen, farmers, shudras and tribal communities, and among higher castes too it was nothing alien. According to *The Census Report-1891*, though it was prohibited in upper castes, still, a custom called *nata pratha* (relationship of men and women who were married or widowed) came into existence. As it slowly gained social acceptance, it gave rise to the new caste known as *natrayat rajputs*.[68] Over a period of time, this custom was pretty common in tribes. *The Census Report-1891* states that "Naata marriages were regarded as legally solemnised and were popularly known as *dhola byaah*, gradually some of the Kshatriya clans started accepting them.[69]

The state often played a crucial role in the formation of castes, it is said that the King Nahar Rao Parihar, took an oath of feeding one lakh Brahmins, on the inaugural ceremony of the foundation of a lake *(sarovar)*. But only eighty-thousand Brahmins turned up. In order to fulfil his oath, he gave Brahmin status to whoever came to attend the ceremony.[70] Another reason for such ethnic mobilites was religious 'diversification'. By that time, Jainism, Buddhism and Islam had gained popularity but during the Bhakti Movement, a remarkable transformation in the socio-religious landscape took place. New, inclusive Hindu religious reforms and devotional movements were being embraced. To attain spiritual illumination without puritannical and bigoted dictates, and to alleviate the pain of loss and suffering after Muslim invasions, people of other castes turned towards Jainism, according to Jain Prashnottar, this trend continued till 1518.[71] The upper-caste Jains employed services of Brahmins, to look after their temples and perform rituals, which led to the establishment of a new caste.[72] Haribhadra Suri, a Jain saint, introduced Jainism to upper-caste Kshatriyas and thus formed a new caste.[73]

As the Sultanate forces came to power in the middle ages, it did alter the religious scenario of India. Preferably those who belonged to higher social ranks, were converted to Islam—either at will, or by force. The process of conversion occurred throughout several centuries. In western Rajasthan, there are quite a few aristocratic Kshatriya Muslims, who originally belonged to higher-caste Hindu Kshatriya communities[74]. New Hindu sects emerged as the result of the Bhakti Movement in Rajasthan too. The sect Bishnoi (also known as Vishnoi), originated from Jats. Followers of Bishnoi are found in the

Western Thar Desert and northern states of India. The Bishnoi sect was founded based on 29 tenets, by Guru Jambheshwar (1451-1536), also known as Jambhaji. Similarly, Saint Jasnath on the basis of nine ethical principles developed another sect known as Jasnathi Jat. Likewise, in the name of Pipa, Pipavanshi darji whereas in the name of Namdev, Namdev darji were some of newly-developed sects[75].

As we can see, before colonial rule, Indian society had a fairly liberal structure, where there were many instances of intermingling of race, culture, caste and creed. Formation of new sects or communities based on economy, or changing nature of religion, was the order of the day. In the recollections of Nagar Brahmins, the ideals of the *varna* system caused caste-based discrimination in the society, and encouraged a strict adherence to the caste-related rules. Some rules were strictly followed by the society and also at times, they were modified, or even rescinded to fulfil more important needs of the hour. Earlier, few rules were compromised and fewer norms, violated. Later non-compliance with caste restrictions and Brahmanical orthodoxy became more common. It was a unique society where there certainly were some rules and boundaries and anyone who wouldn't abide by them could attract dire consequences, but at the same time, religious changes and new movements were on the rise. However, caste-hierarchy still divided the society. People would ask Brahmins for approval or suggestions, if they saw someone failing to comply with dominant religious traditions. Then based on their understanding of scripture and ancient sacred teachings, the nonconformists would be forgiven, punished, or socially ostracized.

But now in the twenty-first century, things have changed. Many things have improved, while some have worsened. Egregious instances of honour killing and caste-based issues have sneaked into ordinary life. In medieval society, the varna caste system might be racial in origin, whereas the jati profession-based caste system was not. Although people followed the profession of their ancestors—it was not always the case. For example, if all Kshatriyas formed nothing but warrior clans, they would have only contributed to the armed defence of the nation. Instead, they have formed a cluster of multi-ethnic communities and have contributed to various spheres of economy in India. Their primary duty was to take up arms and fight, if they failed to do so, they were expelled by their peers and had no choice but to take up new professions, and form their own groups. Only Brahmins, despite their changes in livelihoods claimed purity and ability to look after religious matters, still, they were no more considered as sacred as they were earlier. Although they had a monopoly in performing rites and rituals, higher-caste Kshatriya groups would assume this role too, according to local needs. This is evident from the *Census Report of Marwar 1891*. It is stated that Jagirdar Brahmins had no idea of sacred rituals and scriptures, they would often invite other Brahmins and seek their help in such performances. They would also give them *dakshina* (money and other things as gifts). Many upper-caste Kshatriyas would invite Brahmins to grace occasions like birth, death, pilgrimages etc. with their blessings and used to donate money and land. The villages that were donated to the priests were exempted from land taxes.[76]

4

Even before colonial rule, Brahmins had not enjoyed monopoly in day-to-day life or activities even if dogmatic textual references would prescribe so. In fact, most groups of Brahmins were neither fanatic nor orthodox, their status in the society was neither too high nor did they ever insist on having so. Their knowledge of rites and rituals, preaching, or other traditional activities, earned them respect in the society without them being required to impose discriminations whatsoever. Brahmins who were close to prosperous and politically influential families were powerful whereas those living in smaller towns and villages, were weaker than any farmer or merchant community. Only a few Brahmins were able to properly study scriptures. Some would impart informal education through religious discourses in forms of simple stories and fables, based on the scriptures, while some other Brahmin groups chose different occupations such as agriculture and trade for greater profit. Smriti, (Sanskrit: 'Recollection'), including Purana, or any works of Hindu sacred literature, were passed down as a basic type of knowledge framework. Based on this framework, values and life skills were taught, but they were never accepted as an unalterable basis of social rules. 'Brahmanical supremacy' must be an invention of certain members of the community, with the connivance of British rulers. The British were unaware of the cultural diversity of the country. So, they went through Brahminical doctrines and dogma, and used them to understand the society. Later, the leftist historians did the same, and criticized those ideologies, and traditions, without caring to fathom the breadth of the knowledge offered through the spiritual heritage, and only focusing on the narrow, bigoted elements, though they had no connection with daily life of the common people. It is obvious that Brahmins used those teachings and texts as a tool to percolate their ideals and values for creating an idealistic society, while taking little notice of the social realities and practical applications. Purushottam Agrawal, the secular academic and theologian, has rightly termed it as the colonial "Brahmanical fantasy". He observes that Brahmanical supremacy, since eternity, has not been a universal truth, but has been the outcome of a 'Brahmanical fantasy', which has been accepted as a historical truth, by colonial rulers.[77] It was assumed that Brahmins are the topmost caste of the society. By donating them properties, one earns spiritual merit, and by seizing their land, one is condemned to hell for six million years.

Such assumptions were further reinforced through orthodox literature and strict customs. Two important seventeenth-century Brahmanical texts have been found, which date back to the period of Raja Samudra Sarovar in Udaipur. Those are *Rajprashasti Mahakavyam,* a text in admiration of the King by Ranchhod Bhatt, a Telangana Brahmin and *Rajratnakar Mahakavya* by Sadashiv. There are implications that King had only two important tasks—to wage wars and to donate.[78] On the contrary, according to Ranchhod Bhatt, during festivities at Rajsamundra, forty-six thousand Brahmins received donations.[79] Generosity towards Brahmins was thus validated and it was considered to be a privilege of the rich, to be able to donate to Brahmins and earn spiritual merit. Their respect was ritualistic, their admiration, an obligation. This, however, had an adverse impact on the economy. During the last phase of medieval period in Mewar, about twelve percent of the land went into the hands of Brahmins and Charans.[80] Their villages were now regarded as the *tamba-patra* (the State order issued on the copper plate) villages and were exempted from revenue, but only a few were benefited from such donations. Gradually common people confined themselves only to formal and symbolic donations to the Brahmins, therefore most of the Brahmins shifted to new means of livelihood such as cultivation, trading and other jobs. Shyamaldas in *Vir Vinod* (published in 1886), commented on the condition of Brahmins thus:

In nearly all of Rajputana and especially in Mewar, poor Brahmins who had received land in *udak* (a ritual of pouring water as a funeral rite) had turned into full-time cultivators and became oblivious to religious knowledge to such an extent that they forgot how to utter prayers as common as Gāyatrī Mantra. For the sake of preserving their distinct identity, they would wear a sacred thread *(janeu)* at the time of performing marriage rituals to be recognized as Brahmins. Those residing in populated regions, engaged in jobs, businesses, and different sorts of activities to earn a living, and many of them depended on *bhiksha* (food or other resources acquired by asking for alms) for their survival. However, some of them used to interpret *panchang* (Hindu astrological daily calendar), some slightly more educated would prepare birth-charts *(janampatri)*, year charts etc. in order to make a living, and in case, if some were more knowledgeable, they would turn into *kathavachak*, the narrator of holy texts such as Puranas, but few among thousands were capable of actually reading or fully understanding Vedas. Those who actually could, lived a highly cloistered life, among their own, avoided contact with the public and were not much interested in contributing towards enlightening the society in general.[81]

Even in the *Census Report of 1891,* it is concluded that "During this period, Brahmins were left with little knowledge and Marwar was left with very few Brahmins."[82] The report also reveals the same about priests as well.[83] This was also true for Brahmins associated with the upper-caste Kshatriya families.[84] Clearly, the society to which Meera belonged, had little intrusion of Brahmins in everyday life. Their intervention was only confined to the performance of rituals on a limited number of occasions that they were asked to attend—such as worships, birth, marriage and death etc. Their presence was also a matter of convenience and availability on such occasions. The masses were slowly losing interest in elaborate rituals, so the performances became more symbolic than substantive. In order to fulfil the popular demand, Brahmins started to simplify long, ostentatious rites and rituals. Some communities chose to be completely free from the authoritarian clutches of the Brahmins. Some of the tribes, neither invited Brahmins to perform rituals for them, nor extended their hospitality for Brahmins to live among them.[85]

Bishnoi (also known as Vishnoi), a Hindu sect who reside in the Western Thar Desert and northern states of India, never allowed Brahmins to foray into their affairs. They even went to the extent of refusing to eat Brahmin-cooked food; they never allowed Brahmins to touch their food[86]. Daily routine of the ruling class was formulated by Brahmins.[87] It is recorded there that Brahmins had great significance in the lives of *samantas* (ruling elites) and prosperous gentry. Rituals were performed for them before they retired to bed, and there was also a custom of early morning recitation of sacred texts. Worships, rituals and charity were regularly observed. However, in sharp contrast, in other texts, (i.e. composed by non-Brahmins) and the folk tales, the daily life of samantas is depicted as being free from any interference from the Brahmins, rather, their lives were full of luxury and earthly pleasures. There is a detailed description available in the text such as "Kinchi Gangey Nimbavatro Dopehro" "Ramdas Veravat Ri Aakhadi Ri Baat" and "Rajan Raut Ro Baat Banav"[88]. The samantas, as depicted in the above-mentioned texts indulged in hunting, love-making, consumption of wine and singing. An elaborate description of the ingredients required in love-making is given in "Kinchi Gangey Nimbavatro Dopehro". There is little mention of influence of Brahmins or religious rituals in these texts. It is also suggested that a passionate blue-blooded pleasure-seeker should follow "Gangey Nimbawat" as his role model, if he intends to express his luxurious satisfaction: *Pheri hi koi rajair maangar huey su en bhanti aisey maanjyo.*[89]

During this age, Brahmins were hardly a controlling authority. As suggested before, their significance had reduced to the performance of religious rituals. The authority of the king, his requirements, commands, interests and conveniences were placed above the rituals recommended by the Brahmins. State orders were of paramount importance; the role of the State was conclusive in determining or dealing with castes and creeds. It is said that King Nahar Rao Parihar had declared twenty thousand non-Brahmins as Brahmins by compelling them to wear the holy thread *(jeneu)* on the foundation-laying ceremony of a lake. When Hammir, the ruler of Mewar, to fulfil his political interest, married the widowed daughter of Maldev, a traditional priest disapproved of this idea and deemed it as anti-religious. Hammir, in turn, dismissed the priest and appointed another Brahmin from the village Sisodia as the priest[90]. For centuries, the rulers of Mewar appointed the Naths as their traditional priests at Ekling Dev temple, but when their actions were called in question, their services were dispensed with.[91] Over time, Brahmin priests became more practical and rational in the medieval period, they began to modify their procedures and methods, to appease high-class Kshatriyas, by meeting their needs and convenience. Along with religious rituals, they aimed at arranging the costumes, refreshment etc. for the clientele.[92]

5

During Meera's lifetime, women were at liberty to revel in pleasures of life but the privilege of liberty was contentious. It was not exactly the ideal society in terms of status and conditions of women, as pointed out by cultural resurrectionists, but it was also not stagnant as perceived in the Western sense. To feminist thinkers, the society was purely patriarchal. These polar differences in perception and portrayal, rise from their tendency to judge the society either based on the medieval-era religious doctrines, as social 'ideals' for men and women, or to completely ignore the ideals and make generalization based on limited, verifiable social 'realities'. It would be unreasonable to say that women were seen merely as men's possessions and were only subjected to suppression and patriarchal tyranny, without ever enjoying any rights. Men might just be 'possessive', owing to the political unrest of that time. However, women did have their say in the social and political affairs and enjoyed some freedom of actions and expressions. Gender discrimination did exist though. In upper castes and especially in Kshatriya communities, the birth of a son was a happier occasion of celebration than the birth of a daughter, because it was easier to pass down hereditary rights to sons. The amount spent on the celebrations at the birth of a daughter was far less than that of the son. In the eighteenth century, around the year 1760, royal archives recorded that on the birth of a son the expenditure incurred on recovery of the mother and celebrations was Rs. 7135 whereas in 1705, the expenditure on daughter's birth was just Rs. 102 and eleven annas.[93] The birth of a daughter was considered to be a concern, in the sixteenth-century prose, it has been pointed out, *jassu ghar beti avi, putti laagi chinta avin*[94] (When a daughter is born in a house, worries follow her.) But such views were not shared by all sections of society. Some communities would marry off their daughters in exchange of wealth and they often celebrated the birth of their daughters. In the *Census Report-1891* it is recorded that sons were termed as *dobka* and daughters as *tarka*, *dobka* means the cause of the sinking and *tarka*, the cause forward.[95] The report further states, that the girls' family members would demand a hefty sum for their mature daughters.... "Therefore, were ecstatic on the birth of daughters as compared to the birth of sons".[96]

There was a tradition of celebration of marital engagement during Meera's times. In the Kshatriya ethnic community, the proposal for marriage was known as *tikaa*. It was sent from the bride's family to the bridegroom's along with the priest. The gift items along with tikaa for the family of the bridegroom were in accordance with the social status of the bride. In 1761, Gaj Singh, the ruler of Bikaner, in his daughter's *tikaa* ceremony with the ruler of Udaipur gave gold and silver-plated coconuts, fourteen silver and eleven gold-plated *supari* (betel-nuts), diamonds and jewel-studded crown, twenty five pairs of clothes, one elephant, ten horses, sweets and one hundred rupees cash".[97] The practice of *tikaa* was also prevalent in non-ruling aristocratic classes as well. However, among cultivators, traders, craftsmen and other lower castes, instead of tikaa, the proposal was sent from the bridegroom's family to the bride's family members, in a custom known as *reet.* During *reet*, the bride was given a fixed amount of money along with clothes etc.[98] This ritual of engagement was socially sanctioned and those who violated it, were punished by the state or by the society. Matrimonial engagements were of two kinds: *ekewada* or *dowada.* In the former, the guardians would accept someone's daughter for marriage without giving their own daughter, whereas in the latter, an exchange of daughters among two families was permissible; it was possible only among the families having equal social prestige. In *ekewada* the family of the bride would send a palanquin (dola) or would get married to *khanda* (sword). In such a tradition the word of honour was important. Once an engagement takes place, it should not be broken; there was a popular saying: 'parni chutey par maang nahi hutey'. Although in society in general, marriageable age was between eight to twenty-one years, among Kshatriyas child marriages were prohibited. Marriages usually took place in girls and boys between sixteen and twenty-one years of age.[100]

Marriages and engagements were never a choice of the bride or the groom, the decision was taken by the elders of the household, such as the father or elder brother etc. Often Charans and Bhats were engaged in finding a suitable match[101]; there are certain records where it has been mentioned that the girls opposed the decisions taken by the elders. In the 1660, Charumati, the princess of Kishangarh, disobeyed her father and invited Raj Singh, the ruler of Udaipur for her marriage. The sister of Surat Singh, the ruler of Bikaner opposed her marriage to the ruler of Marwar.[102] Polygamy was a common practice, but then again it was not prevalent in all communities. It was confined to the ruling dynasties, also their nobles and officials. Perhaps, the ruling clans felt that polygamy would enhance their reputation and status. The ancestors of Rana

Sanga, on an average, had fifteen to thirty queens.[103] Sanga had the largest territory under his rule therefore he had married royal princesses of Hada, Chauhan, Kherar, Devra Tanwar, Solanki, Waghadia Chouhan, Sankhla, Ideria Rathore that comprised his legion of twenty-eight Queens.[104] Among his descendants, Udai Singh had twenty, while Vikramaditya and Ratan Singh had four each. After Udai Singh, Rana Pratap had fourteen queens.[105] Among the ancestors of Meera, Jodha too had married Hada, Bhati, Sankhla Hulan, Songara, Waghela and several other royal princesses. His inheritors Satal had seven, Suja, four and Ganga had nine queens[106]. Maldev Ganga Singh's son had twenty-five queens[107]; following the footsteps of their rulers, some of the *jagirdars* (fief-holders), trustees and priests practised polygamy while the rest of the society followed a single marriage norm.[108]; besides, some of the jagirdars etc. would also have concubines from Paswan and Khawasan communities. According to the Queens' Journal, Maharana Sanga had two Paswan concubines, before Sanga, Lakha had five concubines from Khawasan and Kheta had two from the Paswan community.[109] The influence of Gulabrai (the mistress) on Vijay Singh, the ruler of Jodhpur is well-known in Marwar.[110]

In several Kshatriya clans, women often became the means for fulfilling political goals. Matrimonial alliances were often sanctioned to strengthen political allegiance. Such family treaties played a vital role in political relations between Mewar and Marwar-Merta. Hansabai, the sister of Rathore Ranmal of Mandore was married to Maharana Lakha, the ruler of Mewar. Mokal, the son of Hansabai and Lakha became the ruler of Mewar.[111] Similarly, rulers in Mewar and Merta became allies due to matrimonial ties. Gorjayadevi, the sister of Rana Sanga was married to Viramdev, the elder son of Rao Duda, the ruler of Merta,[112] and Meera, daughter of Ratan Singh, younger brother of Viramdev, was married to Rana Sanga's elder son Bhojraj.[113] In order to reclaim his territory from Lajja Khan Pathan, Solanki

Rao Surtan Hara Rajot, who had taken refuge in Mewar married his beautiful daughter with Prithviraj, the elder son of Raimal, the ruler of Mewar.[114] A marriage decision was usually taken by the father or the brother of the suitor. The priests and the chieftains would travel with a coconut as a token for a marriage proposal which was accepted based on the value or prestige and ancestral heritage. Age was usually not a barrier in such marriages. Many times, very young girls were married to elderly rulers. Maharana Lakha, the ruler of Mewar, married Hansabai only when his son Chunda refused to marry her and later their son Mokal became the ruler of Mewar.[115] On several occasions, the beauty of rajput girls would attract perils. Listening to the fame of their beauty, *samantas* (chieftains or princes) would first express their wish to see them in person though it was against the convention, but its refusal would even lead to war. For instance, Jaimal, the son of Raimal insisted on catching a glimpse of Taradevi, daughter of a refugee king Rao Surtan Hara Rajot of Toda and on resistance attacked Badnor.[116]

Maldev, the ruler of Jodhpur extended a marriage proposal to his sister-in-law, the daughter of Jhala Jait Singh and threatened the father with dire consequences unless he accepted this offer. Jait Singh married his daughter to Udai Singh of Mewar, which provoked Maldev to attack Kumbhalgarh.[117] Due to polygamy, the life of the queens in the palaces was bitter and full of conflicts. In order to flaunt their dominance and control, and to see their progeny ruling, they were constantly engaged in scheming and plotting. It was a period when conspiracies for domination occurred between Hada and Rathore queens. Karmeti, the Hada queen, was tough. Since she earned favours of Rana Sanga she took hold of the *Jagir* of Ranthambore for her sons Vikramaditya and Udai Singh, in spite of all the resistance from Ratan Singh, Sanga's successor. She also went to the extent of conspiring with an arch enemy of Mewar, the Sultan of Gujarat. Perhaps her malicious conspiracies led to political instability and the decline of Mewar.[118] Due to polygamous marriages, the queens had a formal relationship with their husbands. They seldom met their husbands to share their affection. In order to meet their husband, they sought help from messengers, clowns, or a place of retreat etc. Inside the palaces, there were endless ups and downs in the lives of women, their dignity depended on their paternal lineage and inheritance. A queen's relationship even with her husband depended on the same factors. Another important aspect was the husband's displeasure due to the queen's betrayal or mischief. If queens annoyed their kings, their status and facilities were cut down. The quality and quantity of food too could be affected. Rana Sanga got his son killed for betrayal and punished his mother too.[119] Perhaps Meera was also accused of violating royal traditions and was stripped of her rank and honour.

Married women often suffered due to their husbands' indifference towards them and the ill-treatment they might be subjected to while living with their in-laws. Ramabai, daughter of Maharana Kumbha had a difficult time with Mandlik, the ruler of Girnar. Prithviraj, her nephew reached Girnar with his forces and rescued her. For the rest of her life, she lived in Mewar.[120] Similarly, when Prithviraj's sister Ananda Bai was ill-treated by her husband, Rao Jagmal of Sirohi, Prithviraj went to Sirohi and compelled Jagmal to repent by touching Ananda Bai's feet.[121] Also when Meera had a difficult time living in Mewar, her uncle Viramdev called her back to Merta.[122] Meera's poetry suggests so as she says, *Kay jo mahra babosa ney bega leba avey* (Go and tell my uncle to come and take me away with him).

However, security and dignity of married women from royal or feudal families were in a precarious position due to constant struggles and twists of fate, therefore they always maintained separate means for their long-term sustenance and expenses. They used to have adequate savings, gold, diamonds and jewels to survive in times of uncertainty and turbulence.[123] Women's modesty and her 'honour' were of utmost importance in elite families. In case of any dispute concerning a woman, it was a tradition to keep it aside from discussion or formal mediation. Its reference or mention was avoided in written records such as *khyats* or *bahis*. During the reign of Ratan Singh the dispute arising from Alauddin Khilji's intention to see Ratan Singh's Queen Padmini or Meera's unwavering devotion to Krishna, which was quite a contentious issue, get little to no mention in khyats or *bahis* of that period.[124]

There were some unique customs and traditions related to marriage, determined by clan hierarchies, and they continued with some variations during reigns of different clans. For instance, grooms did not travel to marry women belonging to clans of lower rank. Feudal lords of lower status would send their daughters in palanquins known as *dolas* to the suitors having higher status. Such marriages were called *dola* marriages. The royal family of Mewar had a higher status, therefore other less influential royal families would arrive at their doorstep with a view to marriage, but Udaipur never followed this custom. In case of having equal status, both the royalties would camp within a hundred miles-radius of their respective territories to solemnize the marriage, Jodhpur and Jaipur performed their marriages following this custom.[125]

The society was not backward in terms of preserving honour and respect for women. Women had a decent level of social privilege with meagre restrictions. In all sections of the society, there were laws and customs to maintain women's honour and dignity. Women had an important role in their respective communities. Although it may seem that women of feudal families had limited opportunities, having been confined to their palaces and havelis, in reality, they formed powerful units, instrumental in the struggle for power. The women had a great deal of influence on both—social and political life.[126]

James Tod, the British officer and scholar, was an admirer of the martial qualities and values of Rajput clans, and perhaps due to this reason, he might have had a leaning towards the community while recording early history of Rajasthan. However, he does have a fair and balanced approach, in his accounts, "Rajput women are described as virtuous, affectionate, and devoted, taking part in the control of the family, sharing with their husbands the dangers of war and sport, contemptuous of the coward, and exercising a salutary influence in public and domestic affairs."[127]; they earned respect with their dedicated service as wives, consorts, mothers and guardians. Rani Hansabai, wife of Lakha Singh, the third Maharana of Mewar, changed the course of history by ensuring her son Mokal as Lakha's successor. Rani Karmeti, Rana Sanga's queen, enjoyed a controlling influence in political affairs. Conspiring along with her brother Surajmal, she took over the territory of Ranthambore for her sons Vikramaditya and Udai Singh, though it was against the wishes of Sanga's heir Ratan Singh. Mewar fell into political chaos as a result of her conspiracies. Not only the queens, but also the *paswans* (the mistresses and concubines) used to interfere with politics. Gulabrai, the paswan of Vijay Singh, the ruler of Jodhpur had an important role in state of affairs, with an influence stronger than that of the queens.[128] In case of the untimely death of a king or a vassal, the minor successor would be under the custodianship of the widow. The history of Rajasthan has many instances of this. Ganga Bai, the widow of Rai Singh (ruler of Bikaner) looked after the administration of the state during the reign of her son Sur Singh. The widow of Jaswant Singh, ruler of Jodhpur reclaimed the succession rights for her son Ajit Singh from the Mughals.[129] Rajmatas (King's mother) used to oversee the functioning of the state and they occupied a dominant status in the palace. At times, servants and maids, i.e., *badarans* (maids who looked after the arrangements in the inner quarters for women in the palace) used to act exclusively on the Rajmata's advice. While going on pilgrimages, Rajmatas would also travel to other states and develop diplomatic ties with them.[130]

Respecting women was part of the culture during Meera's time, especially in the Rajput clans. However, Alexander Kinloch Forbes, the Gujarati language scholar and British colonial officer made an unsubstantiated claim that unlike in Europe where it was a tradition to respect women, while in India, Hindu women neither got the deserving honour from men, nor was it expected of men to respect their women.[131] Kumkum Sangari and other researchers have cited elaborate instances of gender-based discrimination, and oppression against women in a male-dominated society.[132] However, they relied only on doctrines and scriptures to make such interpretations and it is obvious from various references that the society was not governed by scriptural diktats—it rather made use of certain guidelines from the scriptures. Tod, on the other hand, has noted that no caste or clan in the world has ever honoured its women as much as Rajputs.[133] Kshatriya rulers retained paternal identity (i.e. surname etc.) of their women even after marriage. They were addressed in their in-laws' house by the paternal lineage such as Sisodia, Rathore, and Chauhan etc.[134] During the medieval period, fights over succession were common, still, women's honour and dignity were on priority. Parita Mukta inferred that after a battle was fought, the winners used to mistreat women of the defeated Rajputs and exchanged them like lands or properties[135], which is highly debatable. Rajputs not only respected the women but often laid their lives to protect their honour. When Maharana Raimal's son insisted on meeting Taradevi, the beautiful daughter of Solanki Harrarajot and even invaded Badnor, Ratan Singh, a maternal uncle of Taradevi killed him in the battle and he also lost his own life. Maharana Raimal, did not say a word to Harrarajot, for he knew that it was his son's fault.[136] Maharana Mokal was killed by Paswania sons of Kshetra Singh, Chacha and Mera. Kshetra

Singh (Kheta) was Mokal's grandfather. He had two sons - Chacha and Mera - from Paswans (concubines). Chacha and Mera were slain by Ranmal (Mokal's maternal uncle) to avenge Mokal's murder. Then, Ranmal wanted to capture and exploit the women of Chacha and Mera's family and put them in the homes of the Rathods, which was opposed by Mokal's brother Raghavdev.[137] Rajput men, on either side of a battle, honoured their women with solemn gravity. When Rao Surtan of Sirohi, put a leash on the internal power struggles from Devra Kalla, he ensured the protection of Kalla's women.[138] Rao Maldev of Jodhpur, who annexed Merta and several other kingdoms, was never known for humiliating any women.[139]

People often labour under the impression that the women in medieval India were helpless, vulnerable, stuck inside a patriarchal framework, expected to carry out a stringent gender-based role. However, historical records never concur that it is entirely true. Indeed there were deep-seated concerns for women's safety and self-sufficiency, and the society did empower women by making provisions for them. In the ruling clans, women enjoyed economic independence to some extent. There were several arrangements for economic sustenance of queens, daughters, sisters and even paswans, even for times, when their closest male protector would be no more. The queens were given fiefs on occasions such as their marriage. There were almost no restrictions on how they should spend their earnings. The queens used to make generous donations, go on pilgrimages, build i.e., water tanks and structures. Maharana Sanga had given Meera, his daughter-in-law, the parganas of Mandal and Pur for managing her expenses. Meera used to extend charity to saints, from the revenue from her fiefs and spend her earnings on pilgrimages besides paying maids and servants.[140] In the 1662, Gaj Singh, the ruler of Jodhpur, offered the administrative control of seven villages to his Queen Pratapadey along with a handsome sum of money.[141] To empower the ruler's daughters and sisters, they were given fiefs on lease, to make profits from. The evidence of the same is recorded in the stamp issued during the reign of Maharana Raj Singh.[142] Even if the women had to return to the paternal homes, they were free to use their properties and no regulations would get in the way. Fiefs were not only allotted among feudal women but also to *paswans* and *khawasans*. Besides fiefdom, the queens were also allowed to use a fixed quantity of foodstuff and a fixed amount of money from the royal treasury. During festivals, the quantity and the amount would often increase[143]. Women were also preferred while sharing out properties. In some Rajput clans, women were a determining factor in division of property *(Lugayain re larey)*. If a person has two wives and five sons, the property would be divided on the basis of the number of wives.[144] Women in the other sections of the society also had some rights for their maintenance and entitlements over the possessions. The society as well as the administration used to protect their rights. There were some traditional provisions regarding *stree-dhan* (woman's property) which included gifts, jewellery, and land etc. a woman obtained from parents and relatives at the time of her wedding. Women had an indisputable right over their stree-dhan, and this custom was strictly followed by most people from all walks of life. A woman's maintenance and dignity was her husband's duty, and in case he passed away, she was the one and only owner of his property. The widow then was looked after by her children. A childless widow had the right to adopt, and in this matter, she was free to take decisions. Unmarried, married and widowed—all women received the benefits of some social security provisions. Sexual assault against unmarried women was seen as a heinous crime and was punished severely. Marital relationships were blessed with social, religious and moral sanction. Violators were punished by the state and administration. Married women, and especially mothers, enjoyed a great deal of respect in the society. Although polygamy was permissible for men, the first wife was always entitled to more respect. There were also arrangements for protection and maintenance of divorced women.[145]

Widows during Meera's times had limited opportunities to participate in social gatherings. However, they were not vulnerable, neglected or uncared for. The society and the administration gave them the right to their husband's property. Moreover, the children and relatives of the widows were entrusted with their maintenance and security. They might have had limited social engagement, but they knew their rights. The rules and customs prevalent during Meera's time had some symbolic significance as well. A widow had to spend nine months in seclusion within the house as a bereavement period when she would sleep on the floor, eat simple meals, and then her paternal relatives would help her overcome her grief and loss.[146] After that, she could live with her in-laws and in case any conflicts occur, she would return to her parental house. Surprisingly enough, widows were allowed to remarry. In Meera's time, most communities encouraged remarriage of widows. Many widowed daughters of the royal families chose to live in their parental houses, with unmitigated honour and pride. Maharana Raimal of Mewar had given Ramabai, his widowed sister, the pargana of Jawar, she lived in Mewar throughout her life, and built a temple in Jawar[147], often gave alms, and went on pilgrimages. Chandra Kunwari, daughter of Maharana Ari Singh, spent her days of widowhood in Mewar. She also influenced the politics of Udaipur and Jaipur. A silver coin in her name, Chandori was introduced.[148]

Of course there was no 'complete freedom', but to a certain extent, women were entitled to live on their own terms; they enjoyed some independence, wielded their influence in important areas, and this liberty was also socially sanctioned. In forming marital ties, the parents' or guardians' wishes were of utmost importance but there were exceptions too. Charumati, the princess of Kishangarh disobeyed her father and invited Maharana Raj Singh I of Mewar to protect her honour and prevent his father from marrying her off to Aurangzeb against her will. The sister of Maharaja Surat Singh of Bikaner refused to marry the King of Narwar, and went against her brother's wishes[149]. Although scriptures and religious customs insisted on a life-long single marriage for women, during Meera's period, women were allowed to remarry. Most castes in the society including Jats, Gurjars, Maalis and Bishnoi had the practice of *nata*, a tradition allowing women to be remarried—either in the case of widowhood or because of general incompatibility in the previous marriage. Nata marriages provided freedom and choice to a woman to be with a more compatible partner, with social approval, and the women's rights and respect in the relationship were no less than those of married women.[150] Even though marrying within one's own caste was the general rule, inter-caste marriages also existed. Initially, when a woman of a different caste would marry a man, she was considered to be 'intruding' into the house, but it gradually gained social approval over time. Inter-caste marriages were approved among the elites of the society (i.e., feudal lords). Jagirdars, the people in administration, used to have mistresses, concubines from paswans, paddayatan, and khawasan etc. This practice too was socially recognized and women more or less had similar civil rights as those of the married ones.[151]

It was a time when the barbaric practice of *sati* was accepted in society but, it was neither mandatory nor ubiquitous. Trying to find some corroboration of their own preconceived notions and beliefs, colonial historians and neo-feminist thinkers have interpreted the society's history in their own way. In Sadashiv's *Rajratnakar Mahakavya* written during the period of Raj Singh (1652-1680), there is no mention of *sati*[152] whereas, it would have been enthusiastically mentioned, if it actually was performed far and wide. Forbes's argument really went wide of the mark when he pointed out that among Rajputs "it was almost inevitable".[153] It is true that some women committed *sati* after the death of their husbands, owing to a crushing feeling of economic and political insecurity, a pressure of attaining the ultimate virtue of sacrifice as an ideal wife, or in later times, to avoid a fate that could be worse, in the hands of invaders. Earlier, it was rather a 'choice', than a compulsion. It might be true because we cannot find any authentic record depicting queens performing *sati* starting from the reign of Hammir to Rana Sanga. Among twenty-eight queens of Sanga, none had committed *sati*.[154] However, during Meera's lifetime, this custom sneaked into the royal family. Sixteen queens of Prithviraj (the elder brother of Rana Sanga) performed *sati*[155] in front of Kumbh Swami temple in Kumbhalgarh where the final rites of Prithviraj were also performed. A cenotaph is still there to honour the sacrifice of Prithviraj's sixteen queens. Queens of Ratan Singh and Vikramaditya, Meera's brothers-in-law, committed *sati*, whereas none of the twenty queens of Udai Singh did it; Meera too continued to live after her husband's death. Only one out of the fourteen queens of Maharana Pratap became *sati*.[156] In the wake of post-medieval period, there was a considerable increase in such cases in the region of Mewar and Marwar. In this period, even paswans, maids, khawasans and concubines willingly turned into *sati*, because their lands were confiscated by the administration (khalsa) which would then go under the new ruler[157]. The custom of *sati* expanded into *jauhar* when insecurity reached its peak, and feudal lords approved this custom. Usually after the annexation of kingdoms, women and children were captured by the winning forces as trophies and were distributed among the chieftains to be exploited as they wished. In order to protect women and children from a painful life of humiliation and oppression, the custom of *sati* gained importance in the feudal society. In the event of defeat, queens and the wives of feudal lords would commit the unthinkably tragic act of mass self-immolation (i.e., throwing themselves in a massive pyre) known as *jauhar*. Rani Padmini is believed to have committed *jauhar* along with hundreds of other women after the invasion of Alauddin Khilji on Chittorgarh and the defeat of her husband Ratan Singh.[158] Hadi Rani Karmeti, Meera's mother-in-law, committed *jauhar* following the attack of Sultan Bahadur Shah of Gujarat on Chittorgarh. Since Meera had already left Chittorgarh, she lived, or else she too would have ended her life the flames of *jauhar*.[159]

During Meera's time, there is no record regarding female infanticide or neonaticide. Reports of this practice emerged from the latter half of the medieval period and it continued all through the colonial period. The practice grew sporadically in many communities in colonial India, later to be criminalized in modern India. During the British rule, Colonel James Tod, and Kinloch Forbes, both tried to find out the reasons accoutable for the extensive practice of female infanticide among the ruling Rajputs; many resorted to this practice to escape the escalating expenditures associated with ostentatious weddings. It was an economic burden especially on the bride's family, when a girl would reach marriageable age. Rajputs adhered to their customs and traditions with solemn reverence. According to Tod, most branches of Rajput had disintegrated and had settled at new places so the trails of their family lineage had disappeared. Even then, they somehow refrained from mixing up their progenies.[160] This was a challenge for a clan which migrated to a new place, to look for a prospective groom belonging to a different clan and lineage, either equal or higher in social status. If a girl's family failed to do so, it brought shame and dishonour. The intense social pressure of marrying girls off to respectable suitors, combined with dowry demands contributed to the evil practice of female infanticide. It must be noted that, by this time, marriages had become an expensive affair whereas the economic condition of Rajputs worsened after resolving many internal conflicts and countering ceaseless invasions and conquests from the outside. When a marriage took place, charans used to gather around the house of Kshatriya Rajputs to collect gifts known as tyag. Failing to satisfy their demands of gifts, would mean dishonouring the community. According to the *Census Report-1891*, the *tyag* given by Rajputs to charans was an elaborate affair and was widely advertised in the region because no limit of tyag was fixed, therefore thousands of charans used to come and stay there, which would often lead to quarrel. Poorer Rajputs were unable to get their daughters married. The report also reveals that this was one of the main causes of female infanticide. It gradually became a rule that if any Rajput chief would marry, his son he would ensure a tyag of 100 out of 1000 (i.e. 10% of his income) from his fiefdom out of which 6% would be given to charans and 4% to bhats and dholis except for the above tyag, which should be distributed among those who came to attend the marriage.[161]

Bhim Singh of Mewar donated rupees one lakh to his court poet as *daan* (alms), despite his state's unstable economic condition.[162] Generous *daans* were given away to maintain social status and to display economic power. All this escalated to such an extent that it resulted in the social menace of female infanticide; Forbes too had observed that even in upper caste Rajput families, infant girls were killed. The sinful act, he believed, was triggered by the custom of spending excessive wealth in the marriage of the daughter.[163]

In medieval India, women were allowed to socialize and travel, but they also had to abide by certain customs and rules, which, again, were never static. Meera's long pilgrim journeys and her interactions with saints and ascetics were considered an inappropriate disobedience, by a section of the society, while it was regarded as divine courage and virtue by another section of the society. The women of the ruling classes had to obey their fair share of disciplines. Certain conventions were an inseparable part of the clans' identity, culture and pride, so the women followed them to the hilt. The duty of maintaining propriety and security at the inner quarters of the palaces in Mewar was assigned to 'Dyodhathakur' and 'Mehta of Dyodhi'. Queens had their own groups of workers who would look after their distinct, individual needs. Besides revenue gains from fiefs, a fixed monthly amount was paid to those women; they also possessed *stree-dhan*. They were free to spend their wealth as they wished.[164] Paswans, padtayans, khawasans and maid servants too used to live in the palaces with the queens. Widows of the chieftains could return to their paternal homes if they were deprived of means of subsistence. As noted earlier, women of feudal families were allowed to go on pilgrimages, attend devotional gatherings and religious discourses. Maharana Kumbha's widow daughter Ramabai was a Krishna devotee. From her fiefdom earnings, she built a Ramaswami temple at Jawar and a temple of Damodar, the incarnation of Vishnu, at Kumbhalgarh. It has been recorded on the stone inscription at Jawar that the temple was built by the beautiful Ramabai, who was an art lover and a Krishna devotee.[165]

Temples were also constructed at the inner quarters of the palaces. There is a temple of Jaanrai ji, (as Krishna was known in childhood), royal women considered him as their favourite deity. There is also a temple of Pitambarrai ji (a temple of Vishnu). These temples were held in high regard and were a great place for worship.[166] Women, as discussed earlier several times, often braved all odds and undertook pilgrimages. Meera was not the only pilgrim devotee hailing from an aristocratic family, there are several instances of other women going on such sacred journeys.[167] Before her, Mokal's Queen and after her, Maharana Jagat Singh's mother went on religious excursions to Dwarka. Some measures of vigilance and discipline were in place; women were allowed to interact with sages and saints within reasonable limits. In Udaipur, the new capital of Mewar, a dharamshala was built for sadhus where women of the royal family would come to attend religious discourses.

6

During Meera's time, the general population enjoyed some rights to express themselves or speak their opinion. The practice of seeking shelter from the authority figures was not commonplace[168] but Mewar was an exception. In special circumstances, villagers were allowed to choose their own leader for the protection of their lives and properties. If a jagirdar was unfair or had no qualms in exploiting villagers, the villagers would often lease their land to someone else (i.e., tenant farmers), which was known as *bhompatta.* This practice in Mewar was known as *rakhwali* (guarding), and it was sanctioned by the ruler. Tod has provided details of three such lease deeds. The first lease deed was written in favour of Maharaja Kushal Singh (1750) by the people of Dungla village. The second was in favour of Rawat Fateh Singh of Amet (1758) by the people of Amli village. The third was in favour of Maharaj Jorwar Singh of Bhinder (1800) by the villagers from Dungla.[169] The common people communicated their feelings (i.e., opposition of applause) in a number of ways. Farming communities followed the custom of *gadhotra*, when they took a stand against the unrestrained, exploitative behaviour of the state officials. The villagers would flee en masse, emptying the land, and while leaving, they would paint a donkey on the stone of their threshold. Once the village was abandoned, they shrunk from the idea of even drinking some water in that region. To avoid the loss incurred by *gadhotra*, farmers were often appeased[170] and were rather encouraged to be vocal about their own challenges and any ill-treatment they received from jagirdars and officials. The rulers used to take necessary actions and measures on such complaints. This method of tenant farming was very effective. Here are two examples of protests made by the Jats of Marwar as explained in the *Census Report -1891* :

1. During the peaceful reign of Maharaja Man Singh ji, jats have come into conflict with the ruling jagirdar, they elected

Choudhary Harnath to negotiate with the ruler. He arrived with a gold coin, a one-rupee coin, and a paisa. When the king wanted to touch the gold coin, Harnath said it was not for the king and when he tried to pick the one-rupee coin, again Harnath interrupted him. The king wanted to know what he was trying to prove, Harnath replied that all he could gain was the last one paisa. The king wanted to know who used to take the one-rupee coin and the gold coin. Harnath answered that *jagirdar* used to seize the gold coin and *hawaldar* used to pocket the one-rupee coin. Then Harnath presented Rs. 5000/- to the king; in turn, the jagirdar was removed from the post.

2. The jats of Kuchera were unhappy with Karanji Kupawat. When Maharaja Man Singh died, the villagers turned into *bhadar* (shaved off beard and head as done after loss of a relative, king or jagirdar). Then, they reached Jodhpur (erstwhile capital of Marwar) and registered their complaint that Kupawat had not been allowing them to bhadar, by insisting that the villagers were his subjects, so they should bhadar only if they lost Kupawat. Using sharp sarcasm, they went on to the extent of adding that Kupawat had abused their women, and since he was a short man, the villagers started having short-statured children, who would be unable to reach the handle of plough. In a sneering remark, they requested for a Rathore jagirdar with an agreeable physique, so that there would be no birth of short children in their village. As a result, Karanji was removed from Kuchera and was given the village of Basani.[171]

Villagers would often use popular phrases to express their anger, joy or anxiety; that turned into age-old adages, known as *aukhaney* and remained popular through generations. The common people never forgave Udai Singh for killing his father, Rana Kumbha. Even after he ascended the throne, the folk condemned his act in *aukhana* which continued for centuries.

Uda baap na marije, likhiyo labhey raaj
Des basao Raimal, saryoo na eko kaaj.[172]

(Udaa, you should not have killed your father because the claim to the throne depends on one's fate, the country went to Raimal, and you gained nothing).

For many years, the folk phrases condemned Vijayvargiya, a merchant, a Gurjar Gaur Brahmin and a Brahmin from Dahima community who conspired to kill Meera. Curses were hurled against the trio. The common people's anger and hatred echoed against them generation after generation through these *aukhaneys*. It is believed that the Vijayvargiya (a merchant community) could not sustain further because Meera's curse fell on them. There is a description of such an *aukhana* in *The Census Report-1891*,

The Vijayvargiya engaged in selling perfumes and medicines and were often called *gaandi*; they did not work for the state. It is said that in 1600 samvat, Deepchand Vijayvargiya came to Jodhpur from Delhi and became Dewan. The Dewan of the Rana offered a bowl of poison to Meera by informing her that it was a divine nectar. Although Meera was unharmed, and their vile attempt failed, people despised the cunning, murderous trio as popularised in this aukhana :

Singh sirrup na banyo beejo, daav, ghaav na kagad teeja,
Jo tu raja chatur sujaan, aita na chotta mat jaan.
And
Bijabargi banyo dujo gujar gaur
Teejo miley jo dahimo karey tapro chaur.[173]

Certain historical events too become part of the collective folk memory, for instance, after the assassination of Rathore Ranmal, his son escaped and the arrival of Chunda from Mandu is recorded in this aukhana :

Chunda ajmal avyaa, Mandu ho dhak aag
Jodha Ranmal marya bhag sakey to bhag.[174]

Folk tales, local legends, and narratives may not always be in accordance with historical records, but they mirror the perceptions, experiences, worries, fears, dreams and hopes of the common people of the time period. Some academics may choose to reject them but we cannot forget that these stories and sayings are an important part of the history themselves and are certainly based on some truth, some socio-cultural realities. Truths can be altered, by embellishment, exaggeration or by omission, especially when passed along traditionally, but it would be illogical to consider them totally unhistorical. In order to trace the element of truth in traditional stories, a 'sensitive reading' is required. Highlighting the importance of legends and folk narratives, Purushottam Agrawal, the notable academic, points out, "Legends are not merely rumours, they do not even indicate lack of logic. Legends emerge from cultural semiotics and it is difficult to understand any society without comprehending the grammar of legends".[175] Karan Chand Panwar of Ajmer could sense the extraordinary supremacy and charisma of Rana Sanga on listening to the legend, that while "Sanga was sleeping, a snake shaded his face with its open hood".[176] There are many devotional tales etched in the folk memory, recognizing the divine, saintly qualities of Meera. Nothing happened to Meera even when she was given a bowl of poison. Lord Krishna appeared instead of Meera's husband on her bed. The presence of a lion forced Rana to leave Meera unharmed when he actually wanted to kill her. Meera merged into the statue of Lord Krishna in Dwarka. These traditional stories confirm that Meera was adored by the common people. When Vikramaditya's reign ended, Mewar started accepting Meera with great honour and respect. Perhaps this compelled Maharana Udai Singh to send a group of Brahmins to Dwarka to request Meera to return to Mewar. Later the mark of respect for Meera went on rising. Legend has it that Maharana Jagat Singh had a dream in which Lord Jagannath commanded him to build a temple for him in Udaipur where he would reside. There is a mention of Meera in the inscription of the temple.[177]

7

Yet another misconception about Meera's society is that it was inherently discriminatory and chaotic, which added to the disadvantaged status of women of that time. In reality, the society was driven more by self-discipline and less by any intervention from the administration. Rajput clans were dutifully loyal to core values like honour and sacrifice. Even the hard-core warrior clans were not savage or unpredictable. It is true that they became financially weaker but they were rather non-competitive and non-critical towards the mercantile classes. In Mewar and Marwar, merchants flourished and started climbing the social ladder. Especially Mahajans who were engaged as Ministers, workers and subordinate officials, gained wealth and power without using swords and armours. The influential ones among them constructed many magnificent temples and buildings. Ranakpur in Marwar, Dilwara in Mount Abu, in Chittorgarh and Kumbhalgarh and in several other forts, Jain temples are still far more resplendent and stand out against the Hindu temples constructed by the then rulers. Adjacent to the fort of Sirohi there is a group of fourteen Jain temples which have a majestic architectural design, known as Derashrei. Historian Gaurishankar Hirachand Ojha, has generously praised these temples, "There are several other temples of Shiva and Vishnu here, but none is (more) commendable among them".[178]

During the reign of Maharana Pratap, it is said that Bhamashah, one of his generals, was very wealthy, and he supported Maharana Pratap by providing him funds during times of crises.[179] Despite belonging to the ruling class, most of the rulers were debtors of the mahajans (the moneylenders). The *Census Report of Marwar-1891* clearly states the fact: Rajputs are often debtors to the mahajans because they had no clue about the account books and therefore often immersed in debt of the mahajans and the mahajans would charge heavy rates of interest, that too arbitrarily.

The same was the condition of jagirdars. They too had little idea of how to keep financial records and depended on their kamdars that indirectly relied on Mahajans. In old times, the jagirdars used to loot the residences of Mahajans every two-three years to settle their accounts but now due to stricter law enforcement, there was a decline in such incidents...The jagirdars under debt have been benefited by the department of repute.[180]

More than ever during this period, the winning Rajput groups were reasonable towards the defeated rulers. They were known as *bhomia* and their lost territory was called *bapoti* (inherited from father's side) or *adyapi* (since time immemorial). They were even exempted from seeking any sort of lease on their land. They were the sole owner of their land and were not under obligation of any kind to lay their claim on the fiefdom. No decree was issued against such lands, nor would they have to pay any taxes to *jagirdar khalsa* (i.e., under the direct control of the state), thus and so they would actually remain non-tax paying landowners.[181] This kind of virtuous attitude of the winning ruler towards the defeated one is exemplary and has no equal throughout the history of medieval India.

8

New, simple, unpretentious forms of devotion emerged across northern India during the medieval age.[182] Most devotional aspects of classical, institutional and ethical values entered the belief system of the general population. The concrete and the abstract were worshipped alike. New beliefs were introduced in ancient doctrines. Intense loving devotion to deities, idols was expressed and even incarnated human forms like adolescents, or youths were worshipped. Devotion was made free from the arbitrary imposition of rigid religious rules. Every devotional form had their own distinct ideology, had a large following including a variety of sects and sub-sects but they were not hostile towards each other. The rulers, as well as the masses honoured them. Simple devotional activities were encouraged i.e., *satsang, hari kirtan naam-simaran, teerthatun, niyampalan* etc (religious gathering, chorus singing, rotating beads, pilgrimages, daily routine etc). Saint devotees promoted these activities and it was said anyone could gain spiritual merit by immersing in the love and devotion of God. People who were closer to ascetics and saints were given more importance in the society. Since communication was very difficult, saint-devotees played a crucial role in promoting new movements even in the illiterate folk, in simple, local languages. Generous hospitality, prayers, purposeful service too were regarded as channels of devotion. Singing of prayerful songs in chorus *(kirtan)* was prevalent. Members of a group would meditate with a selfless, collective fervour, without requiring any kind of formal religious education. During Meera's lifetime, pilgrimages slowly gained social importance in Mewar and Marwar; Pushkar, Prayag, Haridwar, Shukar and Dwarka were popular religious destinations.

Embarking on a religious journey was a magnificent occasion for celebrations and kith and kin, saints and hermits—all were invited for feasting. Pushkar, Haridwar or Prayag were also visited by those who had suffered a recent death in the family. Often all the members in the family and especially the older ones counted beads *(naam-simran)*, even amid daily household chores. Following the daily devotional routine *(niyam palan)* was one of the challenging practices yet it was a popular one. People used to regularly visit the temple in the morning, take charanamrit with holy basil (tulsi) leaves, followed by having food or observing fasts. People in *grihasthashram* (family men) wore a necklace strung with small beads (i.e. vaishnav rosary) or *kanthi* and lived a life of saint-devotee by abstaining from telling lies or stealing, being kind to all, having patience, never troubling others, honouring saints and devotees etc.—which merged into a soothing, blissful life away from greedy worldly pursuits. It is said that Rao Duda was a sanctified Vaishnav[183] (the worshiper of Lord Vishnu). One of the salient features of the devotional movements rising during this time was that they were free from any caste or creed allegiances. Thanks to the continuous efforts of saint-devotees, the idea that all men and women are equal before God began to be accepted by the masses. Some of the beliefs and concepts were rehearsed through recitation of epics, storytelling during the fasts. Simple, oral narratives and folk tales were more commonplace. Good character traits, sacrifices, rebirth, charity, etc. slowly turned into spiritual and religious merits and the path of devotion became more inclusive, liberal and popularized.

In Marwar, there are traces of Shaivism, Jainism and Vaishnav but such denominations were not yet popular in this region. The rulers of Mewar respected all devotional beliefs but traditionally they worshipped Lord Shiva as Eklingji and regarded themselves as the custodian *(dewan)* of Lord Shiva. The actual ruler was believed to be *Eklingji* the Lord.[184] Therefore, in the orders issued from the state it was specified in the beginning *Eklingji parsadaatu dewaanji aadeshatu*[185] (i.e., …as instructed by Eklingji and executed by his dewans, the orders...") But it would be unreasonable to say that rulers of Mewar never accepted other religious beliefs. Some scholars suggest that Meera's in-laws were Shaivites, who followed the religious traditions of the *Shakta* sect, therefore, it was a cause of tension between Meera and Mewar since Meera's own family were worshippers of Chaturbhuja, an incarnation of Vishnu[186]; this is highly debatable that Meera's relationship with her in-laws became sour because of this reason. There are several instances in the history of the ancient Mewar when Lord Shiva was worshipped along with Lord Vishnu and this custom was favoured by the rulers. There are some fifth-century stone inscriptions, that confirm so, within the vicinity of Chittor. There is a stone caption from the year 426., in Devanagari script, which mentions the popularity of Vishnu worship in the region.[187] In inscriptions from 532 AD, there is also a mention of two Vishnu temples of Chittor.[188] During the reign of Aprarjit of Gohil Dynasty in 661, it is recorded in the stone engraving that the Vishnu worship was a popular form.[189] Vishnu worship was at its peak during the reign of Maharana Kumbha. He had built the magnificent temples of Kumbha Swami and Aadi Varah in Chittor. In Kumbhalgarh under his support, Kumbha Shyam temple was built, which is now popular as Mamadev temple. He also constructed seven reservoirs in the name of Vishnu which are located in Sirohi district. He also erected yet another temple of Kumbha Syam in the Achalgarh fort at Mount Abu. Kumbha also put together a Vishnu temple in the premises of his traditional Lord Eklingji which is now a popular temple built for Meera to worship Krishna[190]; in one of the stone scripts of Kumbhalgarh dated 1460, Chittor is described as a Vaishnava religious destination. An ancient Vishnu temple of the Lord Charbhuja is located in Garhbor. According to the engraving, the restoration work was completed in 1444.[191] As stated in some hagiographies, several saints from the Vallabh sect were in touch with Meera. In the last phase of the Bhakti period, the sect had a considerable influence in Mewar.

During the reign of Raj Singh, a nation-wide campaign was led by Aurangzeb to raze down idols in temples. This compelled the Vallabh sect devotees to relocate the idols to Nathdwara, Kankroli etc. Maharana Jagat Singh honoured the high priest of Vallabh sect of Kankroli as a Vaishnav Guru of the royal family of Mewar.[192] Brahmins too had a significant influence on Mewar in different spheres of life. They were trusted servants, cooks, and were also involved in performances of rites and rituals, they were *gurus* (i.e. teachers), soothsayers, doctors and many more.[193] But their interference was neither ubiquitous nor indispensable. The nobility of Mewar had a great respect for Brahmins, and gave them donations. However, this does not prove that Brahmins had a controlling influence on their lives. To the rulers and the nobility, the importance of comfort, luxury, profit and contentment was paramount, and in case of any intrusion, they would become indifferent to the diktats of Brahmins. In comparison with Marwar and specifically Merta, Brahmins had a greater influence on lives in Mewar. Both Marwar and Merta had attained statehoods later than Mewar did, so the influence of Brahmins was not traditionally established in those regions, and their interference with daily routines of ruling gentry was limited. The inclination towards the path of devotion grew to such an extent that several feudal lords turned into saint-devotees in the Marwar kingdom. Mallinathji, Pabuji, Gogaji, Harbhuji, Mangliya, Meha, Ramdev and other saint-devotees were Rajputs. Pabuji was an ancestor of Meera and Harbhuji influenced great rulers like Rao Jodha and Rao Duda (Meera's grandfather).[194] Since Mewar was an age-old state, the rulers here were far more cognizant of the importance of their folk deities and religious culture than those in Merta.

During Meera's lifetime, Mewar was on the verge of collapse, and was naturally skeptical about people from outside. Marwar and Merta had to cope with a lot of challenges of their own. Since Merta was a newly recognized state, its rulers faced teething problems in gaining stability. Naturally, the kingdom offered a fertile ground for a new sect to flourish to motivate, inspire and unite its common people. Some saint-devotees were elevated to the status of folk deities because of the thriving influence they had on the society.[195] Bhakti movement was pioneered by Ravidas and Kabir, the legendary mystic poet-saints. Upon receiving support from humanist rulers, devotees like Dhanna Bhagat, Pipadas and others gained popularity as well.[196] The rulers of Marwar not only were open to the new Hindu religious movement, but also were highly enthusiastic about its proliferation. They participated in *satsang, kirtan* and hospitality of saints. In Marwar during that time, saint-devotees were so much respected that new forms of devotion were accepted without any significant obstacles. Among Jats, Dhanna and Karma Jatani rose to prominence as saint-poets and earned a great legion of followers. Dhanna was a disciple of another saint-devotee Ramananda. *The Census Report-1891,* points out :

Karma Jatani was a famous saint, her *kichada* (porridge) too was popular, and it is also said that even today Karma's kichada is offered to Lord Jagannath (the deity) as *bhog* (offering to gods before distribution among devotees)[197] Katariasar, a village in Bikaner, became famous due to Jasnath ji, a great saint-poet hailing from the Jats, his followers were known as *Jasnathjis.* Similarly, the disciples of Vaishnav devotee Dhanna Jat called themselves *Dhannabanshi Saadh.*

In *The Census Report-1891* it is stated, among the disciples of Ramananda, Dhanna Jat was a great saint, he inspired the people of his community to follow the path of *dharma* (the righteous way of life) as led by sadhus. His followers were known as Dhanabanshi Jats. It should also be noted that several Jat groups showed affinity with Ramavat sadhus in Bikaner and Marwar.[198]

Among the contemporaries of Meera, another folk saint Jambhoji Panwar, who was born in a Rajput family, was the founder of the Vishnoi sect. He specified twenty-nine commandments to lead a disciplined life for his adherents. Rao Duda, Meera's grandfather was one among his followers. In *The Census Report-1891* there is a detailed account on the religious literature of Bishnois. It is acknowledged:

Rao Jodha was ruling Jodhpur. His son Dudaji was defeated by the Muslim invaders in 1545 samvat in Ajmer and had lost his territory of Merta. While he was travelling towards

Bikaner to seek refuge at his brother's place, on the way he saw Jambhaji at a well near Pipasar, and witnessed animals obeying his gestures. He was surprised at the sight and thought that the man was miraculous, for he could even control animals. Then he saw Jambhaji walking away, so he decided to follow him. In a while, he noticed Jambhaji riding a horse, but still, Rao Duda was unable to reach him, despite the fact that he was riding a horse himself. Then Rao Duda also made up his mind to walk and as he reached Jambhaji, with folded hands he asked his name. It was the first time that Jambhaji had uttered anything in twenty-four years of his life, (Since birth he was dumb) Dudaji narrated his tale of agony to Jambhaji that his Muslim foes had captured his territory of Merta, which he must reclaim. Jambhaji gave him a wooden double-edged sword made of kair, and a rabbit. Jambhaji instructed him to reclaim Merta and get the rabbit incarcerated at the entry gate of Merta and assured that he (Dudaji) would become the ruler for sure.[199]

The tradition of Vaishnav was embraced in Meera's ancestry. Her grandfather Rao Duda, her uncle Rao Viramdev and her brother Jaimal were ardent Vaishnavites. They worshipped incarnations of the four-armed Lord Vishnu such as Charbhuja, Thakurji, Raghunathji, Gopalji among others. Mertiyas had founded a Charbhuja temple at Garhbor in Mewar; many Mertiyas along with their wives became saints.[200] Rao Duda, throughout his life, was a worshiper of Charbhuja. He built a huge and magnificent temple of Charbhuja Nath in Merta in 1475.[201] Charbhuja Nath Ji was their cherished family deity.

There were many faith-based groups in the region of Marwar. It is interesting that groups such as Jogi Saadh, Nath, Jangam, Bairagi and several others came into existence during the Bahkti period. These groups in Marwar are known as 'Khat Darshan' (i.e. forgiveness). They have their own distinct law enforcement system. Sidhas and Naths were held in great esteem in Marwar, following branches of these sects flourished in this region—Maanath ji, Baal Nathji, Ratanath ji and Jasnath ji. The unique geographical location of Merta-Marwar was highly responsible for the emergence of many sects and beliefs and over the centuries they developed strong roots in the folk and traditional culture and became part of the masses. Gradually Merta became a well-known religious centre, linking the north and the south. It was not far from Pushkar, which has been one of the most popular pilgrimage sites in north-western India. The groups of saints who travelled to Dwarka, Mathura and Pushkar used to pass through Merta and sought support and shelter from the rulers. During their stay, they would deliver religious discourses.

9

It can safely be concluded that the overall society during Meera's times was quite different from that seen through post-colonial and feminist lens. It was neither static and stagnant nor too progressive and liberal. It gave Meera respect, acceptance and support that she needed to develop herself as an ardent devotee and to gain spiritual satisfaction. Respect and reverence for Meera's valour and indomitable spirit seeped into the deep recesses of the culture and she became not only a popular name, but also a philosophy, a quest for devotional discovery. Meera's life was unique, unorthodox and made some authority figures uncomfortable, but the society did not dishonour her. How could the society in which she lived be stagnant and oppressive? It was indeed a fairly open and evolving society that, despite relying on religion and scriptures, also modified traditions and customs based on their shifting experiences and arising necessities. The orthodox Brahman-approved model of the caste system had no direct influence on the day-to-day lives of the region. Classes and castes blended in times of crises, new beliefs and denominations emerged, and some castes and creeds faded away in the sands of time. Occupations or social life were not led by a dogmatic caste system. The image of a society stifling under tyrannical Brahman monopoly has been profusely exaggerated and is highly debatable. Such claims have mostly been based on texts written by conservative Brahmins and therefore most of them are a portrayal of their subjective ideals, not social realities or actual practices. Brahmins were only required in performing traditional religious rituals. Most Brahmins lost touch with the ancient, original scriptural sources of knowledge, they were not able to decipher them or transmit the knowledge. Their exclusivity or their proficiency were not so much different from those of other superior castes in society. The pieces of evidence associated with the daily life of the masses, themselves bear witness to the fact that the caste system was not an eternal salient feature of the Indian society.

Both Mewar and Marwar at this point of history were on the brink of collapse due to unending attacks and political intrigues. Constant invasions robbed the regions of peace and security; whereas conflicts, jealousies, deception and struggles for power existed within the walls of the palaces. Occasionally due to widening rifts between clans and communities, their principles diverged and resulted in diverse strata of percepts and practices. Mewar was a well-established state with a long, glorious past, so the masses loyally adhered to traditional values and heritage, on the contrary, since Merta was a new-born state and was free from any allegiance to long-established values, so there was a possibility for creating new ones. Rajput clans in general laid importance on the core ideals such as fierce loyalty, honour, pride and protection to refuge-seekers, but the ruling families were not completely free from treachery, deception, hostility, and revenge. The political uncertainty, insecurity, festered over time and took a toll on interpersonal relationships. Unlike in common perception, women during this phase were not passive and submissive, they played a pivotal role not only in the family but also took part in state of affairs. Matrimonial alliances were often established for political and economic benefit, which, often combined with practices like polygamy and dowry became reasons for women's suffering. Women's honour and dignity was of paramount importance, yet, there were certain restrictions on their mobility, autonomy and even economic independence. Widows led a different kind of life, they were not completely neglected and uncared for. Although barbaric practices like *sati* existed in the society, it was neither so popular nor mandatory. Public opinions were considered important for the ruler as well as the society in general. There were channels for the masses to let out their angst, joy or empathy—through formal complaints or informally, through spreading popular phrases that developed later into folklores and legends. Popular versions of lives of devotees and the rise of new sects and movements of the medieval period in northern India spread far and wide orally, ritually, and seldom in writing. This was indeed far more a stronger trend in Marwar and Merta than in Mewar perhaps because of the fact that the wealthy and influential classes of Mewar were far more attached to their long-established values and standards.

Some religious movements, involving relatively new beliefs and practices, were welcomed by feudal lords in Marwar and Merta, allowing them to thrive and grow in the regions. Folk saints and devotees rose from even cultivator communities, and later they were accorded with divine status. Courage, fervour and devotional aura as perceived in Meera's poetry were nothing supernatural or otherworldly, but were certainly of outstanding sincerity of expression and poetic merit. The fairly dynamic society in which Meera lived, offered her generous space and a fertile ground to grow and thrive. The society also provided her safety, respect and autonomy. She was a daughter of a *jagirdar* who had an unstable and disputed territory consisting of twelve villages and parganas under his charge, she was married to

Bhojraj, the eldest son of the most influential ruler of his times in northern India–Maharana Sanga of Mewar. Her marriage too was, to a certain extent, a political matrimonial alliance. Mewar was among the largest and one of the earliest states of India. Wars of succession led to growing bitterness within the palaces; Meera felt insecure, isolated, and to an extent, vulnerable, and she sought complete refuge in the path of devotion and turned her mind towards Lord Krishna, her only deity. Her religious adherence and poetic flair helped her cope with certain injustices around her. A sense of deep melancholy, and profound yearning, which is ubiquitous in her life and poetry, were not because she felt muted, or suppressed, but because of the demise of loved ones and looming, unstable socio-political climate. She was not an ascetic wayfarer, roaming with a stringed instrument in hand, rather, frequent unrest in Mewar and Merta never allowed her to anchor herself in one place. After losing her father-in-law and husband, she went to Merta, but again, she left Merta following attacks by Maldev. Along with Rao Viramdev she wandered across the Ajmer-Shekhawati region and later set off to Dwarka but, there too, she might have missed the bygone days, and felt torn up by the roots.

Notes and References

1. James Tod, *Annals and Antiquities of Rajasthan,* ed. William Crooke (Delhi: Motilal Banarsidass Publishers, reprint edn. 1971, London: 1st edn. 1920), 2:323.
2. Ibid.
3. Kumkum Sangari, *Meerabai aur Bhakti ki Aadhyatmik Arthaneeti*, Hindi trans. Anupama Gupta (New Delhi: Vani Prakashan, 2012), 45.
4. Parita Mukta, *Upholding the Common Life: The Community of Mirabai* (Kolkata: Oxford University Press, 1997), 69.
5. Purushottam Agrawal, *Akath Kahani Prem ki: Kabir ki Kavita aur Unka Samay* (New Delhi: Rajkamal Prakashan, 2nd edn. 2010), 88.

6. Romila Thapar, *Bharat ka Itihas,* Hindi trans. (New Delhi: Rajkamal Prakashan, 12th revised edn. 1989), 205 & Gopinath Sharma, "Rajasthan" in *The Delhi Sultanat,* eds. Mohammad Habib and Khaliq Ahmad Nizami (New Delhi: Macmillan, 1st Hindi edn. 1978), 61.
7. Romila Thapar, *Bharat ka Itihas,* 208.
8. Ibid., 213.
9. Sharma, "Rajasthan," 61.
10. Gaurishankar Ojha, *Udaipur Rajya ka Itihas* (Jodhpur: Rajasthani Granthagar, 1997, 1st edn. 1928), 68.
11. Ibid., 98.
12. Ibid., 116.
13. Ibid., 233.
14. Tod, *Annals and Antiquities of Rajasthan,* 2:323.
15. Ojha, *Udaipur Rajya ka Itihas,* 386.
16. Shyamaldas, *Vir Vinod,* Part-2 (Delhi: Motilal Banarsidass, 1986), 1:1.
17. Ojha, *Udaipur Rajya ka Itihas,* 359.
18. Shyamaldas, *Vir Vinod,* Part-2, 1:2.
19. Muhnot Nainsi, *Nainsi ri Khyat,* ed. Badriprasad Sakaria (Jodhpur: Rajasthan Prachya Vidya Pratishtan, 1984), 3:44.
20. Muhnot Nainsi, *Marwar Ra Pargana ri Vigat,* ed. Narayan Singh Bhati (Jodhpur: Rajasthan Prachya Vidya Pratishthan, 1994), 3:44.
21. Ibid., 45.
22. *Udeibhan Champawat ri Khyat* (Manuscript), Accession no. 15675 (Jodhpur: Rajasthan Prachya Vidya Pratishthan), 574.
23. Hukum Singh Bhati, *Rajasthan ke Mertiya Rathore* (Jodhpur: Rajasthani Granthagar, 1986), 70.
24. Gaurishankar Ojha, *Jodhpur Rajya ka Itihas* (Jodhpur: Rajasthani Granthagar, 1997), 287.
25. Har Bilas Sarda, *Maharana Sanga* (Jodhpur: Suryanagari Prakashan, 2008), 96.
26. Nainsi, *Marwar Ra Pargana ri Vigat,* 3: 51.
27. Shyamaldas, *Vir Vinod,* Part-II, 1:1 (Foot note no. 2).
28. Tod, *Annals and Antiquities of Rajasthan,* 1:707.
29. Bhati, *Rajasthan ke Mertiya Rathore,* 164.
30. Ojha, *Udaipur Rajya ka Itihas,* 330.
31. Ibid., 392.
32. Ibid., 321.
33. Ojha, *Udaipur Rajya ka Itihas,* 280.

34. Ibid., 281.
35. Nainsi, *Marwar Ra Pargana ri Vigat,* 3:45.
36. Ibid., 46.
37. Sarda, *Maharana Sanga,* 28-32.
38. Ibid., 31.
39. Ojha, *Udaipur Rajya ka Itihas,* 347.
40. Nainsi, *Marwar Ra Pargana ri Vigat,* 3:53.
41. Ojha, *Udaipur Rajya ka Itihas,* 347.
42. Ibid., 353
43. Ibid., 361.
44. Ibid., 341.
45. Gaurishankar Ojha, *Sirohi Rajya ka Itihas* (Jodhpur: Rajasthani Granthagar, reprint edn. 1997), 205.
46. Nainsi, *Marwar Ra Pargana ri Vigat,* 3:46.
47. Ibid., 324.
48. Shyamaldas, *Vir Vinod,* Part-II, 1:61.
49. Ojha, *Jodhpur Rajya ka Itihas,* 271.
50. Ojha, *Udaipur Rajya ka Itihas,* 30.
51. *Report - Mardum Shumari Raj Marwar, 1891 - Marwar Census Report - 1891(Rajasthan ki Jatiyon ka Itihas evam Riti-Riwaj),* ed. Rai Bahadur Munshi Hardayal Singh (Jodhpur: Rajasthani Granthagar, 2010, 1st edn. 1894), 417.
52. Ojha, *Udaipur Rajya ka Itihas,* 330.
53. This observation is made by Superintendent Munshi Hardayal Singh, on the instruction of the then ruler of Marwar and it was included in *The Census Report of 1891*. He also added an editorial to the report on the origin of several castes, their customs, and traditions (*Report- Mardum Shumari Raj Marwar 1891 AD,* p. xxi). This report was prepared on the basis of prevailing customs and traditions of the existing castes and their daily routine. A unique element of the Report is that Brahmin Literature was totally kept aside.
54. Shrikrishna Jugnu & Bhanwar Sharma, eds., *Srimad Eklingpuranam,* (Delhi: Aryavart Sanskrit Sansthan, 2011), 240.
55. M. N. Srinivas, *Aadhunik Bharat Mein Samajik Parivartan,* Hindi trans. (New Delhi: Rajkamal Prakashan, reprint edn. 1992), 21.
56. *Report - Mardum Shumari Raj Marwar, 1891 AD,* 19.
57. Ibid., 65.
58. Ibid., 83.
59. Shyamaldas, *Vir Vinod,* Part I, 1:195.
60. Ibid., 195.

61. *Report - Mardum Shumari Raj Marwar, 1891 AD*, 130.
62. Shyamaldas, *Vir Vinod*, Part-I, 196.
63. Rajendra Prasad Bhatnagar, ed., *Mewar ka Rajya Prabandh evam Maharana Raj Singh Kaleen Do Bahiyan*, (Udaipur: Surya Prakashan Sansthan, 1987), 76.
64. *Report - Mardum Shumari Raj Marwar, 1891 AD*, 493.
65. Ibid., 99.
66. Ibid., 108.
67. Ibid., 112.
68. Ibid., 42.
69. Ibid., 44.
70. Ibid., 160.
71. Ibid., 407.
72. Ibid., 320.
73. Ibid., 230.
74. Ibid., 66.
75. Ibid., 75.
76. Ibid., 200.
77. Agrawal, introduction to *Akath Kahani Prem ki: Kabir ki Kavita aur Unka Samay*, 8.
78. See: Ranchhod Bhatt, *Rajprashasti Mahakavyam* (Udaipur: Sahitya Sansthan, Rajasthan Vidyapeeth, 1973) & Sadashiv, *Rajratnakar Mahakavya* (Jodhpur: Rajasthan Prachya Vidya Pratishthan, 2000).
79. Bhatta, *Rajprashasti Mahakavya*, 34.
80. Dharampal Sharma, *Mewar Sanskriti evam Parampara* (Udaipur: Pratap Shodh Sansthan, 1999), 112.
81. Shyamaldas, *Vir Vinod,* Part-I, 185.
82. *Report - Mardum Shumari Raj Marwar, 1891 AD*, 138.
83. Ibid., 155.
84. Ibid., 200.
85. Ibid., 131.
86. Ibid., 98.
87. See: Ranchhod Bhatt's *Rajprashasti Mahakavya* & Sadashiv's *Rajratanakar Mahakavya.*
88. Narottamdas Swami,ed., *Rajasthani Sahitya Sangrah,* Part-I, no. 27 (Jodhpur: Rajasthan Prachya Vidya Sansthan, 1997).
89. Ibid., 18.
90. Sharma, *Mewar Sanskriti* evam *Parampara*, 66.
91. Ibid., 13.
92. Ibid., 92.

93. Shashi Arora, *Rajasthan Mein Naari ki Stithi* (Jodhpur: Hindi Sahitya Prakashan Mandir, 1995), 20.
94. *Rajasthani Sahitya Sangrah,* Part-I, 21.
95. *Report - Mardum Shumari Raj Marwar, 1891*, 223.
96. Ibid., 428.
97. Arora, *Rajasthan Mein Naari ki Stithi*, 24.
98. Ibid., 26.
99. *Report - Mardum Shumari Raj Marwar, 1891 AD*, 24.
100. Ibid., 24.
101. Ibid.
102. Arora, *Rajasthan Mein Naari ki Stithi*, p.39.
103. See: Devilal Paliwal, ed., *Mewar ke Raja, Raniyon, Kunwaron Kunwarion ka Haal* (Udaipur: Sahitya Sansthan, Rajasthan Vidyapeeth, 1985).
104. Ibid., 6.
105. Ibid., 9.
106. Ojha, *Jodhpur Rajya ka Itihas*, 260.
107. Ibid., 326.
108. Arora, *Rajasthan Mein Naari ki Stithi*, 57.
109. *Mewar ke Raja, Raniyon, Kunwaron Kunwarion ka Haal,* 3-7.
110. Arora, *Rajasthan Mein Naari ki Stithi*, 63.
111. Ojha, *Udaipur Rajya ka Itihas*, 266.
112. Kalyan Singh Shekhawat, *Meera ki Pramanik Jivani* (Jodhpur: Rajasthani Sahitya Sansthan, 2006), 28.
113. Ojha, *Udaipur Rajya ka Itihas*, 358.
114. Ibid., 334.
115. Ibid., 265.
116. Ibid., 333.
117. Ojha, *Jodhpur Rajya ka Itihas*, 290.
118. Sarda, *Maharana Sanga*, 72.
119. Alamshah Khan, *Meera: Loktatvik Adhyayan* (Udaipur: Sanghi Prakashan, 1989), 72.
120. Ojha, *Udaipur Rajya ka Itihas*, 339.
121. Ibid., 341.
122. Shekhawat, *Meera ki Pramanik Jivani*, 43.
123. Arora, *Rajasthan Mein Naari ki Stithi*, p.71.
124. Khan, *Meera: Loktatvik Adhyayan*, p.33.
125. Arora, *Rajasthan Mein Naari ki Stithi*, 40.
126. Ibid., 77.
127. Tod, *Annals and Antiquities of Rajasthan*, 1:744.
128. Arora, *Rajasthan Mein Naari ki Stithi*, 90.

129. Ibid., 83.
130. Ibid., 86.
131. Alexander Kinloch Forbes, *Sanskritik Gujarat,* Hinditrans. of *Rasmala* by Gopal Narain Bahura (Jaipur: Publication Scheme, 1993), 25.
132. Sangari, *Meerabai aur Bhakti ki Aadhyatmik Arthaneeti*, 51.
133. Tod, *Annals and Antiquities of Rajasthan*, 1:744.
134. *Report -Mardum Shumari Raj Marwar, 1891*, p.20.
135. Mukta, *Upholding the Common Life: The Community of Meera Bai*, 69.
136. Ojha, *Udaipur Rajya ka Itihas*, 333.
137. Ibid., 282.
138. Gaurishankar Ojha, *Sirohi Rajya ka Itihas* (Jodhpur: Rajasthani Granthagar, 1997), 225.
139. Ojha, *Jodhpur Rajya ka Itihas*, 285.
140. Harinarayan Purohit, "Meera Prakaran," *Parampara* (Special Issue on Vidyabhushana Harinarayan Purohit), no. 63-64 (1982): 69.
141. Arora, *Rajasthan Mein Naari ki Stithi*, 80.
142. Bhatanagar, *Mewar ka Rajya Prabandh evam Maharana Raj Singh Kaleen Do Bahiyan.*
143. Arora, *Rajasthan Mein Naari ki Stithi,* 72 & Sharma, *Mewar: Sanskriti aur Parampara*, 75.
144. *Report - Mardum Shumari Raj Marwar, 1891 AD*, 21.
145. Arora, *Rajasthan Mein Naari ki Stithi*, 71.
146. Forbes, *SanskritikGujarat*, 141.
147. Ojha, *Jodhpur Rajya ka Itihas*, 339.
148. Arora, *Rajasthan Mein Naari ki Stithi*, 81.
149. Ibid., 39.
150. See: Arora's *Rajasthan Mein Naari ki Stithi* and also *Report – Mardum Shumari Raj Marwar, 1891 AD*, 47.
151. Ibid., 44.
152. Neerja Bhatt, "Rajratanakar Mein Itihas aur Sanskrit" in *Rajratnakar Mahakavya*, 3.
153. Forbes, *Sanskritik Gujarat*, 219.
154. *Mewar ke Raja, Raniyon, Kunwaron Kunwarion ka Haal*, 1.
155. Ojha, *Udaipur Rajya ka Itihas*, 342.
156. *Mewar ke Raja, Raniyon, Kunwaron Kunwarion ka Haal* p.7.
157. Vasumati Sharma, *Rathore Rajvansh ke Riti-Riwaz* (Jodhpur: Maharaja Man Singh Pustak Prakash Shodh Sansthan, 2000), 28.
158. Gaurishankar Ojha, *Udaipur Rajya ka Itihas*, 190.

159. Kalyan Singh Shekhawat, ed., *Meera Granthavali*, (Delhi: Vani Prakashan, 2nd edn. 2004), 1:29.
160. Tod, *Annals and Antiquities of Rajasthan*, 2:741.
161. *Report - Mardum Shumari Raj Marwar, 1891 AD*, 345.
162. Tod, *Annals and Antiquities of Rajasthan*, 2:742.
163. Forbes, *Sanskritik Gujarat*, 113.
164. Sharma, *Mewar Sanskriti evam Parampara*, 65.
165. Gopinath Sharma, *Rajasthan ke Itihas ke Srot* (Jaipur: Rajasthan Hindi Granth Academy, 1973), 156.
166. Sharma, *Mewar Sanskriti evam Parampara*, 11.
167. Neerja Bhatt, "RajratanakarMein Itihas aur Sanskrit", 72.
168. Ramsharan Sharma, *Bhartiya Samantvad*, Hindi trans. (New Delhi: Rajkamal Prakashan, 1994), 33.
169. Bhatnagar, *Mewar ka Rajya Prabandh evam Maharana Raj Singh Kaleen Do Bahiyan.*, 79.
170. *Report - Mardum Shumari Raj Marwar, 1891 AD*, 93.
171. Ibid., 57.
172. Ojha, *Udaipur Rajya ka Itihas*, 326.
173. *Report - Mardum Shumari Raj Marwar, 1891 AD*, 440.
174. Ojha, *Udaipur Rajya ka Itihas*, 290.
175. Agrawal, *Akath Kahani Prem ki: Kabir ki Kavita aur Unka Samay*, 145.
176. Ojha, *Udaipur Rajya ka Itihas*, 744.
177. This folk narrative is at the entrance gate of the temple. The copper plaque certifies in favour of Meera: *Poorvshri chitrakoote kshiti viditgriovdhshen. Devanshey shino mrin medpaat dwish dassahdhara – durg san mool bhumao. MeeraragyeeSheersath Stadanunrip Jay Singh pushtyadhwriitya sheesshein swasthpita-sanwadyypurrey mandirey swarnshringey.*
178. Ojha, *Sirohi Rajya ka Itihas*, 22.
179. Ojha, *Udaipur Rajya ka Itihas*, 463.
180. *Report - Mardum Shumari Raj Marwar, 1891 AD*, 22.
181. Bhatnagar, *Mewar ka Rajya Prabandh evam Maharana Raj Singh Kaleen Do Bahiyan*, 76.
182. Satish Chandra, *Madhyakalin Bharat*, Hindi trans. (New Delhi: NCERT, 1993), 32.
183. Khan, *Meera: Loktatvik Adhyayan*, 41.
184. Ojha, *Udaipur Rajya ka Itihas*, p.32.
185. Bhatnagar, *Mewar ka Rajya Prabandh evam Maharana Raj Singh Kaleen Do Bahiyan*, 21.

186. Parita Mukta, *Upholding the Common Life: The Community of Meerabai,* 56 & Madhu Kishwar & Ruth Vanita, "Poison to Nectar: The Life and Work of Mirabai," *Manushi,* no. 50-51-52 (January-June 1989), 75.
187. Sharma, *Rajasthan ke Itihas ke Srot,* 46.
188. Ibid., 47.
189. Ibid., 49.
190. Ojha, *Udaipur Rajya ka Itihas,* 323.
191. Sharma, *Rajasthan ke Itihas ke Srot,* 141.
192. Sharma, *Mewar Sanskriti aur Parampara,* 16.
193. Tod, *Annals and Antiquities of Rajasthan,* 2:323.
194. Khan, *Meera: Loktatvik Adhyayan,* 41.
195. Ibid., 41.
196. Ibid., 42.
197. *Report - Mardum Shumari Raj Marwar, 1891,* 62.
198. Ibid., 304.
199. Ibid., 94.
200. Bhati, *Rajasthan ke Mertiya Rathore,* 176.
201. Purohit, introduction to *Meera Brahit Padavali,* 1:.4.

Chapter - III

Religious Narratives

As suggested by various religious narratives, Meera was a unique saint-devotee, the only one of her kind. In traditional historical sources such as khyat, bahi, twareekh and the similar texts, there is little to no mention of Meera, therefore most of the information regarding her life and character is available in her poetry sung through generations, along with Hindu devotional literature. Most religious narratives acknowledge her as a saint-poet, they also recognise that she was strikingly different from other devotees of her time. One can understand that how an extraordinary mind, surrounded by a legion of queens and royal relatives, where she actually had to tiptoe on the brink of propriety and face subtle tyrannies day in and out, where there was no immunity from jealousies and dark secrets, she could not but seek refuge in the path of devotion, in her defiance of the materialistic, ambitious socio-political milieu. Her pristine, unwavering devotion, and her use of the regional language added the mass appeal she deserved. A number of devotional sects of the Braj-mandal region tried to accord her the status of a saint, to assimilate her in their respective groups, with a view to promoting their own ideologies and commandments. They supported the exceptional image of the 'woman' saint devotee, who renounced her royal ties to seek God. Many dimensions were added to Meera's image to popularize her, some of which were accepted by the general public, and some were dismissed. Most established sects and institutions were at their wit's end to see Meera's growing fame, not being able to decide whether to eclipse her devotional legacy or to deem her as one their own. They could neither outdo her mass appeal, nor could emulate her aristocratic lineage. To outshine Meera was a real challenge. Those who tried to incorporate Meera as one of their fellow adherents, focused on the practices and principles they and Meera had in common, in turn, overlooked her bold and confident feminine vision. Some even rejected Meera as a saint devotee on the basis of her feudal lineage.

In order to discover a truthful portrayal of Meera, we need to closely examine the religious narratives regarding her life. It must be noted that devotional poetry, anecdotal and religious accounts of Meera's life can be used to recover history; those records do chronicle her as a woman of extraordinary grit and resolve, combating patriarchy and a plethora of stereotypes.

1

Meera's character is depicted in several early sixteenth-century religious narratives. There is a mention of Meera in 'Vyas Vani,' a poetic epic composed by Shri Hariram Vyas in 1555, who was a follower of Shri Hit Harivansh Mahaprabhu (the founder of Radhavallabh sect). Among other saint-poets of her time, Meera is mentioned in the two couplets of Vyas Vani.[1] The reference suggests that Meera was not only a saint devotee herself but also a woman who strongly admired and supported other saint-devotees. In this work, many saints' characteristics have been depicted, but nothing to set them apart from their peers, but regarding Meera it is said, *Meerabai binu kau Bhaktini ko pita jaan ur lavey.* (i.e. who else other than Meera will, like a father, adore the devotees?).

Meera had steadfast respect for the saints and devotees of

her time, as reflected in her poetry. Meera is believed to have had extended warm hospitality and honour to Hariram Vyas, the devotional poet, as reflected in certain hagiographical sources of Vallabh *sampradaya.* Over the course of time, Meera herself became a saint-devotee. However, they do not dwell on Meera's love for Krishna, which in the later period, became the subject of a lot of religious biographies. The popular accounts of her life might have been built on traditional oral narratives.

A trusted, relatively unbiased source that sheds light on Meera's life and her times is *Bhaktamal,* a poem in the Braja language written by Guru Nabhadas ji, a disciple of Guru Shri Krishna Payhari, of Ramanandi sect. A contemporary of Tulsidas, Nabhadas, in his work *Bhaktamal* of 316 stanzas (chappey) has written on the lives of over two hundred devotees. This is an important piece of medieval India's literature, considered next to the Ramcharitmanas of Tulsidas. *Bhaktamal* also continued to be a popular text among its contributors and readers over 2 or 3 centuries. It inspired new works with similar titles. As the year of its first publication was 1594, which coincides with Meera's living years; its commentary on her character is highly plausible. *Bhaktamal* acknowledges her profound devotion in Nabhadas's verses, *Bhakti nissan bajaya ke kaho te na laji* (Upon proclaiming her devotion loud and clear she never felt ashamed). Here, we learn about some details of her life.

(1) Meera embraced the path of Krishna bhakti and never prioritized family 'honour' in the eyes of the society. (2) Meera was bold, unyielding and (3) the vicious accused her and conspired to kill her. She drank a bowl of poison accepting it as a divine nectar and nothing happened to her.[2] Nabhadas embellished some of her traits which added to her mass-appeal as a saint-devotee. He suggested that Meera's love for Krishna was *gopiwat,* similar to that of cowherd women who obtained the grace of Lord Krishna. This analogy might have been made to fit her image within the prevalent, much-familiar imagery

of devotion. Contrary to the popular perception that Krishna worship is similar to the love of Gopis towards Shri Krishna, there is no such claim in Meera's poetry. Meera's miraculous survival after drinking a bowl of poison might not be true. Not everything in the biographies of medieval ecclesiastical leaders or saints are hard-edged facts, rather they were seasoned with divine qualities to gain greater mass appeal. Nabhadas presented some incidents of Meera's life as supernatural and mysterious.[3] This is also true that Meera's living days were not too far from the time when *Bhaktamal* was composed. Moreover, Galta was not far off from Merta-Chittorgarh. So, he might have come to know about the feudal woman's strong will and devotional determination and gave her a deserving mention. Nabhadas also reveals her brave and bold character which was admired and much talked about in her time. He does recognise that Meera's defiance against social expectations were not for the sake of greater self-empowerment, but for the sustenance of her deep love for Shri Krishna. There is a possibility that during Nabhadas ji's period, tales of Meera's resistance and courage were popular among the masses, therefore in *Bhaktamal,* Meera as a brave, rebellious and inspired woman eclipses the image of Meera as a saint. However, in the later editions of *Bhaktamal,* the image was transformed, where her tranquil, soulful devotion was brought to the fore. Dhruvdas of Radhavallabh sect composed *Bhakt Namavali,* which emphasizes on Meera's pure devotion. Dhruvdas states, *Prakat bhakti ki khaani*..., for Meera and also, *vimal hiyo* or *trin sam ganyo sansaar* (i.e. empathetic heart, regarded the whole world of no avail to her). He sheds light on different aspects of Meera's personality. He even believes that Meera was not displeased with her relatives, because they had realized their mistake and they had repented.[4]

Priyadas, a disciple of Nabhadas of the Ramanandi sect, made a detailed commentary on *Bhaktamal,* titled it *Bhaktirasabodhini,* which further enhanced Meera's saint-devotee image. Priyadas was also a follower of the Chaitanya sect and had faith in Chaitanya Mahaprabhu, the legendary saint who propounded the Hare Krishna movement. After Nabhadas ji, Priyadas contributed a great deal to Meera's life history. He cites plenty of evidence to substantiate that Meera had been a devotee since she was a child. This is also aligned with A. K. Ramanujan's theory on the five phases in the lives of women saint devotees—an early submission to God, abstaining from marriage, revolting against social norms and changes and marrying the soul with God. Priyadas includes almost all these phases to narrate Meera's life[5]. He states that :

(1) Since childhood, Meera had been in love with Krishna. Her engagement and marriage were against her will. (2) Immediately after her marriage, Meera refused to worship a goddess, who was an ancestral deity at her in-laws', which annoyed her mother-in-law and infuriated Rana so much that he wanted to kill her. (3) Meera's sister-in-law tried to convince her but she refused to renounce her love for Krishna. The familial discord reached its peak when she was offered a bowl of poison and persuaded to consume it. (4) Rana drew his sword to kill Meera, and in turn of events, he spared her life. (5) A fellow sadhu proposed to have intimate relationship with Meera, but she rejected. (6) Akbar along with Tansen (one of his courtiers) visited the Krishna temple. (7) In Vrindavan, Meera had a meeting with Jiva Goswami, the paramount scholar from the Gaudiya Vaishnava school of Vedanta tradition, and broke his vow of abstaining from seeing a woman's face. (8) Due to Rana's ill will and resentment, Meera left the palace, lived in Dwarka and worshipped only Krishna. Rana, finally, had sent a delegation of brahmins to Dwarka to request Meera to return to Mewar. (9) Meera, upon being insisted and asked repeatedly, went into her Krishna temple and dissolved into the idol of Krishna.[6]

Priyadas's portrayal of Meera as a saint-devotee was different from that of Nabhadas. He chronicles the key events in her life in his own way. Priyadas's depiction of Meera does not show a character with undaunted courage and resolve, in the face of an authority figure. Rather, her refusal to worship devi was nothing unusual. This behaviour was quite common in the medieval India's sects of Krishna devotees, who would worship no one but Shri Krishna. Priyadas believes that all misery and suffering of the devotees would vanish once they seek refuge in Lord Krishna. Complete submission to God is the sole way to have relief from worldly pains, according to Priyadas. If we are to believe Priyadas, we can see that Meera chose to submit herself to Lord Krishna, so she could pull herself through the harrowing ordeals including the political unrest, self-exile from her homeland, and hostility of her in-laws. She did not even flinch from drinking poison, because it was presented to her as a devotional offering, and still, she lived, and also became in fact, immortalized in the folk memory. Similarly, Rana tried to get rid of her, but he could not, he had to return, mortified. However, Priyadas also incorporates some miracles into Meera's life events, to make her tales of devotion even more appealing to the common people. It was one of the salient features in the devotional biographies of that time, so, the lives of similar other devotees were also depicted in the same manner.[7] To reinforce her saintly image further, Priyadas shows how Akbar the great visited Meera along with his courtier Tansen, to have the opportunity to see Lord Krishna himself. As per tradition, women devotees had to 'prove' their allegiance to her deity. A perverse sadhu who sought intimacy with Meera was at once declined, which reflects Meera's steadfast loyalty to her Lord. Since Priyadas was also a follower of the Chaitanya sect, he might have tried to reconstruct her image accordingly, but was not very successful in doing so[8]. Priyadas recounts in detail how Meera met Jiva Goswami, which shows another instance of her unyielding nature. Meera wanted to have an audience with Jiva Goswami who refused to see her. Jiva Goswami informed her that he would not allow a woman's presence anywhere near him. Mirabai sent her reply that everyone in Brij was a woman, except for Lord Krishna. Everyone but her Lord were gopis (cowherd women, admirers of Krishna). Jiva Goswami was able to fathom Meera's devotion to Krishna, and immediately corrected his mistake by meeting her in person. This shows a woman's confidence and strength of character enabling her to fearlessly penetrate into the glass walls of male-dominated sphere of religion.

In 1660, *Dadupanthi Bhaktamal* by Raghavdas depicted Meera's life and character, however, this text was influenced by Nabhadas's *Bhaktamal.* Raghavdas's *Bhaktamal* was written from the point of view of a liberal Nirgun Panthi. There were several other free-thinking saint-devotees included in his work. It must be noted that he uses the word 'Ram' instead of 'Krishna' to describe Meera's devotion. We should also note that interchanging 'Ram' and 'Krishna' were not unconventional those days as both deities were worshipped with equal fervour. In his work, Raghavdas has a more pragmatic approach than Nabhadas. His work reveals three key factors in Meera's life. First, Rana became her enemy because she was mingling with sadhus, without a concern for the family's reputation, so he attempted to kill her. Secondly, the society was not in favour of ignoring traditional norms and supporting Meera, and third, Meera, despite being a woman, made her presence felt in religious congregations and devotional activities.[9] According to Raghavdas, the aristocracy, the erstwhile society and the religious authority were against Meera but she stood firm facing all three, against all odds. Meera faced a number of challenges but then, of course, was successful in cementing her name in the most revered saint-devotees. Chaturdas had included an interesting reference of her association with sages and hermits, in his commentary on Raghavdas's *Bhaktamal.* According to Chaturdas, a king suffered from a stomach disease, and he sent a delegation of brahmins to implore Meera to return to Mewar from Dwarka. He commanded, *Ley kari abhu mohe jibabhu...*[10]' (Go and get Meera and save my life).

2

Meera was a bit different from other saint-devotees of her time but she honoured them. Still, she never expressed her allegiance to any formal sects or denominations like the Vallabh sampradaya. However, there are several references to Meera's life in texts of Vallabh sages. In medieval India, outside Braj (Vrindavan) region, different sects of Krishna devotion were flourishing including Vallabh, Radhavallabh, Chaitanya, Nimbarka among others. These schools of devotion not only had their own philosophies, but also developed their own rites, performances, music, and art forms. No historical records suggest that they were hostile to each other, but a subtle rival undertone is clearly manifest because sometimes they tried to brand any influential individuals, who might just be favourably disposed towards their devotional sect, straight away as their 'fellow followers'. Meera's devotion had a great mass appeal because she rejected the power play and ambitions despite hailing from an aristocratic family, and she did not conform to patriarchal dictates, in spite of being a woman in medieval India. So, her circumstances were unique, much like her devotion. She was not keen on accepting established institutions or values, she was unmediated by conventional forms of devotion or intermediaries. Her love for her God was impassioned and liberal; ethereal yet grounded. Her feudal lineage enhanced her popularity; something which was hard to contest by her contemporaries. So, Vallabh sampradaya tried to assimilate her into their sect in order to share her fame. Meera could never have agreed, and perhaps, due to this reason, they wanted to shame her a few times. This is evident in *Chaurasi Vaishnav ki Varta* and *Do Sau Bavan Vaishnavan ki Varta (Discourse of Eighty-Four Vaishnavites* and *Discourse of Two Hundred and Fifty-Two Vaishnavites).* They were compiled by Har Rai, a disciple of Goswami Gokulnath (1551-1663). A common feature of these works is that Meera is considered undeserving of any praises, whereas the disciples of Vallabhacharya and his son Vitthalnath are described as noble pioneers of their sect and worthy of exalting descriptions. It is obvious that they made some scathing remarks only to belittle her. In *Chaurasi Vaishnav ki Varta* there are mentions of three such disciples who try to lower her dignity and insult her.

Ramdas, the first priest, challenges Meera to a discourse, he renders a song of Mahaprabhu, instead of Meera's deity Thakruji, Meera does not consider any other leader as her deity, so she implored him to sing another devotional song on Thakurji. As a result, Ramdas is furious and hurls abuse at her by calling her *daari raand* (i.e. promiscuous woman) and vows never to see her face in life again. He cries, *Jo raand tero acharya ji mahaprabhu par samatav nahin jo humko tieri virti kaha karni hai*[11] (promiscuous woman, why should I serve you?) Krishnadas, in the second incident, heads a panel of eight friends, and they reach Meera's village after a pilgrimage from Ranchodji Temple in Dwarka. There, he stays with Harivansh and Vyas of the Radhavallabh sect. Krishnadas refuses Meera's hospitality because she is not a disciple of Mahaprabhu Acharya. He also refuses to take the gift for Shrinathji that Meera wishes to give.[12] Govind Dubey, the third, a Sachora Brahmin, stays at her place for a religious discourse but the moment he gets a message from Gosain ji, he leaves instantly and does not pay heed to Meera's request to stay.[13] In *Do Sau Bavan Vaishnavan ki Varta* there are two incidents related to Meera's life. Ajabkunwar Bai, Meera's sister-in-law, wants to have a *darshan* of Lord Krishna in Merta by the grace of Mahaprabhu Vallabhacharya. Ajabkunwar Bai expresses her desire to be consecrated by Vallabhacharya himself but Meera opposes this idea. Finally, Ajabkunwar Bai moves on and becomes an adherent of the *Pushti marg* (the path of nurturing the soul, the system propounded by Vallabhacharya). Here, Meera, who was not interested in monopolies of dominant sects, is shown to have no influence over her in-laws. The second incident is related to a sister of Jaimal whose residence was located next to that of Haridas Bania. She became a disciple of Mahaprabhu as suggested through a letter. Interestingly, in this work, there is no mention of Meera as Jaimal's sister.[14] Thus Vallabhacharya devotees put a lot of effort to show Meera belonging to their sect, and when they failed, they left no stone unturned to tarnish her reputation. This makes it even more obvious that Meera had an enviable mass appeal which resulted in jealousies and false claims. Ramdas, Meera's family priest too was annoyed with her for her stubborn love for Thakurji instead of Mahaprabhu. However, this reported incident is quite contrary to Ramdas's known character, and there might have been some other reason for his discontent, but the followers of the Vallabhacharya sect promoted the incident in such a way, that it seems Meera was single-handedly responsible for infuriating the family priest. Krishnadas Adhikari's meeting with Meera is likely to be part of a pre-planned conspiracy. He reaches Meera's village when Harivansh and Vyas are already there. So, it may seem that Krishnadas was sent with an ulterior motive. In some works of literature, Krishnadas is even described to be shrewd and quarrelsome, capable of conspiring and harm, who would go to any extent to triumph over his opponent[15]. In *Do Sau Bavan Vaishnavan ki Varta,* there is a clear, deliberate attempt to devalue Meera's fame. Meera's devotion is shown to be too weak to persuade her family members into her path, and secondly, Jaimal's sister, the mystery woman who lived under a veil, chose to become a disciple of Mahaprabhu Acharya. It seems that Meera, in spite of her lack of interest in being confined to any single sect or creed, later gave in and became a Vallabhacharya devotee. This implication might have resulted from a spiteful rivalry.

Meera's devotion was restricted by no sectarian boundary, class, or creed, so the common people could relate to it one way or the other, and to embrace it. In the later years, her pure faith, absolute submission and unsuspecting innocence were admired by not only the masses but also more progressive groups of the Vallabhacharya sect. Later *pushtimargiya* devotees themselves mentioned Meera in their texts as a honourable, powerful devotee of Krishna. Bhakt Nagaridas, alias Jaswant Singh Rathore, the ruler of Kishangarh was among one of Meera's descendants, and interestingly, a *pushtimargiya* devotee. He included some of Meera's devotional verses in his work *Pad Prasang Mala* and also added events related to them. There are six devotional verses and the same number of events, which he uses to highlight her saintliness and devotion. Nagaridas refers to Meera's marriage to Rana, her refusal to consummate the marriage and also her denial to become a *sati* on Rana's death.[16]

Similarly, Dayaram (1767-1852), yet another disciple of Vallabh sect from Gujarat praises Meera in relation to the religious principle of *pushtimarg*. His texts *Meera Charitra* (Character of Meera), *Bhakti Vel* (Religious Time) and *Chaurasi Vaishnav* (Eighty-four Vaishnavites) shower accolades on Meera as a saint-devotee. However, there is hardly any mention of historical evidence regarding Meera's life. In *Meera Charitra* there are eighty lines which clearly associate Meera with the Vallabh sect.[17] According to Dayaram, Meera was a daughter of Jaimal and she was married to the Rana of Udaipur.[18] These two assumptions have no historical relevance. It is true that Jaimal was one of the sons of Maldev of Jodhpur who also embraced the Vallabh faith, perhaps this is why, in order to relate Meera with the Vallabh sect Dayaram perceived that Jaimal was Meera's father. In *Bhakti Vel* and *Chaurasi Vaishnav*,

Dayaram refers to two events of Meera's life. One related to the bowl of poison which was sent to Meera and the other, Ramdas was the family priest.[19] Since Ramdas was one among the eighty-four disciples of Vallabhacharya he might have been mentioned intentionally.

3

During the latter half of the seventeenth century, Meera was accepted as a saint-devotee, by nearly all devotional sects and institutions. Some elements of imagination were added to Meera's character in her biographical sketches, her image as an ideal, saintly Krishna devotee was brought to the fore and her struggle as a woman against the gender biases and patriarchal norms, became an increasingly overlooked subject. Brahamdas, a Dadupanthi Charan, poet and a devotee, described Meera's character in his *Bhaktamal* (1759). Like many other texts, this work also emphasizes Meera as a saint-devotee who took spiritual refuge in Lord Krishna. Brahmadas states, *Kaaj isa maharaj kariyee, jiye kaaj isaa maharaj karayee* (It is true that a devotee is helped and protected, this responsibility is carried out by Shri Bhagwan, accordingly He works).[20] Mahipati, a saint belonging to Varkari movement of Maharashtra in his book *Bhakta Lilamrita* (1774) said that Meera was given poison by her father and she drank it, due to which Sarangapani Krishna's body turned blue.[21] Similarly, Seepinama, another saint of the same sect, in his work *Meera Charitra* focuses on Meera's image as a devotee. He also points out that she had a devotional streak since childhood. It is also stated that Krishna had already married her, so she objected when her parents wanted to get her married.[22] "Meerabai ki Parchi" (1798) by Sukhsaran, a follower of Ramsnehi sect, gives an account of the previous birth of Meera. Sukhsaran cites Srimad Bhagavata Purana, recalling that a Brahmin's wife from Barsana was in love with Krishna, because of her unquenched thirst for divine love, she was reborn as Meera in her next birth. Sukhsaran also alludes to some supernatural events in Meera's life. He says that Meera saw Lord Krishna instead of Rana on her bed, and that a lion compelled Rana to flee from her presence and also, she was visible in every temple of Chittorgarh at the same time[23]. Radhabai, a resident of Baroda, in her work *Garba Meeran Mahatamya* (1843) dwells on the saint-devotee image of Meera. Radhabai puts forward the notion that Meera's mother had left her and her brother tried to get her married. She also echoes that Rana offered Meera poison which actually turned into divine nectar and Rana could see Meera in ten or twenty palaces, all at the same time.[24]

Based on her biographical sketches, it is safe to say that Meera was not a saint-devotee, in the traditional sense of the term. Many religious literature along with oral legends have added to her fame as a saint-devotee over centuries. Even after she passed away, the religious narratives about her life grew for over two hundred years. These narratives explore her character as a devotee and sometimes a historical woman, who struggled to assert herself in a male-dominated family and religious life. To cope with unending grief, loss and instability, she immersed herself in devotion. There were repeated failed attempts by many devotees to make her part of their own sects, or to dwarf her image, and at times, to surpass her popularity. The devotional literature also reveals that a lot of influential religious sects mushroomed in medieval India, a time, rife with disorder and conquest. However, by the latter half of the seventeenth century, the groups shed away their differences and disputes, and Meera was given due recognition of a legendary saint-poet. Meera's fame as a Krishna devotee is unmissable in these narratives, some legends about her were genuine and correspond with verifiable historical records, and many were steeped in supernatural ardour, and mystic religiosity which kept on adding more and more to her mass appeal.

Notes and References

1. *Itno hai sab kutumb hamaro,*
 Sain, dhana aru nama, Pipa, Kabir, Raidas, chamaro.
 Roop sanatan ko sevak Gangal Bhatt, sutharo,
 Surdas, Parmanand, meha, Meera bhakti, vicharo.
 Brahman rajputra kul uttam teu karat jaati ko garo,
 Adi ant bhaktin ko survasu Radhavallabh pyro.
 Ansoo ko Haridas rasik, harivansh na mohi bisaro,
 Iti path chalet syam syama kai byashi buron bhavein taro.
 Vihaarihi swami binu ko gave.
 Binu harivashi Radhavallabh ko ras riti sunwae,
 Krishnadas binu girdharju koo ko ab laad ladave,
 Swarath, parmarath Jaimal binu ko sak bandhu khave.
 Parmananddas binu ko ab leela gaye sunave,
 Surdas binu pad rachna ko kaun kavi kahi aave.
 aur sakal sadhun binu ko abyeh kalikaal katave,
 Vyasdas in sab binu ko abtan ki tapati bujhave. – Hariram Vyas, *Shri Vyas Vaani - Sampurna* (Vrindavan: Shree Hit Ashram Satsang Bhumi, 2013), 40, http://www.ras-lila.com/vyas-vani.html.
2. *Sadris Gopi prem pragat, kalijughin di khayo.*
 Nirankush ati nidar, rasik jas rasna gayo.
 Dushitin dosh vichari, mrityo ko uddin kiyo.
 Bar na bankon bhyo, garal amirt jyon piyon.
 Bhakti Nissan bajaye ke kahu te nahi na laji.
 Lok laaj kul shrinkhata, taji Meera girdhar bhaji. - Nabhadas, *Shri Bhaktamal -Shri Priyadasji Praneet Tika- Kavit Sahit*, ed. Sitaram Sharan Bhagwan Prasad Roopkala (Lucknow: Tej Kumar Book Depot
 Pvt. Ltd., 3rd edn. 2011) 712.
3. Hazari Prasad Dwivedi, *Hazari Prasad Dwivedi Granthavali* (New Delhi: Rajkamal Prakashan, 1981), 3:391.
4. *Laaj chandi Girdhar bhaji, kari na kachu kul kani,*
 Soee Meera jag vidit, pragat bhakti ko khani.
 Nrityat nupur baandhi key, nachat le kartar,
 Vimal hiyoo bhaktini mili, trin sam ganyoo sansar.
 Bandhuni vish takon diyon, kari vichar chit aan,
 So vish phiri amrit bhyo, tab lagey pachitan.
 Lalita hoo laee bolike, taason ho ati het,
 Anand so nirkhat phirey, Vrindavan ras khet. - Nabhadas, *Shri Bhaktamal*, 713.

5. Nancy M. Martin, "Meerabai: Shastron Mein Ulekhit, Jivan Mein Rupayit," *Rangayan*, January-March 1997, 9.
6. *Merto janmbhoomi, jhoomi hit nain lagey,*
Pagey girdharilal pita hi ke dhaam mein.
Rana ke Sagai bhai kari byah samanhi,
Gayi mat boodi ya rangeeley ghanshyam mein.
Bhanwrey parat, man sanwary sarup maanjh,
Tanwarey si avey, chalibey ko pati gaam mein.
Poonchey pita-mata, pat aabhran lijey ju,
Lochan bharat neer kaam daam mein. (471)
Devou girdharilal, jo nihaal kiyo chahoo,
Aur dhan maal sab rakihyoo uthay ke.
Beti ati pyari, preeti rang chadhyo bhari,
Roey mili mahtari, kahi lijey ladaye ke.
Dola padhraye drig drigso ladey chalin,
Sookh na samay jaye, pran pati pay ke.
Pahuchi bhavan saasu dui ke garan kiyo,
Tiya aruvar ganth jori karyo bhaye ke. (472)
Debi pujaybey kon, kiyo le upay sansun,
Var pe pujayen, puni badhu, piyi bhakhiye.
Boliju bikayo maatho, lal girdhari haath,
aur kaun naiye, ek vahee abhilakhiye.
Badhat sughag yakey pujiy tatey pooja karon,
Karo jin hat sees payen pey rakhiye.
Kahi bar-bar tum yehi niradhaar janoo,
Vahi sukumar jaye vaari pheri nakhiye. (473)
Tab to khisani bhayee, ati jari bari gaiyi,
Gayi pati paas yeh badhu khi kaam ki.
Abhi jawab diyo kiyo apmaan mero,
Aagey ko parman karey kbharey swas cham ki.
Rana suni kop karyo ghar yo hiyo marriboee,
Dayee thori nyari dekhi, reejh mati baam ki.
Laalin ladavey gun gayeke malhavey,
Sadhu sang hi suhavey, jinh lagi cha syam ki. (474)
Aaye kae nanad kahey, Gahey kin chat bhabhi,
Sadhunison het mein kalank laagey bharie.
Rana despati laajey, baap kulreeti lajey,
Maan lijey baat begi sang inivarey.
Laagey pran saath sant, pavan anant such,
Jason dukh hoye, tako nikey kari tariye.
Suni ke katora bhari garal pathaye diyo,

Liyo kari paan rang chadiyon yon nihaariyo. (475)
Garal pathayo tou sis seel rey chadyo,
Sang tyag vish bhari, taaki jhaar na sambhari hai.
Rana ne lagayao cha, baithesaadhudhiga dhar,
Tabahi khabr kara Mauro, yahi dahari hai.
Rajai giridharlal, tinahi saun rang jaal,
Bolat hansat khyaal kanpari pyaari hai.
Jay kai sunai, bhai ati chapali,
Aayo liye tarwar, deyi kivaar kholi nyari hai. (476)
Jakey sung rang bhiji karat prasang nana,
Kahan veh nar gayo, vegi dayin batayen.
Aagey hi birajey, kachho to soun nahi laajey,
Aabhun dekhi sukh sajey, aankeh kholii darsayeei.
Bhayo kisaano rana likhyoo chitrabhit maano,
Ulat pyan kiyo nekoo man aayei.
Dehkyon hun pey prbhaav mein na bhidyoo jayeei,
Bina hari kripa kaho kaise kari payee. (477)
Vishyi kutil ek bhesh dhari sadhoo liyo,
Kiyo jo prasang mosso aang sang kijyeei.
Agyaa mo to dei aap laal girdhari aho,
Sees dhari layii kari bhojan hun lijey.
Sanatani samaj mein bichaye sej boli liyo,
Sank ab kaun ki nisank ras bhijey.
Seit sukh bhyo vishey bhaav sab gyo,
Nayo pyan ayei mokon bhakti daan dijey. (478)
Roop ki nikayi bhoop Akbar bhai hiye,
Siye sang Tansen dekhibey ko aayo hain.
Nirikhi nihal bhyo chabi girdharilal,
Pad sukh jaalek tab hi chadyon.
Vrindavan ayee su Jeev Gosain ju su milijhali,
Tiya mukh dikhibey ko pan chutayo hai.
Dekhi kunj-kunjlal piyari sukh punj bhari,
Dhari ur maanjh aay dekh ban gayo hai. (479)
Rana ki malin mati dekh basi dwaravati,
Rati girdhari lal nit hi laryee.
Laagi chatpati bhoop bhakti ko saroop jaani,
Aati dukh maani, vipr shreni le pathayeei.
Begi lekey avo moko pran dei jeevavo,
Aari gyo dhrano dei binti sunayee.
Sun vida honey gayii rai rancchod ju peyi,
Chado rakho heen leen bhayi nahin payee. (480) - Priyadas, *Shri Baktamal*, 714.

7. Dwivedi, *Hazari Prasad Dwivedi Granthavali,* 3:392.
8. Martin, "Meerabai: Shastron Mein Ulekhit, Jivan Mein Rupayit," 9.
9. *Lok beid kul jagat sukh, muchi meeraan shree hari bhaje.*
Gopin kee see preeti, reeti kali-kaali dikhaee.
Rasikarai jas gai, nidar rahee sant samaee.
Raannai ros upaee, jahar kau pyaalo deenhaun.
Rom khusyau nahin yek, maanni charanaammrt leenhaun.
Naubati bhakti ghuraee kai, pati so giradhar hee saje.
Lok bed kul jagat sukh, muchi Meeraan shree hari bhaje. (214)
- Raghavdas, *Bhaktamal - Chaturdas ki Tika Sahit* (Jodhpur: Rajasthan Prachya Vidya Pratishthan, 1965), 99.
10. Ibid., 100.
11. *Atha Meeraan bai ke purohit Raamadaas, tinakee vaarta*
So ek din Meeraabaee ke shree thaakurajee ke aage raamadaasajee keertan karate hue so raamadaas jee shree aachaary jee mahaaprabhun ke pad gaavat hute, tab meeraan baee bolee jo doosarau pad shree thaakurajee ko gaavo tab raamadaasajee ne kahau meeraan baee so jo are daaree raand yah kaun ko pad hai. yah kaha tere khasam ko moond hai jo ja aaj se terau muhadon kabahoo na dekhoongo. tab tahaan se sab kutumb ko lai ke raamadaas jee uthi chale tab meeraan baee ne bahutero kahyau raamadaasajee rahe naaheen. paachhen phiri ke vaako mukh na dekhyo. aise apane prabhoon son anurakt hute. so va din te meeraan baee ko mukh na dekhyau, vaakeen vrtti chhod deenee, pher vaake gaanv ke aage hoy ke nikase naaheen. meeraabaee ne bahut bulaaye pari ve raamadaas jee aaye naaheen. tab ghar baithe bhent pathaee soee pheri deenee aur kahau jo raand teron shree aachaary jee mahaaprabhun oopar samatv naaheen jo hamako teree vrtti kaha karanee hai. – Gosvami Gokulnath, *Churasee Vaishnavan ki Vartaa* (Nathdwara: Shrividya Vibhaag, 1970), 140 (The text of this work is authentic. But the author of this is disputed. There is a presumption in Vallabh Sect that Goswami Gokulnath narrated the *Vaartaas* and those were scripted by Harirai. The work begins like this: *Vaarta Shree Gokulnathji Prakat Kiye taakaun bhaav Shree Hariraiji kahat, so likhyate.*).
12. *Atha Krshnadaas Adhikaaree, tinakee vaarta*
So ve krshnadaas shoodr ek ber dvaaraka gaye hute so shree ranachhor jee ke darshan kariken tahaan te chale so aapan meeraabaee ke gaanv aaye so ve krshnadaas meeraambaee ke ghar gaye tahaan harivansh vyaas aadi de visheshasah vaishnav hute so kaahoo ko aayai aath din kaahoo ko aaye dash din kaahoo ko aaye

pandrah din bhaye hute tinakee vida na bhee hutee aur krshnadaas nen tau aavat hee kahee jo hoon to chaloongo. tab meeraabaee ne kahee jo baitho tab kitanek mohar shreenaathajee ko den laagee so krshnadaas ne na leenee aur kahau jo toon shreeaachaary jee mahaaprabhun kee sevak naaheen hot taate teree bhent ham haath te chhoovenge naahee so aise kahiken krshnadaas uhaan te uthi chale. -Ibid., 239.

13. *Govind Dube Saachora braahman, tinakee vaarta*
    Aur ek samen govind dube meeraabaee ke ghar hute tahaan meeraabaee son bhagavadvaarta karat atake. tab shree aachaary jee ne sunee jo govind dube meeraabaee ke ghar utare hain, so atake hain, tab shree gusaee jee ne ek shlok likhi pathaayo so ek brajavaasee ke haath pathaayau tab vah brajavaasee chalyau so vahaan jaay pahunchau, ta samay govind dube sandhya bandan karat hute tab brajavaasee ne aayaken vah patr deenon so patr baanchi ke govind dube tatkaal uthe, tab meeraan baee ne bahut samaadhaan keeyo, pari govind dube ne phir paachhen na dekhau. - Ibid., 109.

14. (i) *Shree Gusaee jee ke sevak Ajab Kunvar baee, tinakee vaarta-*
    So ve ajab kunvar baee medate mein rahatee hate, meeraambaee kee devaraanee hatee aur uhaan ek din shree gunsaee jee padhaare jab ajab kanuvar baee koon saakshaat poorn purushottam ke darshan bhae. jab ajab kunvar shree gusaee jee kee sevak bhae aur asht prahar shree gunsaee jee ke charanavind mein chit kagyo rahe jab gusaee ji padhravein lagey tab ajab kunvar baee koon moorchaa aaee tab gusaee ji vaki aisis dasha dekh ke chaar din unhaan birajey aur ajab kunvar baee kun paduka jee padhraey diye tab ajab kunwar baee shuddh pushtimaarg kee reeti pramaanen seva karan laagee aur shree naath jee ajab kunvar baee ke sang nity chopar khelate. Aur ajab kunvar baee kee man mein aesi hati jo shreenathjee sadaev ihaan biraaje to aachoo. – Goswami Gokulnath, *Do Sau Bavan Vaishanava ki Varta* (Mumbai: Shri Venkatesh Press, 1996), 130 (The text of this work is authentic. But the author of this is disputed. There is a presumption in Vallabh Sect that Goswami Gokulnath narrated the *Vaartaas* and those were scripted by Harirai. The work begins like this: *Vaarta Shree Gokulnathji Prakat Kiye taakaun bhaav Shree Hariraiji kahat, so likhyate.*).

(ii) *Shree Gunsaee Jee ke sevak Haridaas Baniya, tinakee vaarta*
So ve haridaas baniya merata gaam mein rahate. va gaam mein ek hee vaishnav hate aur va gaam ko raaja jaimal ho so smaart

dharm mein hato aur ekaadashee pahalee karate hate. aur jaimal raaja kee ben ko ghar haridaas baniya ke saame hato. So jab shree gunsaee hee haridaas ke ghar padhaare hate tab jaimal kee ben koon baaree mein soon shree gunsaee jee ke saakshaat poorn purushottam ke darshan bhaye. jab jaimal kee ben ne patr dvaara shree gunsaee jee ko vinatee likhake patr dvaara sevak bhee kaahe ten ve padada mein se baahar nahin nikasate jaansoo patr dvaara sevak bhe. - Ibid., 80.

15. "The discourse is an example of good diplomatic and complex way of negotiations. Shrinathji's priests were Bengali, Krishnadas wanted them thrown out. Before offering the bhog to Shrinath ji, they offered it to the goddess. Then one day when the Bengali people were engaged in worship, they set fire to their huts. When poor Bengalis leaving behind the rituals ran towards their huts, Krishnadas' men thrashed them and when the poor Bengalis came to plead, they said, "Why did you run away from the ritual?" And fired them; when Rupa and Sanatan Goswami tried to give a slight support, they threatened, "You are shudras and yet you ask Brahmins to bow to you, we will see you." - Dwivedi, *Hazari Prasad Dwivedi Granthavali*, 3:392.
16. (i) *Atha anya pad prasang*

Medate meeraambaee tinakon raana ke chhaate bhaee so byaahee, yah jag-prasiddh hain hee, so kitanek din uparaant kaah samen raana ke va bhaee ko dehaant bhayo, aru raana hute so meeraambaee son dukh paay rahe hate, ye vaishnavan ko satsang karate yaaten va samen raana nen kahaee, jo yah ausar hai tum bharata ke sang satee hohu, tab meeraambaee bhagavat rang aage lage rahai, tyaunhee lage rahe ya samen kachhoo kshedamaanee naaheen aru ya baat ke uttar ko ek vishnu pad nayo banaay raana ko likhi pathaayo, pad bahut prasiddh bhayo. so yah pad-

Meeraan ke rang lagyo haree kau, aur rang sab atak paree.
Giradhar gaasyaan, satee na hosyaan, man mohyo dhan naamee.
Jeth bahoo ko naato nahin raana jee, hoon sevag ye syaamee.
Choodo dobado tilak ju maala, seel bart singaar.
Aur singaar bhaavain nahin raana jee, yaun gur gyaan hamaar.
Koee nidon koee bindo, gun gobind ra gaasyaan.
Jin maarag vai sant pahoonta, tin maarag mhe jaasyaan.
Choree karaan na jeev santaava, kaanee karasee mhaaro koee.
Hasatee chadhi gadhai na chadha, ya to baat na hoee.
Raaj karanta narak padesee, bhogeeda jam kai leeya.
Bhagat karanta mukt pahoonta, jog karanta jeeya.

Giradhar dhanee, kadoombo giradhar, maat pita sut bhaee.
Th thaare mhe mhaare ho raana jee, yaun kahe meeraambaee.

(ii) *Punah anya pad-prasang:*
Meeraan baee saun raana bahaut dukh paayen rahai, raana ke ghar kee reetaten inake bhiny reet, yah bhagavat sambandh sat sang vises karen, deh sambandh ko naato vyauhaar kachhu na maanen, raana bahut samujhaay riyo, nidaan ek vish ko pyaloo unkaoon pathayoo, kayo charanaamrt ko naam leken deejiyon, unakein pran hain, charanaamrt ke naam ten pee hee jaayange, so aise hee bhayo, jaani boojh peeyo, raana to inake maribe kee raah dekhat rahyau, aru vah jhaanjh mrdang sang laike param rang son ek nayo pad banaay thaakur aage gaavat bhaye, pad bahut prasiddh bhayo. so vah yah pad-
Raanai joo vish donau, ham jaanee.
Jboojhi charanaamrt suni piyo, nahin bauree bhau raanee.
Kanchan kasat kasautee jaisain, tan rahyo baarah baanee.
Aapun giradhar nyaav kiyo yah, chhaannyau doodh roo paanee.
Raana kotak vaarau jihi par, haun tihin haath bikaanee.
'Meeraan' prabhu giradhar naagar kain, charan kamal lapataanee.
- Nagaridas, *Nagaridas Granthavali*, ed. Kishorilal Gupta (Varanasi: Nagari Pracharini Sabha, 1955), 3:363.

17. C.L. Prabhat, *Meera: Jivanaur Kavya,* (Jodhpur: Rajasthani Granthagar, 1999), 1:67.
18. *Jaimal raathoranee deekaree re, suno medata enu dhaam,*
Roop gun samovad nahee, roodun dharyun meeraambaee naa.
- Quoted by Prabhat in *Meera: Jivan aur Kavya,* 1:68.
19. Ibid., 69.
20. Charan Brahamdas Dadupanthi, *Bhaktamal* (Jodhpur: Rajasthan Prachya Vidya Pratishthan, 1997), 13 & 48-49.
21. Text quoted by Prabhat in *Meera: Jivanaur Kavya,* 73.
22. Ibid., 62.
23. Sukhsaran, "Meerabai ri Parchi," *in Parampara,* no. 69 & 70:17.
24. Text quoted by Prabhat in *Meera: Jivan aur Kavya,* 69.

Chapter - IV

Poetry

At present, Meera is revered in two ways—as a traditional divinely ordained mystic saint, and also by some, as a romantic poet, inspired by bittersweet pangs of love and longing. This results from the heavy influence of colonial historians who relied merely on traditional legends and folklore. Elements of romance and yearning were given greater importance, and her verses were thus enjoyed as something light and entertaining, reducing her history to mere beauty and romance—to match with the scholars' colonial mindset and interests. Historians who idealized her piety and love, often overlooked her feminine strength and revolutionary aspects. Some feminists portrayed her as a vulnerable, oppressed woman trapped in the shackles of a time and society that were deaf to the suffering of women. This assumption is based on orthodox texts, which were as still as stagnant water, and were never a credible mirror of social realities. According to some critics, Meera is not the representative voice of the society to which she belonged. Meera belongs to the margins and not the centre, therefore her voice too is a marginalized one. Carrying her image to such extremes, does not help us understand her work from a balanced perspective. Before knowing Meera the poet, or a holy saint, we should consider her as 'a woman' who used her poetry to combat injustice and barriers stemming from patriarchal norms.

Her protest was neither too extraordinary, nor an embittered fruit of marginalized sentiments. Rather, her poetry reflects a juncture of medieval India which was about to undergo a drastic change in beliefs and practices with a new wave of progress waiting right at the corner.

In a traditional sense, Meera was not a Bhakti poet, she used her poetry as a tool to protest against patriarchal ideologies and constraints. Her protest was clothed in *bhakti*, which is clearly manifest in her verses. To classify her a bhakti poet right from the start, without assessing her context and circumstances may not do justice to her devotion. Even in the twentieth century, her image was established as a saint-poet. In terms of her nature, purpose, and use of language, Meera is very different from her contemporaries, but early researchers failed to observe her uniqueness. Before putting her on a pedestal and idealizing her, we must realize that Meera was a flesh-and-blood woman, with a distinguishing feminine identity, psycho-spiritual needs, and her struggle for dignity and freedom. Her concerns were broad, yet reasonable. In her verses, there is an articulate, direct expression of some of her concerns. Her poetry reveals her corporeal self, torn by divine longing. Unlike works of any bhakti poets of Meera's time, her poetry outlines her quest for identity, her eager anxiety to remove worldly conflicts. Saint-devotees often believe in karma, and do not dispute theories related to fruits of actions, but Meera's poetry has no inclinations towards antique doctrines and pedantic theories. Meera's use of the simple language, tone and expressions resonate with the everyday feelings and experiences of the ordinary people, though she hailed from a royal family, this also makes her different from many of her contemporaries. Those who consider her society to be unprogressive and oppressive, reflecting on some of Meera's verses, completely ignore the fact that Meera was born in the womb of her time, which was impregnated with seeds of forthcoming reforms. This chapter aims at reflecting on salient features[1] of Meera's poetry, which have been overshadowed by her benign bhakti-poet image.

1

Many foreign writers believe that the negation of materialistic, worldly life[2] is at the core of major traditional Indian philosophies, a fact which we cannot deny. It has been repeatedly asserted from times immemorial that our worldly duties are nothing but an illusion. So, many saints chose to turn their face away from such responsibilities completely. This idea has been etched in many scriptures, epics, mythologies and tales, and it was accepted in the belief system of a large section of the population, transforming the way they see life, the world and the universe. Many spiritual seekers, over centuries, renounced all worldly pleasure and lived as ascetics. This is why there are traces of melancholy and despair in works of saint poets, related to the impermanence of beauty, relationships, happiness and human existence itself.

yo sansaar chahar ki baaji, saanjh padyan ud jassi
and
Iss deh kaa garbh na karna, maati mein mil jaasi

(This world is full of chirping of birds, [signifying pleasure & enjoyment], with the evening it will end,

Do not be proud of the body, it too shall merge in dust.)

The same feeling permeates religio-philosophical literature throughout our history. Meera was also subject to the limitations of her time, she was nonetheless different. Meera might have been inspired by some traditions, but she was certainly not tied to them. Her poetry is simple and eloquent, offers a lot of visual and sensory cues, reflecting a range of everyday experiences and underlying sensual awareness. Unlike her contemporaries, she does not negate her feelings and emotions, nor does she deny the mortal world. Saint-devotees believed in a popular saying, the essence of many philosophical discourses and institutions of our nation, *Brahma-satya, jagat-mithya* (Truth lies in God, World is but an illusion). Many devotional songs and poetry reflected the same idea. However, Meera employs imagery drawn from her earthly world. There are invigorating examples of different elements of nature, rivers, ponds, trees, plants, animals, birds, wind, lightning, earth, sky, clouds, rain, forest, sea, castle, attic, clothing, jewellery, etc. Unlike other saint-poets, Meera does not turn a blind eye to her mundane surroundings, rather, draws inspirations from them to enrich her journey within. There are several examples of this such as :

Piya Mohi dursani deejey ho
Ber – ber main terhun ya kirpa kijey ho
Jeth mahina jal bin paanchi dukh hoi ho
Mor asada kurleh ghan chalrak soi ho
Saawan me jhad lagiyo sakhi teejan khelyo
Bhadrvey nadiyan bahey doori jin miley ho
Seep swati hi jhel ti asoonja soi ho
Dev kaati mein pujey mere tum hoi jo
Mangsar thand bhut hi paro mohi bogi
Samhalo ho
Pos mahi pala ghana, abhi tum nihalo ho
Maha nahin basant panchami fagaan sab gavey ho
Phagun phagan khel hain banraav jaiarave ho
Chait chit mein upjie darshan tum deeje ho
Baisaakh banrai phulvey koyal kurlijey ho
Kaag udanvat din gaya bujhun pandit josi ho
Meeran birhan byakul darshan kad hosi ho
(O dear one, meet me,
Persistently I call out, shower grace [upon me],
During summer month in scarcity of water,
The bird is in peril,
During rains peacocks quack...
In rainy season, showers are incessant,

My female friends celebrate teej [festival],
Rivers are overflowing; now do not stay far away,
Seashells will capture pearls in the month of Asoj,
In month of Kartik gods shall be worshipped,
You are my lord, aren't you?
In Mrigashira it would be too cold, envelope me in your care,
Winter months will be cold and frosty,
Now you have to see...
During basant–panchami, all are singing songs of spring,
At the beginning of summer, the heart leaps, grant me a sight of you,
In Baisakh, full of pride, black cuckoo sings
Throughout the day I've kept crows at bay,
Now will enquire the soothsayer,
Meera, suffering pangs of separation,
Is bewildered, when will you meet me, Lord?)

Many of India's saints and spiritual leaders have promoted the repression and inhibition of passionate interests and deprivation of carnal desires. Gradually it became a fixed notion that appetites of the body and senses are anti-religious and salvation can be attained only through abnegation of comforts and pleasures of the world. Before the medieval period, suppression of feelings and senses was a hallmark of a saint-devotee's nature. Medieval saints promoted mastery over the mind and the senses. Works of Kabir and his contemporaries offer a lot of examples of the same idea. Kabir says: *Maimtaa man juaari rey ghat hi maahigheri* (Tether and kill the raging elephant of your mind within your soul). In another example, he expresses his strong dislike for lascivious actions: *Bhagati bigari kamiyaan, Indri karey swad* (In order to feed their carnal appetite, wicked ones have debauched worship). Similarly, Dadu Dayal, the poet-saint from Gujarat, lays importance on having a mastery over the senses: *Dadu panchoon yeh parmo dihikey, inhin ko updesh,* (Dadu knows the five senses, and is well aware of their purposes too). In the last phase of medieval period Sunderdas, a notable disciple of Dadu Dayal, warns against the consequences of lustful thoughts, he says: *Man ko rakt hat ki karey, sat ki chahun deri jayi/ Sunder Latki ru lalachi gatki, vishya fal khai* (No matter how well-controlled the mind is, it may slip from the hand, while gazing at beautiful fruit hanging on branches, one ends up consuming a poisonous fruit).

Meera's poetry, too, calls attention to her deep faith and soulful devotion, rather than to her sensuous life. Her verses at times, represent her devaluation of the body, and rejection of the world as false and superficial, she wants to contemplate on Lord Krishna only, without any distraction. However, she is yet not completely detached from the sensorial, aesthetically pleasing material life. A subdued shade of sensuous and physical impulses can be felt throughout her gamut of poetry. And unlike most saints, she does not rule out such longings. Her verses show that she had shed all inhibitions, and freely developed intense, vigorous feelings for her sole deity. This is clear when she says: *Darsan bin mohe jak na parat hai, chit mero davandol* (Without having an audience with him, my mind is swinging) and also *Aavo Manmohana jee joon thaari baat* (O, my Lord Manmohan! I expectantly wait, please come). She also adds, *Meeran daasi tum charnaan ki miljiyo kaanth lagayein* (Meera is a slave at your feet, embrace me). She wants her divine lover to notice her beauty, and to embrace her when she says, *Saanwariya ke darsan paan, pahar kusumbhi saari* (Wearing a scarlet red sari, I long to see my dark-complexioned beloved).

Referring to her unruly mind, she says, *Yo man mero bado haraami, yun madmato haathi* (My mind is like a wild elephant, unrestrained). While luxuriating in a sensuous downpour, she says, *Rimjihm barsey mehda ho bhijey tan saari ho* (The soft pitter-patter of the rain; it soaks my body and my saree). By submitting her youth to Krishna, she says: *Tere kaaran sanwarey dhan joban waaron ho/ya sejiya bahu rang ke bahu phul bichaye re* (For you alone, beloved, I'll sacrifice my youth on a bed decked with flowers). Similarly, she enjoys gazing at Lord Krishna's beauty she says: *Pal-pal piv ko roop niharoon, nirakh-nirakh sukh pati* (Every moment, I adore my lover's beauty, more I adore Him, more I explore eternal pleasures). Her love for Krishna is expressed openly, without any sense of guilt. She says, *Saakhi mahro Khanudo kalejay ki kor* (Oh, dear one! Krishna is a piece of my heart).

In a folk culture as well, traditional festivals are means of expressing joys and togetherness. Since Meera never denied her womanly side, she indulged in festivities and celebrations, a quality extremely rare in saint-devotees of her time. Her poetry occasionally reflects how she rejoiced, in tune with the trinkets of life. Her unbridled joys have been expressed on occasion of the Holi festival, at a point, she asks longingly, *Kin sang khelun holi* (With whom shall I play holi?) and also she revels in seasonal joys, *Phagun ke din chaar holi khel mana re* (Spring will last for just four days, celebrate it by playing holi). Meera pines for the presence of her sole beloved in the festival of colours. *Holi bin piye laagi khari* (Without the presence of a lover, holi seems to be dull). There are references to Gangaur festival, which is celebrated primarily by married female folks, she says: *Saanwaliya mahrey rangilee gangaur* (Oh! Krishna my Gangaur is so colourful).

2

Meera's poetry reveals her rebellious aspects in the face of the injustice and indignity she faced, which makes her different from her contemporaries. The mystics and hermits of her time would not place so much importance on the vicissitudes of the material life knowing that it's transient and insubstantial. They placed importance on the 'next life' as a result of the actions in the present one. Suffering was seen as evil reaped through bad deeds. Certain section of the society misused this throey by justifying deprivation, discrimination, and sufferings of some classes as heaven-sanctioned penance for their previous wrongdoings. Any kinds of rebellion or defiance, even if done for noble causes and altruistic purposes were deemed unnecessary and even anti-religious. "This theory has few salient features such as the negation of life due to failure; the mind should be immersed in the closet, to promote utter isolation, man felt helpless in the wake of floods and droughts, disease and bankruptcy. Deprived of his power, he was unable to transform Nature and Society in his favour. Eventually, he took refuge in the theory of Karma and Soul and transmigration of soul. If calamities befell on someone, then he would consider it as an inevitable consequence of the laws of Karma. Any attempt to change the social environment was considered as a challenge to the Law of Karma and the judgement of God. It was the duty of man to silently accept the will of God with his head bowed."[3]

The principle deeply affected the thinking of Indian saints and poets, and their voices against the injustices of the feudal system, were thus quietened. The notion of one's future inevitably resulting from one's past actions, or *karma* got deeply entrenched till the beginning of the millenium, as noted by Hazari Prasad Dwivedi, the literary historian; "System and principles of reincarnation and ism related to fruits of action were deep-rooted in the society so much so that even with changing times, poets and thinkers never ever tried to express sense of dissatisfaction against the universally accepted system. Whatever is happening in the world is for definite reason, and there is no scope to question and doubt"[4]. Medieval saint-devotees too firmly believed in 'transmigration' of the soul and fateful 'fruits' of action, so in their poetry, rarely any question was raised against the feudal system. However, Kabir and other poets seem to be somewhat in disagreement with this medieval mode of government, because they prioritized egalitarian ideas. However, in conventional devotion, this trend was negligible. In this respect, Meera's poetry is extraordinary. It directly challenges the selfish, unkind interests of the feudal system, religious institutions and public relations. She has a dauntless, rebellious voice. She is far ahead of Kabir in this regard. Kabir seeks the truth, and raises objections in abstraction, while Meera challenges her enemy face to face. She vehemently opposes the authority and legitimacy of those in power, regardless of future repercussions.

Meera openly criticizes her antagonist, who is none other than the ruler of Mewar. She chastises him, *Tum jaavo Rana ghar aapno, meri – teri nahi sari* (O Rana, go home, you and I can never go along). She expresses her indifference towards honour and riches when she says, *Raano mahro kain kar lesi Meera chhod lai kul laaj* (What on earth can Rana (the ruler) do to me, Meera is not entrapped in community-imposed honour). In another verse, she says, *Sisodhiyo roodhayan to mahro kain kar lesi* (Sisodiya Rana is offended, what wrong can he do to me?). Her revolt against power and submission to love, are felt frequently in her poems. She says, *Raanaji thein kya ne raakho mahsoon bair/ Thein to Raanaji mahrey Isdaa laago, jyon barchan mein kair* (Ranaji what ill will you bear of me, you appear to be *kair* (unwanted and wild) among trees).

And again, *Thaara des mein saadh nahin hain, log basey sab kudoo.* (Your kingdom has no good people, those who live are corrupt and useless). She doesn't even flinch from calling the ruler a fool, *Moorakh raja raaj kart ho, pandit phira bhikar* (Silly is the reigning king, beggars are the learned ones). Her open disregard of prevailing laws is also evident in her poetry, *Ranaji hu ab na rahoongi tore hat ki/ saadh sang mohe pyara lage laaj gayi ghoonghat ki* (Oh! Rana no more shall I be at your command, I prefer the company of saints, I have forsaken my veils of coyness). Her fierce disobedience and defiance is a rare trait in saint-poets, *Raano kahey so ek na manaa mahe, saadh dware nit asi hai maye* (Oh, mother! I'll disobey all of King's commands, every day, saints will arrive at my doorstep). Her aversion to the use of force is so strong that she does not want to reside in her homeland any longer, *Mein to nahi rahoon Ranaji tharo desh mein rey* (I will not live, Ranaji, in your land). Meera expressed her lack of interest in appeasing her family or community by following conventions, *Loklaaj, kul ki marjada ya mein na rakhoongi* (I am not bothered about tarnishing the honour of the family or society).

Meera's poetry reveals her defiance towards prevailing norms that might lead to inequality and might disempower women. She appears to be remarkably unconventional. *Saaji sringaar baandh pug ghungroo, loklaaj taj naachi.* (Well-adorned, with ghungroo on ankles, I dance, oblivious to all social constraints). She does not falter from confessing her feelings, and she makes no apologies for her love, *Koi nindoo, koi vindoo, mein to govind ke gun gaasya* (Let others condemn or support me, I will sing in the praise of Krishna only). She is oblivious to the pride of her social status, rather, she mocks the society and some of its rigid, censorious rules, *Apne ghar ka parda karley, main avala bourani.* She requests everyone to draw curtains on their houses, because she is passing by. In another line, she says, *Meera khaye main bhaie banwari, kaho to bajaun dhol.* (Meera says, I am out of my mind, should I beat a drum?).

3

Most saint-poets of the medieval period do not dwell on their personal identity and worldly interactions in their poetry, whereas in Meera's work, her distinct personality and character are noticeable along with her material life. In conventional devotion, contemplating on birth, family relationships, household and worldly relations are 'unsaintly' and do not have an enlightened outlook. Many saint-poets avoided such issues in their devotional verses. Traditionally, it was thought that the material world has no substance, no meaning, and is a mere illusion, and only the soul is real. Reincarnation is inevitable, whenever evils or bad karma takes place, leading to fateful justice. So,the matter of personal identity was considered irrelevant in attaining liberation. Kabir and Raidas have mentioned which community they hailed from, apart from this, they did not reveal much about their own individuality, worldly attributes or relationships. In Meera's poetry, her worldly suffering, pleasures, relationships, emotions and desire are laid bare. Unlike her contemporaries, Meera is not detached and passive towards things around her, rather, she harbours powerful emotions toward them.

Most saints are oblivious to their individual or local identities, and their poetry does not have any regional allegiance. On the contrary, Meera's poetry is deeply embedded in regional contexts, carries rich flavour of her ancestral homeland, yet has a universal appeal. She is not bound to her regional, religious or cultural backgrounds, but she also acknowledges them through her use of expressions and tone. She states. *Peehar mahro desh Merto. Chandi kul ki kaani* (My parental house is in Merta, I have left my family customs). While leaving behind her parental house, she says, *Saadh sang mohey pyaraa lagey, laaj gayi ghunghat ki/peehar Merta chod apna, surat, nirat doi chatki* (I prefer to be accompanied by saints-devotees; I no more wear the veil of coyness, have left behind my parental home in Merta, and have raised myself above any indulgence or abstinence). On one occasion, she remembers both her parental house at Merta and in-laws at Chittor, *Ek kul Rana tyaroon, apanu, dujo rad rathore/ Teejo tyaroon Rana Merto, chuthoo garh Chittaur* (I have brought salvation to our own, and to Merta's Rana, to Rathores, and also to Chittor).

Meera's verses bear evidence of some familial conflicts, discriminatory frameworks and patriarchal dominance of her time. Meera's relationships with Ranas, the rulers of Mewar, were bitter, which is revealed in her verses. *Sisodhiyo Rana, pyalo mahne kyun re pathayo/ bhali – boori to main nahin kihni Rana kyon hai risayo.* (O Sisodiya, why have you sent me a bowl of poison? I have done you no wrong, so, why are you so hostile?) Not only with the ruler of the State, but her relationship with her mother-in-law, sister-in-law and brother-in-law were not very nurturing or stable, nor was the feudal environment very suitable for her spiritual growth. She says, *Sasuji barji nanad ji barji, Ranoji davadar.* (Mother-in-law, Sister-in-law interfered, and Rana claimed me as his property) and again, *Saas ladey, meri nand khijavay, Rana rahiya risaaye.* (Mother–in–law quarrels, Sister–in–law taunts, and Rana is always annoyed with me). Her relationships with her in-laws are not conducive to her path of devotion, *Saas hateli, nanad chugeli, divar det mujh gaari* (Stubborn Mother-in-law, slanderer Sister-in-law, and brother-in-law rebukes me). At times, she feels alienated, angst-ridden, increasingly separated from her milieu, and the mainstream values of her society, she says: *Miran Giridhar haath bikani log kahey bigadi* (Meera has been sold away to Krishna, people think she has gone astray). Similarly, in another instance, she says: *Log Kahey Miran bhai banwari, nayat kahe kulnasi* (People say that Meera has lost her mind, and stained her family's honour). Like any other woman, she feels intense grief over loss, and she also yearns for love and security. Other saint-poets of her time were not so expressive of their personal grief or hardships. Meera's marital life was a bed of thorns, rife with a lot of constraints, which her verses reveal aptly,

Saasiryo dukh ghana re saasu nanad satavey devar jeth, kutumb kabiloo, nit uth raad chalavey Raja barje, Raani barje, barje sab parivari Kunwar paatvi sovi barje aur saheliyaan saari.

(Living with the in-laws is very demanding, Mother-in-law and Sisters-in-law, pester a lot,

Brothers-in-law and the whole clans quarrel every day,

King and Queen together set restrictions,

Eldest Son of King and my friends too impose limits on me).

When living with her in-laws becomes increasingly difficult, Meera misses her parental home, like any ordinary woman. She says, *Mahrey baboo sa ne kahiyo mahney bega leba aavey* (Go and inform my father, to send someone to take me home).

Meera reached Merta from Chittor, and soon, Maldev invaded the kingdom, and Merta was shattered to pieces. Unable to endure the emotional oppression by her in-laws, Meera decided not to go back, and rather chose a life of a homeless destitute. Despite being from an elite clan, and being a mystic saint, her pain and misery over her worldly loss, are not much different from those of female folks, *Saago snehi mero na koi, bairee sakal jahaan* (I have no dear ones in this world, the whole world is hostile) and also *Yaa bhav main bahu dukh payo, sansaa rog nivor* (I've suffered a lot in this world, (O Lord!) emancipate the world from suffering). Finally, floating along with the passage of time, she travels to Dwarka. She says, *Saadan re sang jaye Dwarka, mein to bhajya ranchod* (Along with other ascetics, I will go to Dwarka and sing devotional songs for Krishna). Interestingly, even after reaching Dwarka and immersing herself in love and devotion of Krishna, she does not completely forget her past. She still feels bitter about the ill-treatment of Rana, and she misses her homeland. Had she been fully detached from all worldly cares, like most of devotees of her time, she would not have said, *Ambaa pakaaya kulhar kairi, nimbura mahrey des/Udaipur ra rana kin widh choryo des, mewari rana kan par choryo des*[5] (Mangoes might have ripened, raw mangoes too might have appeared, but in my land, there only are lemons, O Rana, don't you know, why have I left the kingdom?) On another occasion, she regards Rana as her false husband and Krishna as the real one, she says, *Rana they cho mahra jootha bhartaar, saancha che shri hari sanwara*. Meera's verses reflect her discontent for her family traditions, patriarchy and fruitless relationships that would not give her any dignity or spiritual freedom.

4

Meera shows a command of the familiar language of the region in her poetry. Medieval saint poets have different dialectical flavours and variations in the language, because they hailed from and travelled to different locations. Meera did not write to show a pedantic knowledge of Sanskrit, nor did she have any scholarly pursuits. She relied on everyday words and phrases only to express herself, and to communicate her deep-seated religious feelings. Her language is borrowed from her ordinary interactions with the people of her community, the places where she hailed from, and where she lived. She was not emancipated from womanly cares and concerns, caught in a mesh of relationships, with in-laws and Rana, which entangled her deeper in worldly distractions. She realizes the triviality and impermanence of life as she says, *Jeevno din chaar* (life is too short). She pines after her unattained beloved and her anxiety and restlessness is manifest in her feminine qualities, *Hiyo phatat meri chaati* (My chest might explode). She blames herself for her misfortune, in the line, *Aapana karam ka hi khot, dosh kahin deji hi ali* (The fault is in my deeds, why blame God for it?). There is a creeping sense of apathy towards bodily appetite and elemental needs, *Din nahin bhookh, raine nahin nidra, bhojan bhaawan gayi* (No hunger during day, no sleep at night, I have lost my appetite). Her joys are hampered by ill luck, *Main mand bhaagan, karam abhaagan* (I am an unfortunate one). Her inflamed soul seeks to be one with her beloved, Shri Krishna, she sorely longs for him, *Ubhi dhari arj karat hun, arj karat bhaie bhor* and again *Mere naina baand padi, khay na khootey chor na loote, abke jin taalo dey jaavo, pandar ho gaye kes, rahoongi bairagan hoi ri, adhbich mat chit kajyo, tum bin neend na avey ho, ghayal ki gati ghayal jaane, dhaan na bhavey neend na avey, diyo re liyo tere sang chalego, ghari ek nahin avere aur karam gati tare nahi tare,*

(My eyes are tired, my suffering won't cease even if I eat,
No thief can steal,
Hairs are grey, I'll abstain from all indulgences,
Don't leave me in the middle of my distress,
I cannot sleep without you,
The pain in wounds is known to no one except for wounded herself,
I am sleepless, numb, cannot eat,
...
I cannot find comfort even for a second...),

Similar easy to understand, clear, uncomplicated phrases are plenty in Meera's poetic oeuvre. Her use of language is a lot different from her contemporaries. Strong influences of Mewar and Marwar regions are not so deeply felt in devotional verses of other saints-devotees. This is clearly evident in her expression of joy when she meets her friends with open arms, *Aavo mil saheliyaan, bataan such lijey* (Come together my friends, and let's talk of good old days). Pouring her heart out to the world, she says, *Jhakolo lagyo ji rang girdhar ko aan, and also Meri baat nahin jag chani* (I am not hiding anything from the world). She understands the stigma associated with her love for an idol, but this does not discourage her. Her simple language of the folk clearly conveys her devotional integrity and transparency. Her restlessness can be felt when she says, *Khin aangan khin daagle rey khin khin ubey holi.* (In one moment at the surface, and in the next on the ceiling, and then in the next stand). Many words such as *olum* (remembrance), *oluma* (reproach), *sagpan* (relationship), *ruda* (beautiful), *rijaya* (enchanted), *dikri* (girl), *dagle* (ceiling) are only found in Mewar and Marwar regions of Rajasthan. It is clear that Meera does not borrow pedantic, conventional expressions in her poetry, she is rather influenced by her distinctive culture and rugged linguistic beauty. In Meera's poetry, familiar objects related to a woman's day to day life have been mentioned. The use of symbols and imagery is associated with her material experiences, such as those related to the adornment of the feminine body. Words like *kaakan* (bracelet), *moondro* (ring), *ghaagroo* (skirt, also known as lehenga in hindi), *duladi* (double threaded beads), *dovodo* (a special ornament), *akhota* (ear ornament), *jhootano* (hanging earring, pendant), *besari* (nose ring), *choodo* (ivory bangles), *rakhari* (head ornament) are frequently used in her poetry, which gives a sensuous edge to her mystic subject matter. The following verses indicate this.

Chaalo agam ke desh kaal dekhat darey
Vahan bhara prem ka hauj, hans kela karey
Odhan lajja cheir, dhiraj ko ghagro
Chimta kaakn haath, sumat ka mundro
Kaancho hai viswaas chudo chit ujallo
Dil dulari dariav saanch ko devro
Daanta amrit mekh daya ko bolno
Ubtan guru ko gyaan, dhyaan ko dhovno
Kaan akhota gyaan, jugat ko jhutno
Besari hari ko naam, kaajal hai dharmko
Jihari seel santosh, nirat ko ghungroo
Bindali gaj aur haar, tilak guru gyan ko
Saji sohlaa sringaar, pahri souney raakhri,
Sanwaliya su preet, auran su aakhari
Patibarta ki sej prabhuji padhariye
Gaav Mirabai dasi kar raakhiye.

(Let's go to God's kingdom where death do not dare tread,
Reservoir of His love is filled to the brim,
Where flamingos (free souls) are at play.
Here coverings of shyness, and skirts of virtue wrap us.

Hands are adorned with bracelets of forgiveness and rings of virtues
Mirror of trust,
Brightness in the heart, bracelets made of ivory
The heart is a necklace like an ocean, and the truth embellishes it,
Teachings of Guru are like brilliant turmeric, Meditation washes it clean,
Words of empathy are like gold-plated teeth,
Knowledge, like earrings, honesty in the hanging pendant,
Nose ring like the name of the Lord,
Virtues are ornaments of feet and ghunghru of trust,
Alms for guru is pearl necklaces, also head pendant,
Decked in sixteen bridal ornaments, gold string on the wrist,
I have surrendered to Krishna and have vowed to abstain from others.)

Homely allusions and household affairs are expressed in her poetry such as, *bade ghar taali laagi re* (key to the big house). Meera is not unmindful of her surroundings, she rather admires them by using phrases like *chilariya* (algae-covered pond), *dariyav* (sea), *haaliyan mouliyaan* (contractual labours working on landlord's farm), *sardaar* (squire), *kaam-daar* (manager), *kaam-katheer* (metals of low-value), *sona-rupa* (gold-silver), *huzoor* (God) etc. Her poetry thus uniquely amalgamates her humdrum,mundane existence rooted in Mewar-Marwar with her abysmal spiritual energy and divine vision, which sets her apart from a lot of her devotional peers. It is expressed in the following verse.

Bade ghar taali laagey re
Mahra man ri uundarath bhagi re
Chilerye mahro chit nahin rahe, dawariye kun jaav?
Ganga – jamuna su kaam nahin re, main to jaie miloon dariyav

Haaliyan–mooliyan kaam nahin re, seekh nahin sirdar
Kaamdaraan su kaam nahin re, mein to jaya karun durbar
Katha kathir su kaam nahin re, looha chadey sir bhaar
Sona–rupa su kaam nahin re, mahne hiraan ru bopaar
Bhaag humarey jaagiyo re, bhyo samand su seer
Amrit pyala chandi ke, kun peevey karvo neer,
Pipa ku prabhu parchoo dino, diya re khagina pur
Miran ke prabhu girdhar nagar, dhani milya che huzoor

(My marriage has been arranged with a prestigious house, all my heart's desires are fulfilled. I do not want to go near algae-covered ponds. Why would I go to a small pond to take some water home? (My relatives) are like Ganga-Jamuna, I will merge with the ocean. Neither the field-workers nor the chief of the clan are of any use to me, labourers too cannot serve me. I shall go straight to the royal court. Cheap metals are of no avail, iron too is useless, so are gold-silver, I trade in diamonds alone. My fortune has bloomed, I am now in relationship with the ocean, Who can reject a silver bowl of divine nectar and instead, drink stale water? O Lord! You have miraculously showered (me) with wealth. Shri Krishna belongs to Meera, he is her sole Lord.)

Although many saint-poets used regional languages, self-denying ascetic ideals are predominant in their work. On the contrary, Meera combines earthly experiences with her profound devotional longing, she marries the mortal with the sublime, the temporal with the transcendental.

Other women poets of the medieval period like Daya Bai and Sajho Bai also make use of language commonly used among saints. The symbols and phrases in their work are borrowed from Kabir and others who belonged to the tradition of Bhakti poetry. Most importantly, their verses show their adherence to the devotional pioneers, but reveal very little about themselves as the women of their times. This is obvious that Meera never passively followed spiritual traditions, in contrast to other male or female saint-poets of the period and her mode of communication is "brilliant, sturdy, lively and sharp"[6]. Her verses reflect a full range of emotions including rebellion, her unshakable strength in the face of the opposition, envy, ecstasy, conflicts and worry, womanly desires (i.e. expectations and longings like those of a new bride). Her feminine gentleness, submissive devotion is reserved only for her beloved Lord, *Araj karoon, abla kar jorey, Shyam tumahari daasi* (With folded hands I plead before you Krishna, as I am at your command). Like an ordinary woman, she is prone to envy and insecurity, *Mein buri chaan, thankey bhlii he ghaneri, tum hai ek rasraaj* (I am unvirtuous, you have several 'good ones' at your disposal, you are Rasraaj); this is also evident in the following verse,

Girdhar roosunuji kaun gunhan Khuch ik augun kahro mah mein, mein bhi kana suna Mein to daasi janam-janam ki theey sahib saguna Kain baat su karyu rusnun, kyun dukh paio cho mana, Kirpa kar mohey darsan dijiyo beetey divas Ghana Meera ke prabhu hari, avinashi, tharo hi naanv bhana (O Krishna, which of my wrongdoings displeases you? I need to know, let me be conscious. In this birth, and always, I am at your command. O virtuous one, what displeases you, why are you upset? Many days have passed, kindly give me a sight. O auspicious one, I pray before you.)

Traditionally, women are often portrayed as shedding tears easily and being more vulnerable than men, when in love. Meera too weeps and sobs due to the pangs of separation, and her emotions are intense. *Phaarungi chir karun gal kantha, rahungi bairagan hoi ri.* (I'll tear all clothes, will renounce all material pursuits, clad in a patched robe). A lot of women lose their hunger or sleep, when separated from their beaus. Meera is no different. *Din nahin bhookh raine nahin nidra, yun tan pal-pal chijey re*; (I do not feel hunger during the day, nor can I sleep at night, my body and soul are restless.) Like a damsel in love, she climbs on the rooftop, to watch and awaits her lover to arrive,

Oonchi char-char path niharan roye-roye akhian raati (Climbing high on rooftop, I await your arrival, and shed tears at night). She recalls wiping her tears, *Lekir aanchro asuwan poochey, ughri gaat gayi.* She also unlocks her imagination, and desires to fly like a golden bird, *Ud jaavo maahri sone chidi.* Like other women, she feels exhilarated at the arrival of her lover, *Joseeda ne laakh badhai re, ab ghar aye shyam/ aaj anand umang bhiyo hai, jeev lahey sukh dhaam* (I congrat Brahmans that Krishna has come home, it is a time to sing, dance and celebrate, for all living beings are revelling in his presence). Meera sings auspicious prayers in company of her friends, *Paanch saakhi ekathi bhai milli mangal gaavey ho* (Five dear friends have gathered and are singing auspicious hymns on arrival of their lovers). Women are traditionally believed to have been more inclined towards ceremonies, decorations, rites and rituals, *Ratan karun nyochavar le aarti sajoon ho* (I bestow precious ornaments and decorate for aarti). Thus, in her poetry, her claim on her Divine Love is transparent in tone, mystic in meaning, characterised by physical emotions and agony, yet unwavering in the face of the stigma attached to her unconventional life. Despite preserving her feminine identity, she challenges gender stereotypes, and perils of a woman saint's life. However, Meera's popular saintly image overshadows her feminine qualities including her strength, resilience, longings, and vulnerability which are revealed in her poetry whereas Meera, as an idealized figure embodying devotion, patience, and piety are always admired above all.

Notes and References

1. In this chapter quotes drawn from Meera's poetry are taken from *Meera Brihat Padavali,* ed. Harinarayan Purohit, Vol.1 (Jodhpur: Parachya Vidya Pratishthan, 2006) until mentioned otherwise. All translations are done by the translator.
2. K. Damodaran, *Bhartiya Chintan Parampara,* Hindi trans. G. Sridharan, 1997 (New Delhi: People's Publishing House, 1997), 513.

3. Ibid., 514.
4. Hazari Prasad Dwivedi, *Hindi Sahitya ki Bhumika* (New Delhi: Rajkamal Prakashan, 1997), 118.
5. This section of Meera's verse is not included in the available texts. This is rendered by the folk singers of the Western Rajasthan. This section is cited from the audio cassette *Mystic Love* conceived and directed by Komal Kothari and released by Ninad, Mumbai in 1998. It was rendered by Padama Ram Mahesha Ram.
6. Anamika, *Stritav ka Manchitra* (Delhi: Saaransh Prakashan, Paperback edn. 2001), 164.

Chapter - V

Canonization

Col. James Tod, a British political agent in the Princely States of Rajputana, an influential historian and an officer in the East India Company, disseminated Meera's image of a mystic and romantic poet. Since no undisputed historical records of Meera and her life were available to him, he relied on tales and poetry traditionally passed among families, clans, tribes and villages. There was hardly any mention of Meera in the formal records of *tawarikh, khyat, bahi, vanshavali* etc. So, of course she was presented in many forms. She was etched as a religious figure in folk memory, her devout saintly image overshadowed her history. Devotees claim that she had miraculous, superhuman qualities, while folk legends and lore often admire her sacrifices for her devotional pursuit, and remember her mainly as a woman who renounced luxury and comfort of palaces, and all the privileges of her elite lineage, to live a sacred life. Certain feudal groups may recall her as an unruly woman who stained her family's reputation in the name of spiritual liberation. In the early nineteenth century, Tod's *Annals and Antiquities of Rajasthan,* and also his travelogue, *Travels in Western India,* presented Meera as a romantic and mystical poet. Despite a lack of historical sources to validate this image, she was popularized as a saint and her 'canonization' took place. This image did not assess her with respect to her worldly hardships, constraints or circumstances.

This did not acknowledge her as a mortal being with emotions and frailties. But, Tod's fame and influence gave this image a nearly undisputed legitimacy, and popularity. Several factors were behind this. Tod's preconceived notion of oriental magic, mystery and romanticism, his colonial interests of exerting influence on indigenious communities and his relationship with Rajput rulers.

During the colonial period and also afterwards, many Indian scholars undertook the mammoth task of writing history. A department was established for this purpose. Some leading scholars of Mewar and Marwar were Shyamal Das, Gaurishankar Hirachand Ojha, and Munshi Deviprasad. They diligently carried out the task of recovering history, but their points of view too, were under the influence of European historians, because they also relied on the colonial-era records to make inferences, and they did not tamper with the saintly image of Meera, which was cultivated by Tod, however they rectified some of the factual errors in his work.

1

Although Tod was a British executive, appointed by the East India Company, in some ways, he was different, too. His curatorial knack for research, exploration and collection, a deep understanding of European history and knowledge of the classical tradition of literature and his attachment to Rajputana made him unique and different from his colonial peers.

James Tod was born on 20 March 1782, in Islington. He decided to join the military instead of following the family business. At an early age, he was offered a cadetship in the East India Company. In 1798, he joined the Royal Military Academy, Woolwich. Next, he came to Bengal, where on 9 January 1800, he received a commission in the second Bengal European Regiment. After staying for some time on Malacca and Marine

Island, on 29 May 1800, he was appointed as a Lieutenant in the 14th Infantry Regiment. During his posting in Delhi in 1801, he was given the responsibility of the survey of a canal. Graeme, a friend of his uncle, took Tod along, when he became a resident at the royal court of Daulat Rao Scindia in 1805. This was a turning point in Tod's life, and from here, his scholarly prowess had a new lease of life. He undertook the task of surveying unexplored and undiscovered routes to Agra, Jaipur and Udaipur and completed the task in a timely manner, for which he was appreciated. During this period, he became well-versed with the geography of Rajputana. After Mercer's departure, Richard Strachey became resident in the court of Scindia, Tod was promoted as a captain. After Strachey's departure from the durbar, Tod became the assistant to the Resident-II.

During this time, he spent most of his time collecting geographical information of regions like Sindh, Bundelkhand and areas between Yamuna and Narmada rivers. He came in close contact with the Rajputana. In his treatise written during this period, he has clearly pointed out the atmosphere of fear, terror and devastations in moving terms. Marathas had strengthened their hold on the region, took advantage of the internal conflicts and looted rampantly. Pindaris, under the immunity of Marathas, had converted the entire Rajputana into a desolate waste land. In relation to the plight of Mewar, Tod points out:

Mewar was declining fast towards its destruction, every evidence of civilization was getting wiped out, the fields turned barren, cities were destroyed, people, thakurs and jagirdars were corrupt, while Maharana's family had to struggle to have access to the ordinary facilities of life.[1]

Marquess Hastings, a British General, decided to crush the Pindaris. The East India Company took advantage of Tod's geographical survey, his farsightedness and presence of mind in their conflict with Pindaris and their guardians Marathas.

Tod actively participated in the war.[2] He played a vital role in it, he also received letters of appreciation from other military commanders. After 1817-18, when Rajputana was liberated from the Pindaris and Marathas, most of the Princely States signed a treaty of peace with the East India Company. On reaching Udaipur, the Governor General of that time, pleased with Tod, appointed him as his political representative in this region. Tod focused his efforts on rebuilding the Rajputana states, which were ravaged by the Pindaris and Marathas. On his initiative, several reforms were implemented. In 1819 and 1820 Tod travelled to Jodhpur and Kota-Bundi respectively. He was impressed by the feudal lords of the Rajputana. He acknowledges that Rajputs must be given due recognition in the world because of their accomplishments[3]. He decided to record their history. During his stay in the region, he collected vital pieces of historical evidence related to Rajputs, such as rock inscriptions, khyats, *bahis*, genealogy documents, copper plates, coins etc. He also penned down information he gathered from sources of traditional lores, legends, hymns, from songs of charans and bhats and pedantic texts from Brahmins. He grew an affinity towards the feudal lords of Rajasthan, due to which the higher officials in the company were suspicious of him. Moreover, hard work and frequent travelling took a toll on his health. Eventually in 1822, he resigned from the post and left Udaipur for Bombay (now Mumbai) via Gogunda, Ranakpur, Sirohi, Mount Abu, Chandravati, Siddhpur, Patan, Baroda, Bhavnagar, Palitana, Junagadh, Dwarka, Somnath and Kutch. The research material that Tod had collected during his stay in Central India and the Rajputana, he organized and studied after he reached England from Bombay in 1823. In 1829, a detailed account of the history of Rajputana appeared in *Annals and Antiquities of Rajasthan* Volume-I and in 1832, its Volume-II too was published.

After accomplishing this task, he settled down to write an account of his last journey, but before its publication Col. Tod passed away in 1835. The travel account *Travels in Western India* was published posthumously in 1839. Tod had a flair for seeking and collecting information, and preserving them. Regarding his natural instinct, he notes that the task of exploring the past for a non-industrious person would be tiring and scary, for James Tod himself such engagements were like a favourite past time.[4] During his tenure in Rajputana, he spent a fortune, in order to retrieve antique rock inscriptions, copper plates, coins, manuscripts etc, carried them to England in forty-one boxes and after finishing the two volumes of the *Annals and Antiquities of Rajasthan* and *Travels in Western India,* he donated all of them to the India House and the Royal Asiatic Society.

Tod had a comprehensive knowledge and a clear understanding of European history and classical literature. He was born just before the French Revolution and was deeply influenced by the ideas of Montesquieu, Hume, Gibbon and others.[5] He knew the poems of Coleridge and Wordsworth by heart. Due to his familiarity with the history of Rome, Greece, Syria, Egypt and several other countries, he even did a comparative study of the descriptions, character narratives from Indian history which he carried from India before leaving. Due to his amicable and cooperative nature, the Rajput feudal lords gave him respect and held him in high esteem. His proximity with the feudal system helped him develop a close relationship with the royal families of the Rajputana. Among the Rajputana states, he had special regards for the Rajputs of Mewar. In 1806, along with Daulat Rao Scindia, Tod, for the first time as a young officer met the Maharana of Marwar, he was overly impressed with his grandeur and courteous demeanour. Perhaps due this very reason, he even decided to settle here once. He was overwhelmed by the valour and military qualities of the Rajputana Kings and its clans. According to him: None can match the beauty of ethicality of a Rajput and if one is unable to follow, an experiential proverb would provide him the guidelines.[6]

2

Recreation of Meera's image as a mystic poet, shrouded in magical, saintly charm, and esoteric history, was the result of Tod's *Annals and Antiquities of Rajasthan* and *Travels in Western India.* His sources were narratives of Bhats, Charans, Brahmins and different communities, and also clues in available writings such as raaso, khyat, vanshaava, genealogies. His sources were refutable, so he was prone to factual errors. According to Tod, Meera was the wife of Rana Kumbha (1433-1468), whereas in his travelogue he refers to her as the wife of Rana Lakha (1382-1421). Such contradictions prove that he was unsure in his depiction of Meera and no reliable records were available to him. Also, in the footnotes, he states that it might also be incorrect, because there is a lot of uncertainty on the history of Mewar. Based on new research, scholars have modified this interpretation and pointed out that Meera belonged to the Rathore family of Merta. She was a daughter of Ratan Singh, the fourth son of Rao Duda and grandson of Rao Jodha of Jodhpur. Rao Duda established Merta. Meera was married to Bhojraj, the eldest son of Rana Sanga (1482-1528) Tod's history regarding Meera's birth, marriage and similar such life events are not based on factual evidence. However, it also enhanced Meeera's reputation as an extraordinary saint-devotee, a romantic and mystic poetess. In the *Annals and Antiquities of Rajasthan* Volume-I Tod points out:

"Kumbha married a daughter of the Rathor of Merta, the first of the clans of Marwar. Mira Bai was the most celebrated princess of her time for beauty and romantic piety. Her compositions were numerous, though better known to the worshippers of the Hindu Apollo than to the ribald bards. Some of her odes and hymns to the deity are preserved and admired. Whether she imbibed her poetic piety from her husband, or whether from her he caught the sympathy which produced the 'sequel to the songs of Govinda,' we cannot determine. Her history is a romance, and her excess of devotion at every shrine of the favourite deity...and gave rise to many tales of scandal[7]".

Tod has shared a fascinating reference of Meera in his travelogue *Travels in Western India.* In the twentieth episode, he gives account of places such as Veraval, Aarmara, Gureja, Bet forts of the pirates, Vishnu temple and Krishna temple that Meera had built. He says: "But the shrine which proved most attractive to me, was that raised by a princess of my own land, Mewar, the celebrated Meera Bai, wife of Lakha... to the pastoral divinity of the Suraseni, in his genuine character as the lover of the Nine; and assuredly this Rajput queen was one of the most ardent of his votaries. The productions of her muse are said to have been unequalled by any of the bards of the day, and it is asserted that a sequel to the Gita Govinda or canticles in honour of Kanya, will stand a comparison with the original by Jydeva. This and other odes, descriptive of the spiritual charms of her divine lover, and which still exist, are so fervidly sapphic, as to have afforded themes for no small scandal, perhaps the malicious invention of the regular sons of rhyme, envious of her fame. But since the fact is attested, that she abandoned all the duties of her station, and that her life was passed in excursions to every land in which Apollo (Krishna) was enshrined, where she danced before the god of her idolatry, in the character of one of the celestial nymphs in the mystic rasamandala she afforded some ground for malice to build upon. Her lord and sovereign, however, never having entertained any jealousy or suspicion, notwithstanding, in one of these devotional ecstasies, Murali descended from his pedestal and embraced his devotee, it is but fair to infer that there was no just cause.[8]"

In this way Tod concluded that (1) Meera Bai was a well-known princess of her time, her beauty and devotion were admired by many. (2) Her history is a 'romance'. (3) She was an excellent poetess and her works were praised far and wide. (4) She renounced the comforts of the palace and went on pilgrimages to the shrines of her favourite deity, Krishna (5) Due to her unbridled devotion for Krishna, her songs and dance before the idol, and travelling to far-off places, some denounced her lack of womanly propriety, and her disregard for conventions. (6) Her husband, Rana, however, did not doubt her or chastise her. It is highly possible that Tod deliberately avoided the worldly conflicts and complexity attached to Meera's mortal, feminine identity and womanhood, and bequeathed her with a holy identity, as a mystic, romantic saint poetess. This 'canonization' no doubt had an immense effect on the posterity. Even the traditional records such as histories of clans, *bahis*, khyats and similar other sources who had earlier treated Meera as an outcast, now began to take serious note of her.

In 1886, Shyamaldas mentions Meera with deep reverence in *Vir Vinod* (Delight of Heroes - a history of Mewar). He refuted Tod's claim that Meera was Rana Kumbha's wife. He also commented that Meera Bai was a great devotee herself who respected other saints and devotees. She sang songs and was famous.[9] Clearly, after Tod's 'canonization', Meera's devotion and saintly abstinence started defining her. However, in the footnotes, Shyamaldas does mention that Meera lived during the period of Maharana Vikramaditya and Udai Singh and her pain and sufferings are reflected in her poems.[10] Shyamaldas's *Vir Vinod* is an important work on the history of Mewar and only in a few lines and the footnote, Meera is mentioned. After a few years, in 1898, Munshi Deviprasad did a detailed study of Meera in his work Meerabai ka Jivan Charitra (Life of Meera). He was closely associated with the historical department of Jodhpur state. He also penned some other biographies based on his research. Munshi Deviprasad claimed that his sources are more authentic than those used in *Bhaktamals* and Col. Tod's history. According to him, information related to Meera in the texts written in the medieval period do not correspond with the reality and are based on "irrelevant rumours and hearsays".[11] Some of the incidents related to Meera's life such as her meeting with Tansen and Akbar and her correspondence with Tulsidas, are nothing but "gossips of the innocent devotees"[12] of Meera. Munshi Deviprasad also added that "the majority of her devotees, in order to repay her debt, circulated such entertaining tales regarding Meera."[13] In his work, he has corrected several speculations earlier made on Meera i.e., her husband, father, father-in-law, birth and marriage. Also, some relevant information regarding her paternal lineage of Rathores and in-laws' lineage of the Sisodias, also came to light. However, he also regarded Meera as a saint-devotee and his conviction, too, was based on folk memory instead of historical sources.

Despite his knack for history, Munshi Deviprasad too, had his limitations. First, he was dependent on feudal lords himself, so he was careful of not displeasing his 'patrons' and avoided being critical of them. Secondly, he mainly relied on his correspondence with Gaurishankar Ojha and Shyamaldas[14] who seemed to be pretty impressed with the past of the feudal dynasties, and also with James Tod's work. Munshi Deviprasad in his work, might have rejected some of the incidents of Meera's life as hearsays and tradition rather than the truth, but on the other hand he had to rely on some unconfirmed claims. For instance : 1. Meera Bai, since she was a child, was fond of Giridhari Lal ji (Krishna) and fell in love with his idol. When she went to her in-laws, she carried the idol along with her and after her husband's demise, she surrendered herself completely in the service and worship of the idol.[15] 2. (After the demise of Bhojraj, her husband) Meera Bai did not make any hue and cry over her misfortune but chose to detach herself from the comforts of life in a tender age, she insisted on attaining a perfect nirvana and considered the mortal world nothing more than a dream.[16] 3. (After leaving Chittor) what happened to Meera Bai? There is no historical record of it, but people say that she went on a pilgrimage to Dwarka and one day a group of Brahmins were sent by Maharana to bring her back, she sang *Meera ke prabhu mil bichran nahi keejey* ("O Lord, if you meet Meera once, do not leave her") and merged into the statue of Ranchhod ji" (Krishna).[17] There is no historical consensus on these statements, Munshi Deviprasad too uses "It is said so..." to cite an event, and then narrates it, based on the same folk memory which he earlier rejected as "rumours and gossips". It is clear that some pieces of unhistorical evidence too were used to further reinforce Meera's image as a sacred, spiritual being, a "saint-devotee". Munshi Deviprasad does not allude to Meera's bitter relationship with the authority. Like Col. Tod, Deviprasad too holds Meera responsible for her misfortune, for she had freely mingled with saints and hermits. He states that: "Rana ji decided to hurt Meera Bai because many saint devotees would seek an audience with her, which in turn gave a bad name to the state, so Ranaji had to take strict measures to prevent it".[18]

In 1928, Gaurishankar Hirachand Ojha, the prolific writer, penned *Udaipur Rajya Ka Itihas* (History of Udaipur State). He too enjoyed patronage of the then Maharana of Mewar. Like Col. Tod, Ojha also asserts Meera's fame, "Hardly one could find in India a Hindu, man or woman, who would not be familiar with the name of Meera Bai, and there hardly was a shrine where her devotional songs were not sung."[19] Ojha, however, accepts that Meera never was very attached to the royal family of Mewar (her in-laws). Col. Tod, Shyamaldas and Munshi Deviprasad, all three coincided that Meera's suffering was due to her interactions with the saints, unfettered by the rage of the ruler. It has been stated that "Due to the popularity of Meera Bai's devotional songs, many people used to come to meet her, including the saint devotees from far off places. This was the reason that Vikramaditya was annoyed with her and would often give her various kinds of troubles".[20] In the nineteenth century Col. Tod and later, following his footmark, Shyamaldas, Munshi Deviprasad and Gaurishankar Hirachand Ojha in the twentieth century, created an image of Meera as a popular saint-devotee, which in the course of time was enhanced to a greater extent, by popular forms of media and literature.

3

Tod's history, despite setting a foundation of the recorded history of Rajasthan, has also been criticised for carrying inaccuracies and biases due to his affinity with the feudal lords. Influenced by his imperial ideals, and his colonial prejudices, knowingly or unknowingly, Tod reconstructed Meera as a romantic mystic, a holy saint poetess.

In the early nineteenth century, some European scholars were keen on understanding Indian society and culture. Interestingly, many of these scholars and early historians were, by profession, high-ranking officials of the East India Company, actually posted to make an in-depth study and analysis of their respective regions. They acquainted themselves with the history and traditions of that particular area. During this period, certain European Universities were interested in exploring Indian history and culture. Different western studies conducted in the early nineteenth century have been classified by Amartya Sen, the Nobel awardee Indian economist, as "exoticist, magisterial and curatorial".[21] Their exoticist approach sought to relate India, as a land of 'wonder', magic and non-materialistic concerns. Illustrious scholars like Friedrich Schlegel and others presented India as a land focused on spiritual and religious matters. From a 'magisterial' viewpoint of European scholars, India was primarily a colonized territory, so it must be controlled with a sense of superiority and ownership. James Mill, the Scottish historian, declared that India was a primitive and uncivilized country, so it is expected that the British Empire should stay for bringing about generous reforms. With a 'curatorial' approach, studies were carried out, ultimately leading to the idea that the Indian society and culture were quite ostentatious. In contrast with the exoticist method, there was no emphasis on esoteric wonders or mysticism, and in contrast with the magisterial method, which focused on the administrative needs of the government, the curatorial approach was somewhat an impartial way of looking at India.

Tod was attracted towards Rajputana, out of his intellect and curiosity, in pursuit of understanding its history, he was sympathetic and full of admiration for the society. Therefore, his method is rather closer to the curatorial method. Intellectuals like William Jones, Thomas Colebrooke and several others followed the same path, but Tod's conclusions are characterized by sound reasoning, despite his special affinity with Rajputs. Some of his notions have also been substantiated later by Indian researchers. In the early nineteenth century, Tod proved that India was not a country which lacked a study of its past, and there were sufficient native historical resources. On the contrary, many of his European peers were of the view that India never had any tradition of recording its history. Tod expressed his surprise that some people blindly believed that "the Hindoos" do not have any historical texts. He suggested that before making such illogical assumptions, one should have a look at the private collections of the Jain texts of Jaisalmer and Anhilwara (Patan), which were in possession of the Jain Granth Bhandar (repository), Kings of Rajputana and fief-holders.[22] Tod had a strikingly different belief that India's feudal system was not very different from that of the Europe. While many historians believed that in India, the lands belonged to the king, Tod's understanding was quite different from that. He had a belief that the lands belonged to the masses or the cultivators and farmers.[23] Later Romila Thapar, an Indian historian, also had a similar interpretation.[24] Tod adopted a 'curatorial' method in seeking history. Because of the rational angle of this approach, exoticist and magisterial methods were later influenced by it to some extent. The same is applicable to nearly all the studies carried out with a 'curatorial' approach. According to Amartya Sen, these studies never remained completely neutral; and they had one inclination or the other[25]. Tod's however, also looked at certain portions of the country through the glass of exoticism, and found them "extraordinarily marvelous,"[26] religious, and mysterious. Tod's perspective, however, was also magisterial enough to consider Europeans superior to Indians. In a manuscript, while commenting on the translation of poetry of Chand Bardai he notes that he had mixed with the native Indians and had understood their emotions. However, in his opinion, the Indians were no match to the British, but it could also be judged how the natives had been before the tyranny and repression were inflicted on them. To him, they seemed worth emulating.[27]

Tod's interpretation of Meera Bai, was also influenced by these different perspectives. He was not oblivious to her corporeal experiences, or her worldly struggles. He knew about her tense and embittered relationship with those in power. He knew that there were a lot of ill feelings targeted at her. Therefore, he says, as discussed earlier, "Excessive devotion of Meera gave rise to several hearsays and rumours".[28] To state the reason he clearly points out... "She danced before the God of her idolatry, as though she was one of the celestial nymphs in the mystic rasa mandala, therefore she provided some ground for malice to build upon". He also says, "There was no just cause".[29] He does not elaborate on the issues like her non-spiritual experiences, her loss and sorrows, or her mundane struggle. He sanctifies her, puts her on a pedestal, as a romantic, idyllic, sublime being who has renounced the luxuries of material life, and thus establishes her as a famous religious figure. The approaches of early historians might vary, but they were influenced by each other. Tod's canonisation of Meera was a blend of different approaches. Those who followed a strictly magisterial approach, regarded the Indian society as blindly conventional and stagnant, which justified the British Raj in India, this notion was a severe blunder, a gross injustice. Whenever a dominating class inappropriately exerted their power on the common people here, voices were raised against its monopoly. Meera's life-long struggle in resistance to the whims of the medieval feudal class, especially patriarchy, and gender discrimination, is enough proof the society was constantly evolving. However, Tod ignored this aspect to avoid igniting protest against the authority, and to maintain the importance of colonial rule.

Interestingly, Tod also shared a close relationship with the feudal lords of Rajputana, so he fondly labels them as, "Apney Rajput"[30] (my own Rajput) and for Mewar, "My land".[31] and the fondness was mutual. During his stay in Rajputana as a political agent, he earned remarkable affection and respect of the rulers and he also extended his deep gratitude towards them. In the words of William Crooke, editor of Tod's *Annals and Antiquities,* James Tod scandalously favoured the Rajput kings of Rajasthan and that too especially those from Mewar and Marwar.[32] He was especially impressed with the courteousness, loyalty, chaivalry, and military courage of the feudal lords. In the Introduction of his book he praises the warrior clans, by acknowledging that the struggles of the brave people for their sovereignty through the ages, sacrificing whatever was dear to them for safeguarding the faith of their forefathers, sturdily defending against death and in spite of every temptation, their rights and national autonomy, form a picture, from which it is difficult to contemplate without emotions.[33]

Meera was a daughter of Marwar and daughter-in-law of Mewar, a voice of both devotion, and revolution against state-imposed limitations. She was admired by the masses, so Tod could not overlook her, so, despite giving her a few interesting mentions, he could not empower her character as a rebel, an ideal of confidence and independence, lest her followers be ignited by the same fire of rebellion. He transformed her multifaceted life and identity into a unidimensional love story full of romance and mysticism. For the same reason, Meera hardly had any mention in the memory and history of the feudal lords, but her image of a saint-devotee was acceptable to them as well. Although several narratives point out in the same direction that Meera was heckled in the palace and was persuaded to give up her devotional path, this was overlooked by Tod, as he might not want to displease the lords who thought so highly of him. Tod in his travelogue, presents her as a romantic enigma, surrounded by obscure moral lines, "Her lord and sovereign, never had any kind of jealousy or suspicion… even though Murlidhar (Krishna) descended from His pedestal and embraced His devotee, it is but fair to infer that there was no just cause."[34]

Tod admits that there were many scandalous tales and gossips in the society aimed at Meera but he does not hold any feudal lords responsible for it. He rather puts the blame on her, implying that her lack of regard for conventions (i.e., fraternizing with saints and ascetics) was the root of such scandals. Perhaps, however, there might be another reason Tod did not acknowledge the other admirable nuances of her character. He earlier formed another image of ideal Rajput women in his mind, which was based on flowery exaggerations of charans and bards. While delving into the past of Rajputana, Tod learnt about women who were doting wives, who made herculean sacrifices for the sake of their husbands and children, about women who didn't even flinch from committing *sati*, or *jauhar* and gave up their life to protect the dignity of their husband and family. Tod praised

Rajput women, who upheld high ethics, were affectionate, brave, actively participated in decision-making, never left their husbands during battles, and even chastised them when they committed any cowardly acts.[35] This notion of Rajput women was further engraved in his mind after witnessing the exemplary sacrifice of Princess Krishna of Mewar in 1806 while he was a young English officer.[36] Although girls and women suffered due to polygamy and other patriarchal traditions, also the malaise of female infanticide, Tod has not taken note of such atrocities while writing history. William Crooke, the editor of *Annals and Antiquities* makes a remark that Tod avoided descriptions on practices, customs and festivities etc. while describing different Rajput dynasties.[37] According to E.M. Kelley, during that period, the number of female infants were less than that of a year-old male infants[38] but Tod avoids mentioning any disparities in gender ratio. Meera was completely different from Tod's ideal Rajput woman. Meera was not bothered about preserving her family's honour, nor was she keen on winning her in-laws with dedicated service. After being so sorely criticized by her in-laws, she severed all family ties, and distanced herself from her royal privilege, she was by all means, an unconventional woman, unlike any Rajput women, no matter how influential or virtuous they might be. She refused to commit *sati* after her husband's death. She violated prevalent feudal family norms by falling in love with a deity, going frequently on pilgrimages and meeting people from different walks of life, so she was never praised or respected by feudal lords, so it is also reflected in Tod's depiction of Meera.

Tod was well-versed with classical European literature, where love, romance and adulations were recurring themes, he incorporated the same in Meera's life and character while reconstructing her image. It is safe to say that Tod's image of Meera might not match with her real identity. The image construction was dominated by several factors--Tod's colonial interests, his intention to be on friendly terms with the feudal lords, and his preconceived notions of India as a land of mystic charm, and the valour of Rajput women. Tod's interpretation of Meera was accepted far and wide, and was gradually assimilated in traditional histories and devotional storytelling. Tod was indeed a venerated historian with an enduring legacy, but he might as well have deliberately turned a blind eye to some realistic aspects of Meera's life and character, and his accounts robbed her of her unique identity, her real-life resilience, her quest for emancipation and dignity. Due to Tod's canonization, Meera's became a mystic saint, bereft of any historical contextualization, in a land of wonder and ecstasy.

Notes and References

1. James Tod, *Annals and Antiquities of Rajasthan*, ed. William Crooke (Delhi: Motilal Banarsidass, 1994, London: 1st edn. 1920, 1:546.
2. "Granthkartavishayak Snasmaran" (Memoir of the author) in *Paschimi Bharat ki Yatra*, Hindi trans. of *Travels in Western India* by Gopal Narayan Bahura (Jodhpur: Rajasthan Prachya Vidya Pratishthan, 2nd edn.1996), p.11.
3. Ibid., 2.
4. Ibid., 5.
5. Gopinath Sharma, "Itihaskar James Tod: Vyaktitva evam Krititva" in *Itihaskar James Tod: Vyaktitva evam Krititva,* ed. Hukum Singh Bhati (Udaipur: Pratap Shodh Sansthan, 1992), 185.
6. "Granthkartavishayak Snasmaran," 4.
7. Tod, *Annals and Antiquities of Rajasthan*, 1:337.
8. Tod, *Paschimi Bharat ki Yatra,* 442.
9. Shyamaldas, *Vir Vinod - Mewar ka Itihas*, Part-I, (Delhi: Motilal Banarsidass, reprint edn. 1986, 1st edn. 1886), 371.
10. Ibid., 371.
11. Munshi Deviprasad, *Meerabai ka Jivan Charitra* (Kolkata: Bangali Sahitya Parishad, 1954, 1st edn. 1898), 1.
12. Ibid., 28.
13. Ibid., 28.
14. Ibid., 10.
15. Ibid., 11.

16. Ibid., 10.
17. Ibid., 26.
18. Ibid., 12.
19. Gaurishankar Ojha, *Udaipur Rajya ka Itihas* (Jodhpur: Rajasthani Granthagar, 1996-97, 1st edn. 1928), 359.
20. Ibid, 360.
21. Amartya Sen, *Bhartiya Arthatantra Itihas aur Sanskriti,* Hindi trans. of *The Argumentative Indian* (Delhi: Rajpal & Sons, 2005), 134.
22. Tod, *Annals and Antiquities of Rajasthan,* 1:268.
23. "Granthkartavishayak Snasmaran," 39.
24. Romila Thapar, *Aadikaleen Bharat ki Vyakhya,* Hindi trans. Mangalnath (New Delhi: Granth Shilpi), 11.
25. Sen, *Bhartiya Arthatantra Itihas aur Sanskriti.* 141.
26. "Granthkartavishayak Sansmaran," 37.
27. Ibid., 18.
28. Tod, *Annals and Antiquities of Rajasthan,* 1:337.
29. Tod, *Paschimi Bharat ki Yatra,* 442.
30. "Granthkartavishayak Sansmaran", 32.
31 Tod, *Paschimi Bharat ki Yatra,* 442.
32. William Crooke, editor's introduction to *Annals and Antiquities of Rajasthan,* 1: xxvii.
33. Tod, introduction to *Paschimi Bharat ki Yatra,* ixiii.
34. Tod, *Paschimi Bharat ki Yatra,* 443.
35. Crooke, editor's introduction to *Annals and Antiquities of Rajasthan,* 1: xxxviii.
36. This incident occurred when the condition of most of the princely states of Rajasthan was awfully bad due to mutual rivalry and constant looting of Marathas and Pindaris. Krishna Kumari was the daughter of Maharana Bhim Singh of Mewar. Her marriage was fixed with Maharaja Bhim Singh of Jodhpur. After the demise of Maharaja Bhim Singh, Krishna Kumari was espoused to Maharaja Jagatsingh of Jaipur.

    Daulatrao Scindia, the ruler of Gwalior, who was already indignant with Jaipur, could not appreciate this matrimonial proposal. He requested Maharana Bhim Singh of Mewar to turn out the representative of Jaipur out of Udaipur, which Maharana Bhim Singh did not accept. Enraged Scindia attacked Mewar as there was no other way to bring Bhim Singh around; Bhim Singh had to listen to Scindia. Since Krishna Kumari's first association was with the royal family of Jodhpur, therefore the then Maharaja

Mansingh of Jodhpur considered her relationship with Jagatsingh of Jaipur as his insult. Eventually the forces of Jodhpur and Jaipur ran into each other. Pindari Nawab Amir Khan supported Jaipur in the battle as the result of which Man Singh returned to Jodhpur after being defeated. Jagatsingh sieged Jodhpur, but this time Man Singh bribed Amir Khan. And now Jagat Singh was defeated by the joint forces of Jodhpur and Pindaris. Amir Khan reached Udaipur on behalf of Man Singh and in front of Maharana Bhim Singh, proposed the marriage of Krishna Kumari with Man Singh or to give up her life drinking poison. High and dry Maharana Bhim Singh accepted the proposal to consume poison in order to save the state from hassles.

According to the wishes of her father, Krishna Kumari sacrificed her life after drinking poison. Tod has described this phenomenon in his book in an emotional and poignant language. He compared Krishna Kumari to Virginia, daughter of Veuseus, the warrior of Rome. It is said that Viussius had killed his daughter in front of everyone in order to protect her chastity and virtuousness.

37. Crooke, editor's introduction to *Annals and Antiquities of Rajasthan*, 1: xxxviii.
38. Ibid., 1: xxxviii.

Chapter - VI

Image Construction

Meera's image is based more on speculations and inferences than actually on facts. The reconstruction of Meera's image began right after her death to advertise some religio-political interests. As discussed earlier in this book, being a feudal lady, she was relatively self-reliant and enjoyed some economic independence too, because she was married to Bhojraj, the eldest son of Rana Sanga, the ruler of Mewar, the largest kingdom in northern India. She had been brought up in a traditional environment, she held saint devotees in high esteem, extended them hospitality and charity whenever she could, which is probably why several devotional movements and sects were keen to take her into their fold. In order to show their closeness with Meera they went on to the extent of spreading tales on her life, with an ulterior motive of getting greater approval and admiration from the masses themselves. Meera had a great deal of interactions with saints of her time and she travelled a lot for the same purpose. Even when she was estranged from the feudal class, and was disregarded by her own kind, she did not lose her mass appeal. She did not give in to discriminatory expectations of Rana, who symbolized a stifling moral authority and undeserving political leadership. Her faith, will and determination were admired by the society.

Colonial historians regarded the Indian society as crude, non-progressive, owing to their preconceived notions and authoritarian mindset. Naturally, they ignored Meera's courage and struggle for independence. Early European historians had a monopoly on some theories, which later influenced Indian scholars; therefore, Meera's image of a pious romantic poetess became more acceptable and recognized. With the rise of new printing techniques, publication of newspapers and magazines, cinema, radio and several other modes of mass communication, Meera's image, even during the post-independence era, was promoted in an idealized and unrealistic manner. In early postcolonial years, the mind of the middle-class Indian was still heavily set under the Western influence, despite being aware of India's cultural integrity and pride. On one hand, Western ideologies were still prevalent, yet national consciousness was stronger than ever. Consequently, in this state of insoluble dilemma, Indian intellectuals considered it as their responsibility to recover Indian past and heritage. As a result, the colonial-era image of Meera spread by leaps and bounds in popular books, newspapers and magazines, comic strips, and movies, with little to no deviation from what the European rulers have created of her. The idealized accounts of her life and love fascinated the Indian middle class.

Afterwards, India saw a revolution in industries, technology and communication. Globalization came as a new wave that swept over the world. Commercial campaigns were run to generate interest in people from all walks of life. Big marketers jostled to reach a wider audience, which caused the middle-class to fall into the trap of consumer culture. The market took advantage of the common man's longing for mobility and freedom of choices. While the Indian masses were intrigued by rationalism and scientific thinking, they also advocated preservation of cultural values, and there was a clear tendency to "emphasize religious identity".[1]

Between 2007 and 2015, people in India who considered religion to be very important increased by 11 percentage points to 80%, according to a Pew Global Attitude survey.[2] India offers a diverse kaleidoscope of religious practices and beliefs. However, fierce pride associated the religious past and growing sectarian tension, "enthusiastically supported communal politics in India."[3] Some ancient cultures were brought back through movements like "religious revivalism" while many dogmas and doctrines were modified for the betterment of the society through religious 'reforms'. In a twist of fate, the reconstructed image of Meera had all the ingredients to propagate diof people from different quarters. Her image as a 'saint-devotee' satisfies the desire of the masses to assert their religious and devotional heritage, while a gorgeous tale of poetess of love, romance, mystery and rebellion fulfils the new consumerist demands. Her recently built images are born out of her 'popular' images, which themselves may not coincide and have uniformity. Here an attempt has been made to examine how Meera's image has evolved across new media.

1

In the early twentieth century, when the communication revolution was yet to arrive, books were the most popular way to be educated, enlightened and entertained. Middle class Indians brought home devotional, mythological books for their family, often in order to pass on the traditions and the rich religious legacy. Women and children often enjoy religious tales, and especially heroic mythological legends. The books also help inculcate values in children from an early age, and promote the images of ideal, virtuous Indian men and women, to learn good character traits, with a wider view to attain lasting peace and security in the community. Publishing houses like Gita Press Gorakhpur and Diamond Books seized this opportunity. In 1923, Jaydayal Goyandka, the founder of Gita Press Gorakhpur, established its office in Govind Bhawan, Calcutta, with an objective to spread Sanatan Dharam. The press focussed on publishing religious texts in simple language and at an affordable price.

Their venture was a big success. Gita Press has sold several million religious books till date[4]; the company has published Shrimad Bhagavad Gita, Ramayana, Durga Sapt-shati, Puranas, Upnishadas and also religious biographical sketches etc. In 1930, it also published two volumes of character sketches of ideal pious women in *bhakt nari* drawn from Indian myths and history. The second volume includes vivid character sketches of Shabari, Jana Bai, Karmeti Bai and Rabia along with Meera Bai. Hanuman Prasad Poddar, the lifetime editor of Gita Press, is also the writer of a chapter on Meera Bai. Poddar depicted Meera Bai's personality in accordance with deep-seated Hindu devotional beliefs. He did not reflect on her multifaceted womanhood and her struggle, but presented her as an ideal righteous Hindu woman. According to him, she was a blessing and a pride for "India, Hindu woman and her ancestory."[5] He substantiated his claim in the light of folk memories recorded by Nabhadas, Priyadas etc and added some imaginary inputs of his own. From 1930 to 2001, thirty-nine editions and 4, 62,000 copies were published, the book became a bestseller.[6] Poddar suggests that Meera developed a deep devotion at an early age. He cites an example from a folk narrative about a saint who gave her a 'Girdharlal' (Krishna) idol. He also suggests that Meera held the same idol of 'Girdharlal' in her hand, when she was getting married to Rana, so, she, in fact, was married to Lord Krishna's idol. He further adds that after marriage, Meera's refusal to worship the ancestral deity of Rana's family was justified because she had already been married to Krishna, so she says, "I will worship none, except Girdharlal [Krishna]"[7]. Poddar employs an embellished version of Priyadas' account, with a special focus on the triumph of God. He also presents the event of the attempt to poison Meera with vivid emotions.

She accepted it as a divine nectar. By the grace of God, the poison turned into nectar and Meera was unharmed; God is great, with divine intervention, anything is possible.[8] Though her married life was conventional, it lasted for a short time, and this period of time cannot be validated by historical evidence.

However, Poddar adds some extra zest, to present her as an ideal Hindu wife. He suggests that Meera never displeased her husband, Prince Bhojraj[9], who was also impressed with her devotion, felt blessed and made a temple of Ranchhod (Krishna) for her. To further establish Meera as a model Hindu wife, Poddar adds that Meera suggested that Bhojraj should marry again. Often, she was worried that she was not able to fulfil her homely obligations or her husband's desires. After Bhojraj's second marriage, she could finally breathe a sigh of relief, and entirely devote herself to her almighty God.[10] Poddar leaves no stone unturned in presenting her as a loving, considerate ideal Hindu woman, who, despite being divinely inspired, was not completely oblivious to her wifely duties and also felt a tinge of guilt, failing carry them out. Drawing from Priyadas' account of Meera's meeting with Akbar and Tansen, Poddar, a devout Hindu, reinterprets the incident, and suggests that no Hindu devoted wife would approve a meeting with a male of different religious identity, so, Akbar came to meet Meera in the disguise of a Vaishnav Brahmin[11], otherwise, she would not have interacted with him at all.

Diamond Books, a New-Delhi based publishing house, has published some of the best Hindi literary works besides popular literature (including works of Jaishankar Prasad, Premchand, Vrindavanlal Verma) among others in its pocket edition. In the early twentieth century, it also brought out a series on the lives and poetry of saint-devotees and gurus like Kabir, Meera, Guru Nanak, Surdas and Tulsidas. Giriraj Sharan Agrawal was the general editor of the series. The book titled *Prem Deewani Meera*[12] (Lovelorn Meera) depicts Meera's early life experiences and includes her poetry. To attract target readership, Agrawal also paraphrased Meera's poetry in Hindi. Though the language is simple, the tone is romantic. Meera's character in this work is very different from the one presented by Gita Press Gorakhpur. While the latter portrayed Meera as an ideal Hindu wife, Diamond Books showed her like a love-sick woman pining for her lover, with a great deal of longing and anticipation. Gita Press's Meera is focused on her spiritual devotion and moral awareness, while Diamond Books perceived her differently, because times had changed.

The early twentieth century witnessed a great transformation in the middle-class Hindi speaking society. Though its conservative religious outlook still continued, the onslaught of consumer culture had somewhat altered its thinking and priorities. The middle class suffered from a set of internal contradictions. In the latter part of the twentieth century, globalization and economic liberalization had a dramatic influence on common life. The notion of ideal women changed, into a liberal, bold, self-reliant, and at times, a fierce rebel, where still, in reality, within four walls, women were expected to be obedient and passive. Naturally, the masses craved for a loving woman who defied orthodox norms, instead of a serene feminine deity on a pedestal. So, Diamond Books presented a new image of Meera, different from the one published by Gita Press. They showed her as being insatiably in love, with unwavering loyalty to her Lord, unfettered by social or cultural constraints. The career-oriented, mobility-seeking middle class was often known for great academic achievements, and carried seeds of revolution in order to grow themselves. So, Meera's rebellious character against the ruling elites, as portrayed in the Diamond Books, definitely caught its attention. Diamond Books, depicts Meera this way,

> Krishna had innumerable (devotees),
> (Meera) was worshipper of Krishna' love.

Was an epitome of the pangs of separation,
Was an ocean of joys,
Meera douses intoxicating nectar in her love songs, so longingly,
We shall all be contended if the clouds shower rain,
She never sang to prove poetic merits,
Her songs are natural conveyors of her feelings,
Whenever some feelings arose, she sang,
To enlighten one's soul, one should get to know lovelorn Meera,
To render her songs is to bathe in an intoxicating pool,
Let's search for the pool,
Her songs have thrilling pain and love.[13]

It is clearly an idealized picture of a woman devotee and lacks a realistic appreciation of her character. There is an allusion to the event when there was an attempt to poison her, but it was also overly romanticized. This has been depicted the following way:

She sat beside the statue of Krishna. She remembered him (Sanvalia ji)

An ethereal aura lit her face,
Smile flickered on her lips,
With her eyes closed, she touched the bowl on her lips,

The Panda (a Brahmin) started shivering, his soul went into flames of the terrible sin. Meera sat calmly. Panda fell to her feet,

"I have committed a grave sin,
Oh Queen, It was not a nectar but was a deadly poison.
I was helpless, Oh Queen, What have I done?"
He was weeping. Meera was still in a meditative state.
The maid servant was petrified.[14]

The new-generation middle-class intellectuals are keen on preserving their religious heritage, but they also raise questions and think rationally. Meera's survival even after consuming poison is explained thus,

"This phenomenon can be questioned in the age of science...survival after consuming poison is not impossible. It is also probable that the poison given to Meera was not lethal. "Even today, people may survive after accidental poisoning..."[15]

2

"Meera Bai" in the series Amar Chitra Katha reintroduced Meera to the common masses,[16] following the popularity of which, many comic book publishers came into existence such as Macaw books,[17] Wilco Publishing House[18] and several others. These comic books have played an important role in leaving an indelible, positive impression of Meera on the mind of young readers.

There were many reasons behind the massive popularity of such ventures. During the 1970s and the 1980s, India's economy experienced some hiccups as fruits of sudden development. Positive faith is needed to pull oneself through times of financial crises. In earlier times, the joint family system was accepted by one and all. The responsibilities were shared, to inculcate values and traditions in young members of the family. Earlier, the elderly in the family were the storyteller, and moral guardian. Since the Indian middle class had deep-rooted traditions and culture, it felt a need to glorify the heroes, symbols and stories related to its devotional past, in order to revitalize the nation.

Anant Pai, a great educationist, recognized the importance of moral and ethical leadership in every family.[19] He took up epic Hindu characters, and their glorious tales, seasoned them with ideals and vision, simplified them with graphics to match the level of understanding of young readers, and presented them as Amar Chitra Katha.[20] Apparently the purpose of this product was to enlighten English-medium school children who often considered anything Indian as inferior.[21] The "Immortal Picture Stories", as the name of the series means, celebrated India's own great heroes of history, legends, classics, and folktales. It carries tales of Meera, Nanak, Kabir, Tulsidas, Surdas, Ravidas and several other medieval saints.

Anant Pai adapted Meera's character in accordance with Hindu ideals. Pai's Meera is unique in the sense that he presented her as a saint-devotee without belittling her role as a wife. Moreover, her character here was not reconstructed to provoke readers' excitement, rather was meant to educate. The series acted as a source of knowledge, where legends and myths were made even more interesting with a sprinkle of Pai's own imagination. He largely depended on folk memory and available textual sources. The events of Meera's life covered were her acceptance of Krishna as her husband when she was a little girl, her marriage to Bhojraj, her refusal to worship the ancestral tutelary deity *(Kuldevi)*, Bhojraj's discontent with Meera after Uda complains of her excess devotion for Krishna, her meeting with Akbar and Tansen, the untimely death of Bhojraj, her refusal to become *sati*, tortures inflicted on Meera by Vikramaditya, his attempts to kill her by giving her poison, snake bites, etc Meera writing letters to Tulsidas, her travel to Merta, Vrindavan, Mathura and Dwarka, finally her merging into Krishna's idol. In order to realistically depict Meera's life while also promoting Hindu ideals, Anant Pai carefully mentions a few incidents in such a way that her protest and struggle were complementary to her wifely duties. Meera's submission to Krishna is not an obstacle in her duties as a wife. In one of the episodes, she falls to Bhojraj's feet and it is said that Meera was an ideal Hindu wife and her husband adored her.[22] Anant Pai also asserts that while carrying out daily household chores, Meera would remember Krishna as her divine husband[23].

In order to further establish Meera's role as a good wife, Pai incorporates an imaginary episode, which is neither mentioned in Bhaktmal or any other textual sources. Bhojraj is infuriated to learn that Meera met Akbar, who was a non-Hindu, and orders

her to die by drowning herself, and like any obedient wife, Meera decides not to defy his order. Like an "ideal Hindu wife", Meera. with a heavy heart and tears in her eyes bids goodbye to her friends.[24]

Pai also adds another incident, which was substantiated by no one else. Bhojraj, clad in a saffron robe, reaches Vrindavan to apologize and requests her to get back to Chittorgarh, on his request, Meera returns. In one of the strips, Bhojraj is shown to be saying, "Meera, forgive me. I request you to come with me to Chittor". In response Meera says, "Has Meera ever disobeyed her husband? I shall go to Chittor."[25]

Anant Pai further glorifies Meera by giving a divine interpretation to her romantic introversion and resistance, which otherwise would not have tallied with the image of 'an ideal wife'. It can be inferred from various other sources Meera went to Vrindavan, by leaving the royal family, as a result of constant harassment, scrutiny and stress, but Pai attributes her departure to a divine command. In a picture, Meera drowns, but Krishna saves her, throwing his arms to catch her, saying, "Your relationship with your husband has ended; now you belong to me, go to Vrindavan and reach me."[26]

Pai overlooks the incompatibility between Bhojraj and Meera. Despite ceaseless attempts by Bhojraj to dissuade Meera from her path of devotion, when all are in vain, finally Bhojraj

decides to get a temple constructed for her, as depicted by Pai. A picture shows Meera dancing, and as the text reveals, "Bhojraj was convinced that his wife had lost her mind. In order to make her happy, a temple was built where she could worship the statue of her lover. After a while, a crowd of devotees started gathering around Meera. She would sing and dance before her Lord in absolute love."[27]

3

The unprecedented popularity and commercial success of Amar Chitra Katha inspired several other publishers of children's books to enter into this sphere. Macaw books, a multinational and multilingual publisher, in 2009, published comics in English on several mythological characters such as Ashta-Vakra, Shrawan Kumar, Satyavan-Savitri, Angulimala and Sudama and of course, Meera. The books were designed to feed children's curiosity while also developing a creative flair in them.[28] Similarly, Anant Pai's

Amar Chitra Katha, despite being a commercial venture, was aimed at introducing children to the golden past of India. The target readers of Macaw comics were children from well-to-do backgrounds with a reasonable command over the English language, so the characters in the stories were made more relatable to them. For instance, there is a mention of Meera's early formal education, which, in reality, cannot be validated. There is also a depiction of Meera developing important skills, receiving education of religious texts, music, archery, war strategy, horse riding, chariot and weaponry.[29]

Almost all incidents mentioned in Amar Chitra Katha have also been covered in Macaw's book on Meera. Meera's encounters with Raidas and also with Jiva Goswami in Vrindavan, have also been included here, based on medieval references. Unlike Amar Chitra Katha, Macaw's Meera was not recreated to promote Hindu ideals and values. However, incidents in Amar Chitra Katha that accord Meera the status of an ideal Hindu wife, have been shown here as well. In one of the scenes, Krishna is shown beside Meera.[30]

Some episodes such as her meeting with Raidas or even with Jiva Goswami in Vrindavan were not included in Amar Chitra Katha, but in Macaw Books they are included. It is obvious that Macaw Books did not introduce anything innovative or strikingly original, because the books were designed to emulate the success of Amar Chitra Katha. This too contributed in promoting Meera's image as the ideal Hindu wife, which was already shown in Amar Chitra Katha.

Wilco, the heritage publishing house has brought several titles related to myths, history, gods, biographies, inventions, festivals etc. Its main objective was to educate and entertain readers from all age groups with international-standard books.[31] More or less, its Meera Bai too, is based on Amar Chitra Katha, although the latter's portrayal was more idealized and bigger than life, many of the fictional incidents of Amar Chitra Katha have been used here too. Some new fictitious events have also been added by Wilco, to bridge the gap between certain incidents of her life and rectify some discrepancies. For instance, after the death of Bhojraj, the ruling Rana is jealous of Meera because she may claim the throne, whereas such claims have never been mentioned in the folk memory, ecclesiastical biographies or other textual references. In one of the scenes, Rana tells his courtiers that Meera might be planning to claim the throne.[32]

The work describes how Krishna's idol was given to Meera, in her childhood by a hermit,[33] and how Akbar and Tansen came to meet her in disguise and offered flowers at Krishna's statue. This incident has been shown in detail.[34] Here, Akbar is appreciated, and meeting him was not considered sacrilegious for a Hindu woman. Akbar is depicted sitting in his court and the caption suggests, In those days the country was ruled by Akbar the great, he was kind and cultured." Moreover, he is shown to like and appreciate music.[35]

Anant Pai, in Amar Chitra Katha was rather more cautious; he only suggested that Akbar once came to see Meera.

More films have been made on Meeras' life and times, in comparison with the number of films on other legendary saint-poets like Tulsidas, Surdas, Nanak, Kabir and Raidas.[36] In 1979 Gulzar directed a film called *Meera* starring Hema Malini. The film's songs are composed by Pandit Ravi Shankar and lyrics were of Meera Bai herself. According to the producer, it was a film on Meera's immortal love. The film portrays Meera as a lovelorn, extraordinary woman, it combines elements of romance and spirituality, history and imagination. Gulzar uses a historical approach in a masterly fashion, but the film does not shed light on Meera's rebellious aspects. Here, despite showing Meera's struggle for respect, stability and spiritual fulfilment, she is shown to have placed special importance on family honour and is ready to sacrifice a lot for it. He even depicts the eighteenth century's princess Krishna, who is remembered for her great sacrifice, as a sister of Meera. The film shows that she has been in love with Krishna since her childhood. After marriage, her love for Krishna creates sorrows and sufferings in her life, but there is no allusion to her sour relationship with Vikramaditya or Ratan Singh. As the plot thickens, Meera's ardent, unshakable love has been highlighted, and her rebellious resistance to feudal arrogance of power is overlooked. Not every section of the society was in sync with Meera's ideals and way of living. Gulzar, too shows Meera being chastised in a socio-religious reform sabha, and highlights how societal disapproval was used to curtail rebellious behaviour in women, but here too her image as a romantic 'fanatic' has come to the fore. Gulzar's selection of Meera's lyrics have helped highlight her feelings and emotions. However, verses of Meera that reveal her vocal protest and refusal to give in to patriarchal standards have been omitted.

At present, among all saint poets of medieval times, perhaps Meera is the most recognized, widely sung and known to all. Her songs of devotion are available everywhere, and have been sung by Lata Mangeshkar, Asha Bhonsle, Vani Jayram, Kishori Amonkar, Omkarnath Thakur, M. Subbalakshmi, Sadhana Sargam, Kavita Krishnamurti, Hema Desai, Mahalakshmi Iyer among others. The songs may not reveal much about her real-life struggle, but do convey the mellifluous essence of an extraordinary, romantic devotee's life. Times Music series has rightly stated that "It is the bravery of Meera, the Rajput princess by birth, that has been expressed in devotion and dedication at the feet of God"[37].

It can be safely concluded that in oral narratives, devotional literature, works of colonial historians, even to this very day, in popular films and mass media, idealized tales of her life and devotion are everywhere, though Meera too had a temporal and earthly life, as a woman who had remarkable strength and courage as well as frailties and vulnerabilities. Meera, with her own spiritual identity and values, struggled for emancipation from social and institutional stagnation, in a time and place that were primarily indifferent to women's independence or honouring their choices. In the latter part of the twentieth century, her saint-devotee image was popularized through comics, films, cassettes and CDs, which gained a wider audience and were more accessible than past literature, historical texts and various archives, so the popular forms of her image became considerably accepted through mass media. Aiming at satisfying higher public demands and commercial success, certain changes to Meera's images were made from time to time. Her images also articulated different mindsets, perceptions, and beliefs of their creators. Gita Press and Amar Chitra Katha, presented Meera as an ideal Hindu wife and a saint-devotee, which satisfies religious sentiments and family ideals of the then middle-class, while the Diamond Books focused on her fearless, rebellious love and longing, which reverberates with the modern-day hope, love, and rebellion symbiosis. In Gulzar's film, Meera's image as a saint-devotee and Krishna's beloved is highlighted. Popular forms of literature, soulful songs in CDs and cassettes have also asserted Meera's image of a saint with an unshakable faith in her beloved Krishna. Thus, many images of Meera have appeared because she has an enduring, universal appeal. Her images have been employed in healing, educating and inspiring generations.

Notes and References

1. Pawan Kumar Verma, *Bharat ke Madhya Varg ki Ajeeb Dastaan*, Hindi trans. of *The Great Indian Middle Class* (New Delhi: Rajkamal Prakashan, 2009), 130.
2. Pranav Gupta, Sanjay Kumar, "The Growing Business of Religion in India" retrieved from livemint.com/Politics/2Vpsk1a1j4RwcIg9eKMErL/The-growing-business-of-religion-in-India.html
3. Verma, *Bharat ke Madhya Varg ki Ajeeb Dastaan*, 134.
4. Information is taken from the website of Gita Press, Gorakhpur: www.gitapress.org.
5. Hanuman Prasad Poddar, *Bhakt Nari - 2* (Gorakhpur: Gita Press, 2001), 40.
6. Ibid.,12.
7. Ibid., 20.
8. Ibid., 26.
9. Ibid., 26.
10. Ibid., 21.
11. Ibid., 31.
12. Giriraj Sharan Agrawal, *Prem Diwani Meera* (New Delhi: Diamond Pocket Books Pvt. Ltd., 2003).
13. Ibid., 1.
14. Ibid., 16.
15. Ibid., 18.
16. Anant Pai, Hindi Amar Chitra Katha *Meera Bai* (Mumbai: India Book House Pvt. Ltd., reprint edn. 2007).
17. *Meera Bai* (Mumbai: Macaw Books, 2009).
18. *Meera Bai* (Mumbai: Wilco Publishing House, 2011).
19. Aryank Guha, "Ek Bhartiya Chitrakatha ka Kitab Banana," *Shiksha Vimarsh*, September-October 2009, 30.
20. John Stratton Hawley, *Three Bhakti Voices* (New Delhi: Oxford University Press, 2005), 142.
21. Guha, "Ek Bhartiya Chitrakatha ka Kitab Banana," 31.

22. Pai, *Meera Bai* p.14.
23. Ibid., 4.
24. Ibid., 11.
25. Ibid., 17.
26. Ibid., 13.
27. Ibid., 7.
28. As written in the introductory commentary on the series printed on the back cover of *Meera Bai* published by Macaw Books.
29. *Meera Bai* (Macaw), 12.
30. *Meera Bai* (Hindi Amar Chitra Katha), 16.
31. Quoted from introductory commentin *Meera Bai* (Wilco).
32. *Meera Bai* (Wilco), 13.
33. Ibid., 1.
34. Ibid., 9.
35. Ibid., 9.
36. National film Archive Project no. 689/5/04 (Pune, 1984).
37. Quoted from introductory comment on the C.D. cover of the film *Meera* directed by Gulzar.

Translator's Note

Eugene Nida describes translation as a science, Theodore Savory terms it as an art and Eric Jacobson visualizes it as a craft. A translator is all this and much more. To translate *Pachrang Chola Pahar Sakhi Ri* to *Meera Vs Meera* was to be rational and objective like a scientist, creative and artistic like an artist, trained and hardworking like a skilled craftsman . Yet I would say that my role as a translator is a meagre one, I cannot claim to have any clue of Madhav Hada's creative moods during the writing of the *Pachrang Chola*, I must confess that it was indeed a pleasure and I thoroughly enjoyed reading and translating the book. Among the Hindi literary circles the book has been well received so much that its second edition will soon be out for the book lovers.

Often it is said that we live different lives in different languages. *Pachrang Chola* tended to excite the readers and the critics alike and I do hope the translation too would do the same.

One feels compelled to see it as an adventure with language, which is creative and self challenging. For me translation is a discovery and more so I delved into the text several times. The attempt made through this translation is to enliven the flavours, inhale the sounds, and explore sensitive nuances of each and every word, before searching for rhythm in translation. Often I was apprehensive of being emotionally swept away by the text but on all occasions Madhav Hada came to my rescue, and held me back during the course of our discussions over the text. I realized that the translator's relation with the language of the original text is a play between the ear and the text. For me it has been a process of what T.S. Eliot describes it as "a continual self sacrifice, a continual extinction of personality...." Meera had a universe of her own, which activated her thinking in this sense and led her to the status of saint–devotee among the galaxy of other poets of the Bhakti-movement. She intently listened to the 'still sad music of humanity' along with its celebration of life and blitheness that added a metaphysical dimension to her poetry. Hada explores to comprehend her 'human' aspects of life along with the spiritual ones in doing so he extensively depends on not only the historical sources or even those which are inherent in the internal evidence of her poetry, but he considers vernacular sources as his major concern too. Like an iconoclast he dismantles the age old image/s of Meera that is only as a 'saint-poet'. He reconstructs her alternative image that is more human and full of life.

During the course of the translation at times, a situation arises where the translator confronts the untranslatable and therein lies a challenge, and challenges can never be side lined they are to be met head long and translator is reminded of:

ये मेरा कमाल-ए-गुनाह सही मगर इसको देख मेरे .ख़ुदा
तूने रोका मुझको जहाँ, मैं वहाँ-वहाँ से गुज़र गया।

(See the height of my crime, O God!, I overcame the hurdles, you created for me)

The present effort of translating *Pachrang Chola* is an attempt to reach out to the larger audience and readers of English language. It will bring forth the rich cultural heritage of the vernacular sources used by Madhav Hada to highlight their human vision and lofty ideals and also to bring forth Meera's quest for truth, beauty, liberty, justice and happiness. Eugene Nida, righty remarks, "Translating consists in reproducing in the receptor language the closest natural equivalent of the source language message, first in terms of meaning and second in terms of style". Thus one may say that translation involves trans-creation, it is always rewriting of the original text, 'a meta text'; it reproduces not only what the author in the original language says but what he means....". As one can see *Pachrang Chola Peher Sakhi Ri* (which is highly idiomatic) turns into "Meera v/s Meera" in English which is nonetheless more metaphorical.

If one looks into the etymology of the term translation it is from the Latin 'translatio' where 'trans' stands for 'across' and 'latus' stands for carrying in other words it means to carry across their meaning. But in Indian language especially in Hindi it does not convey the same meaning for it is known as *anuvad* that is to speak later, in Urdu it is *tarzuma* that is to 'reproduce' in Sanskrit it is Vivarthanam that is 'change'. Perhaps due to this P. Lal, an eminent translator from West Bengal described it as 'transcreation'. While translating Hada's "Pachrang Chola" compelled me to 'transcreate' on necessity basis, because my major concern was 'fidelity' to the original thought. G.N. Devy, a prominent linguist, regards it as a "Western metaphysical obsession". He quotes Hillis Miller, thus 'Translation is the wandering existence in perpetual exile' and then goes on to correlate it with the multilingual, eclectic, "Hindu spirit , entrenched in the belief in the soul's perpetual transition from form to form".

Both Madhav Hada and I have undergone the "perpetual transition" because Hada too depended on some of the translations of English texts written by Lieutenant Colonel. James Tod, Amartya Sen, Kumkum Sangari and Parita Mukta in order to prove his point regarding their perceptions where as for me it was 'wandering in an exile in search of a perfection if not paradise'. In *Pachrang Chola* Meera too had to wander from place to place translating her quest of spirit to merge into her 'Krishna' so that the journey of her soul should transcend from 'a form' to 'the form' of the ultimate.

❑❑

Index

C

D

H

I

J

K

N

O

P

Q

R

S

W

Y